Hurt and Revenge

Deborah E Oxberry

Visit my website at www.deborahoxberry.com

First Printing: February 2018

Copyright © 2018 Deborah E Oxberry

All rights reserved.

ISBN-13: 987-1-9802-4093-8

To A and T, for being there and brightening every day

CONTENTS

CHAPTER ONE

'As we commit the body of our sister, Grace, in the sure and certain hope of the resurrection to eternal life through our Lord Jesus Christ.'

The curtains started to close around the coffin, and Enya's 'Orinoco Flow' was piped out of the crematorium's sound system, softly at first then rising as the curtains finished their circuit around the platform, totally enclosing the coffin and shielding it from view.

Sue Robinson paid attention to the words of the song, probably for the first time, "Let me sail, let me sail, let the Orinoco Flow, let me reach, let me beach, on the shores of Tripoli. Let me sail, let me sail, let me crash upon your shore."

Suddenly all Sue could think about was a TV show she'd watched as a child in the 1970's. The Wombles was about a group of walking, talking, furry toys who picked up and recycled litter. One of them was called Orinoco, like the song, and Sue imagined a group of Wombles coming along to recycle Grace's ashes after the cremation had taken place. Sue giggled out loud, and immediately put her tissue to her face and bowed her head. *What am I thinking? This is my mother's funeral for goodness sakes, I shouldn't be giggling like a naughty schoolgirl.*

Sue felt Peter's warm hand in the small of her back. He didn't speak, but the feel of his large hand there was reassuring. He must think that she's upset, but instead she felt a rising euphoria, yes that's the only way she could describe it. She got an overwhelming urge to throw out her arms and start singing, right there in the chapel. But not the Enya song, she wanted to sing the Wombles' song. How did it go again? "Under-ground, over-ground Wombling free, The Wombles of Wimbledon Common are we ..." *What is WRONG with me? Am I having some odd reaction to grief? I'm going to miss Mum, I shouldn't be laughing at her funeral.*

Peter moved his hand from her back and placed it on her arm. 'Come on sweetheart,' he whispered, and Sue realised that the vicar was leading them out of the chapel, and as the chief mourners, they had to follow next, so the rest of the congregation could follow. As the only daughter and son-in-law of the deceased, it was their job to stand at the door, thank everyone for coming, and share memories about her mother. Keeping her head down, she took a deep breath and allowed Peter to guide her to the door.

Sue let out a heavy sigh as the undertaker closed the door of the limousine and her shoulders sagged. Peter looked at her for a minute before he spoke. 'Were you giggling at your mother's funeral?'

Sue blushed. 'Oh God, do you think anyone else noticed?'

'No, I think you covered it up well with your whole handkerchief over the face trick. You looked like you were about to break down. I'm sure no-one else noticed, but you didn't fool me. Terrible acting.' Peter smiled, he was teasing her.

'I don't know what's wrong with me, I feel happy rather than sad. Am I a very bad person?'

'Just exhausted Sue, you probably can't believe that it's all over and you don't have the worry of Grace and her illness anymore. It's relief, don't beat yourself up about it. Now if you'd stood up on your pew and danced and cheered, that might have been inappropriate.'

Sue punched Peter lightly on the arm. He always knew how to make her feel better, and she suddenly drew him into a tight embrace. 'Love you, you old bear.'

CHAPTER 2

Sue cursed as she bumped her head backing out of the cupboard under the stairs, dragging a dusty and battered suitcase right from the back. It was heavy, and she wondered what she would find in it. Grace's house was so small, she wouldn't have believed it could hold so much. But every cupboard, every shelf, the space under the beds, the loft ... they had all been jam-packed with stuff.

I think I'll become a minimalist long before I die, save someone having to do all this sorting out after I'm gone. Sue stopped dragging the suitcase for a moment and thought about who would sort out her stuff when she died. Peter, she supposed, if she died first. But he'd probably just leave it where it was, unless he moved to a new house. Would he move if she died? They didn't have a daughter to do it, or a son. Sue got that hollow, sad feeling she always got when she thought about children, her children. She clenched her teeth, well, she wouldn't have wanted them to do this anyway, clearing out someone else's house was a nightmare.

She looked around. This was the last room to finish, the kitchen/sitting room where Grace had lived most of the time. She'd found some funny things, a set of house keys in the tea pot, and a tea cosy under a pillow in the spare bedroom. Sue was sure they'd made sense in Grace's dementia-addled brain but opening anything could lead to a surprise.

Sue was being very methodical about everything. Three boxes: rubbish; recycling/charity; keep. There was very little on the 'keep' pile. She didn't need things to remind her of her parents. They had always been a close family unit, just the three of them, and she had so many happy memories from when she was a child. She'd kept her mother's engagement and wedding rings, worn and misshapen, but she couldn't bear to part with them. And her Father's copy of 'The Catcher in the Rye.' That was his favourite book. It had been published when he was 15, and Sue wondered if her Father had felt some affinity or sympathy with Holden Caulfield, the sixteen-year old narrator of the book? Whatever he saw in it, it was one of the few books that he re-read throughout his life. The cover was cracked, but the pages still had notes in the margin, in his neat, small handwriting. It seemed more personal than anything else.

Sue suddenly felt tired and slumped into an armchair. She would rest while she looked through the suitcase. The lock was stiff, slightly out of line, but after a couple of minutes it clicked open. Pulling a side table near to her, Sue placed the suitcase on it and lifted the lid. It held photographs and photograph albums. Sue had wondered where they were, she hadn't found any photographs anywhere else in the house, apart from the framed ones her mother had on display: Grace and John's wedding. Sue and Peter on their wedding day. Sue in her graduation gown, with her parents and Peter standing by her side, looking proud and pleased. Peter's graduation, with his parents, Margaret and Joe standing at one side, and Sue at the other, in a hideous blue suit with shoulder pads. It was the height of fashion then, but it made her look practically deformed.

Sue checked her watch. It was 3pm. She only had this room to finish, and then at the weekend she and Peter would load up their cars and make trips to the tip and the charity shop and drop stuff off. The house clearance people were coming early next week to take the furniture, and the decorators and cleaners were coming in the following week to freshen the place up. The house would be ready to go on the market then. The estate agents had suggested a price much higher than Sue had imagined. It would be nice to have some spare cash after the house sold. But she had to get it cleared before that could happen, and she needed to go back to work tomorrow. She'd kept up with some work from home, there were some clients who needed attention *now*, no matter what else was happening. To them, a VAT return or letter from HMRC was much more pressing than packing up your family home and couldn't wait.

Right, I'll finish everything else in here, and then I'll have a cup of tea and look through the suitcase. Sue felt a flutter in her stomach, and a renewed sense of energy. She was going to enjoy looking through the old albums, a bit like watching an old movie that you always enjoyed, even though you knew the plot.

The first album was Sue's birthday book. At one side, there was a photo of Sue, showing her growing from a chubby baby and toddler into a scrawny child, and a leggy adolescent. It went all the way up to her 21st birthday. That was the only photograph where she wasn't shown on her own. Peter was standing beside her.

Opposite each of these photographs there was a collage made from the birthday cards she had received each year. As a little girl, she had loved to help with these, cutting out greetings, pictures, numbers showing what age she was that year. As a teenager, she'd been scathing of her mother's continued insistence on updated the book every year. But now, as she flicked through it, tears pricked her eyes. Grace had compiled this, with love, every single year, even when Sue wouldn't look at the album.

As Sue got to the 21st year, she noticed there were two collages. One was made from her 21st birthday cards, the other was a collage of engagement cards. They'd had a joint party for Sue's 21st and her and Peter's engagement. She hadn't realised her mother had done this with the engagement cards, she'd never mentioned it, and Sue had never wondered what had happened to the cards they had received. There was a handwritten greeting from Pat, her best friend at university. 'A first AND a fiancé – superwoman! Love ya, Pat xxx.'

Sue wondered what happened to Pat? They had been such good friends, and had kept in touch for a few years, but then life had taken over and they had lost touch. Pat had gone to work for a large utilities company, securing a place on their graduate training scheme. Sue remembered getting an invitation to her wedding, but her father was so ill they couldn't go. She wished she still had a friend like Pat, she was good fun and a real rock. This album was definitely going on the 'keep' pile – she looked forward to showing it to Peter when she got home.

An album of her parents' wedding photographs was added to the pile, and a couple of albums showing particularly happy family holidays. The first was the Isle of Man in the 1970's, with one photograph showing acts from a circus walking down a busy shopping street. A man on stilts, higher than the shop windows, and a clown in a checked coat and a cap, with a painted face. There was a photograph of Sue, looking tiny next to the stilt-walker. When she got home her Dad had made her some stilts out of old pieces of wood he had lying around their shed, because she was so fascinated by how the man could walk so confidently, balancing on bits of wood, and she quite fancied towering above everyone else.

One particular photograph, from a holiday in Jersey, also in the 1970's, showed John, her Father, standing in a line-up with 3 other men, all with their trouser legs rolled up above their knees. An attractive blonde woman, wearing a sash (a local beauty queen perhaps) is feeling the knees of an elderly man in a suit, who is standing up straight and smiling as if he's enjoying the sensation. Her Father is next to him, standing with his hands behind his back and looking down at the man's knees. The other two men, standing to her Father's left are also doing the same. Judging in a "knobbly knees" competition by the look of it. Sue tried to remember who had won, but the memory wouldn't come. She smiled and felt a rush of love for her Father. She probably asked him to enter the competition, and he was a good sport, always joining in, even if it was something silly.

Loose photographs were placed neatly in envelopes, and, pulling out some of the larger ones, Sue smiled at a photograph of her parents and Peter's parents on holiday together. Grace and John, and Peter's parents, Margaret and Joe, had hit it off from they first met. Peter sometimes joked that he had to marry Sue because his parents liked her parents so much. They went out for meals together regularly, and in this photograph, they were on holiday together. They'd started to go abroad for holidays then, Spain, Greek Islands, Turkey. After Sue's Dad died, Grace still went on holiday with Margaret and Joe. Sue had made a remark about two being company, three a crowd, but they'd all insisted that it wouldn't be the same if Grace didn't go along. The holidays stopped when Joe had his first stroke, he didn't feel like going away from home then.

After Joe died, Margaret and Grace had a couple of holidays together. When Margaret had her leg amputated, because of diabetes, they went to a hotel in Scotland which had an adapted room, so Margaret could manage in her wheelchair. But by the following year Grace's Alzheimer's disease had got so bad that she was too difficult for Margaret to manage alone.

So, then Peter and Sue took both their mothers on holiday. Margaret increasingly needed help with personal care, but she was still as easy-going as she has always been. Grace had been more difficult as she didn't accept that there was anything wrong with her and so she refused any offers of help. She would head off out of the hotel by herself, and then not be able to find her way back. She would repeatedly ask when they were going for lunch, even though they'd already eaten. And then when they went for a meal she hardly ate, saying the food was 'too sweet' or 'too salty.' Sue and Peter were always exhausted when they got back from these holidays, but they persevered because they knew Margaret, at least, really looked forward to them.

Then there had been that terrible holiday in the Lake District. They had rented a luxury cabin, which was all on the same level, so it would be easy for Margaret to manage. The views were magnificent, and there was a lot to see and do locally. They locked the doors when they were in the cabin, so that Grace couldn't wander off, but one night, exhausted, they forgot to lock the doors out to the patio. Grace disappeared. Sue and Peter searched through the night for her, tramping through the woods and country paths, shouting her name.

Some of the families in the neighbouring cabins came out too, and one of them found Grace's cardigan down by the lake. They knocked on the cabin door, trying to find Sue and Peter to show them the cardigan. But they were both still out searching, and only Margaret was there, waiting anxiously for news.

Eventually, the local police found Grace, she'd been spotted walking along a country lane in her nightgown, and they had picked her up. She was wet, and tired and cold, but couldn't remember where she was going, or why. After thanking everyone for their help, and apologising for the inconvenience, Peter and Sue headed back to the cabin, with a shivering and confused Grace between them. They opened the door and shouted a greeting to Margaret. But there was no reply. Sue and Peter looked at each other, and called more loudly, thinking she was asleep. Peter headed towards Margaret's bedroom, and Sue took Grace into the bathroom to start drying her off.

Sue heard Peter retracing his steps and heading towards the main living area in the cabin. There was a silence, and then she heard him say 'Sue' in a strange, flat voice. There was something about that one word that filled Sue with dread and she rushed along the corridor. There was Margaret, lying on the floor, obviously dead. She was clutching Grace's cardigan in her hand.

The doctor said her heart could have given out at any time, but Sue and Peter both felt that the shock of believing Grace had drowned in the lake might have been the thing that brought it on. That was the last time they took Grace away on holiday. Partly because they couldn't face it after Margaret's death. But also because Grace became confused and distressed even on a visit to their house, constantly asking when she was going home. Later on, she asked that several times an hour, even when she was in her own home. It was one of the symptoms of the disease that Sue found the hardest to deal with. She remembered counting the number of times that Grace asked it each hour. 'Whose house is this? When are we going home?' She found that by counting, she could stop herself from getting irritated, it seemed to work as a distraction. The record was 47 times in one hour. And each time, she replied patiently, 'this is your house in Windsor Avenue Mum. You *are* home.'

Sue stood up abruptly. Looking at these old photographs was making her maudlin. She added the photograph of all four of their parents to the pile of albums that she'd already selected and put the rest in the 'rubbish' pile.

CHAPTER 3

Peter's car was parked in the drive as Sue pulled in. Sue smiled when she saw it, glad that Peter was home. Occasionally he worked late, as his role as Head of History at the local secondary school made big demands on his time. Plus, Peter was conscientious, he really cared about the students, and took his pastoral role seriously, as well as his teaching.

He must have heard the engine because he opened the front door before she was even out of the car. Probably waiting for her to get home. She knew he felt bad leaving her to sort out her mother's house on her own. But while she had been able to take some time off from the accountancy practice where she was a partner, it was very difficult for Peter to take time off during term-time, she understood that. But it didn't stop Peter from wishing he could help. They'd had enough experience of clearing out houses after a death to know that it was draining, both emotionally and physically.

Peter pulled Sue into an embrace as soon as she was inside, and for a few moments she just stood, enjoying the feel of his solid warm body enclosing her. Eventually she pulled away, looked up at him and smiled. 'That was just what I needed.'

'Drink?' 'I've put a casserole in the oven, wasn't sure what time you'd get back. It'll be ready in half an hour but will keep longer if you want a bath or time to unwind?'

'Think I might have a bath, but I don't want to get too relaxed, I must do some work, lots of catching up before I go back tomorrow. At least I got all the main stuff sorted at Mum's. It's all ready for us to start moving things at the weekend.'

'Well done,' Peter said, smiling sheepishly, 'you must have worked hard, I wish I could have helped.'

As they walked into the sitting room, Sue started telling Peter about the photo albums. When Peter was pouring drinks, Sue pulled out the albums and showed Peter some of the funniest photos. Somehow, looking at them together made them seem less sad, and they giggled at the fashions and hairstyles from previous decades.

Sue put down her glass and sat back, with a sigh. Peter looked at her and cleared his throat. 'You do realise that we don't have anyone else to look after now? Just each other. For the first time in how many years? Thirty years?'

'Yes, 32 years since my Dad first became ill, we'd only been married a couple of years. And it's been pretty much non-stop since then. Do you think we'll be able to fill in our time?' Sue grinned to show that she was joking.

'It's our time now Sue, we have earned it, and we deserve it. We must make the most of it. We can finally do the things we've talked about. You can take up painting again, I can brush the dust off my golf clubs. And we can go on holidays, travel.'

'Yes, without worrying about the folks left at home.'

'When did we ever get away without there being some sort of crisis at home? We always seemed to be on the phone, trying to sort something out, or coming back early.' Peter stood up and walked over to the fireplace, where he turned and looked at Sue.

'Let's make a pact, no more lame ducks, we'll only think about ourselves, let's have some fun before we are too old and decrepit.' His voice had an almost pleading quality.

'I don't regret looking after our parents Pete, I really don't.'

'No, neither do I, of course not, we couldn't do differently. We were both lucky to have such great folks. But we were unlucky that they were all ill, one after another. It's taken over our lives. And I wasn't just thinking about them. What about all the other people who have taken up our time? Your friend whose husband was hitting her? Betty, who used to live next door, she was very demanding.'

'Yes, we do seem to attract them. But I always hope that someone will be there to help us when we need it.'

'And where are all our friends now Sue? They didn't rally around when we needed help with our parents, did they? Where were they when we needed help with Grace? Where have they been since she died? Has any one of them asked if they could help you clear out the house? All they've done is send a condolence card, nothing practical.' Peter spoke evenly, he wasn't recriminating, he was just stating facts.

'People have such busy lives though Pete, families, their own parents to look after ...'

Peter interrupted, 'but my point is Sue, other people don't put themselves out like we do. And I'm not saying that they are right or wrong, or that we are. But what I mean is that now, we have a chance, we can do what we want. We are comfortably off, and when we sell Grace's house we'll have a nice nest egg. Let's stop being dutiful and live a little.' He spoke with such conviction and enthusiasm, that a bubble of excitement rose in Sue's stomach.

'Ok then, let's make some definite plans. Where would you like to go for our first holiday?'

'Antigua,' said Peter without hesitation. 'I'd like to go to one of those resorts just for couples. No children, I see enough of them at school. Where they have a cocktail bar in the swimming pool, and you have a private patio and you can lie in bed and look out at the sea. And I want to go for 3 or 4 weeks, and do nothing except eat, drink, sleep, swim and relax.'

'Sounds wonderful,' Sue said with longing in her voice. Then she stopped and thought for a moment. 'We can really do it, can't we Pete? We really can.'

'Of course we can Sue, this is a fresh start for us, a time to have some fun. And it doesn't just have to be holidays. We can do things at weekends too, now that we don't have to be at your mother's all the time. We can try those restaurants that we've wanted to go to, and go out for the day, go to farmers' markets, go away for the weekend.'

'And I think I'll set up a studio in the orangery, the light is great in there.' And I might learn to play the piano, I've always wanted to,' said Sue, her enthusiasm growing.

'The golf club has a new professional and he offers improver lessons. I'm going to book them. And I've still got that list of all the National Trust places that we want to visit. We can expand the list and stay overnight in a luxurious hotel. Perhaps travel on a Friday after work, look around the National Trust properties on a Saturday, then come home on Sunday after a leisurely morning and Sunday lunch at the hotel?' Peter leant forward as he said this, his eyes shining with anticipation.

'We could book a hotel with a spa, and when we get back on the Saturday I could have some treatments, and you can lounge by the pool?' Sue was imagining it now, and her aching body longed for a massage, and the warmth of a sauna. She looked at Peter, smiling broadly, and they both began to laugh.

'And that's only for now, it'll get better,' Peter went on. 'In a couple of years, I can retire, while I'm still young enough to enjoy it. And then we can move to the sea, like we've always planned. We will be comfortably off with our pensions and the sale of this house. Then we can dedicate our lives to fun and relaxation. Unless you want to carry on working?' he said, teasing.

'Me, no, I'm ready to go now. I love accounting, but I've had enough of it. I want to paint, and go to shows, and get a dog .... '

'We must have a dog, remember when we were engaged, we

were planning on buying two Cocker Spaniels and breeding them? But you said you'd want to keep all the puppies.'

'I still might want to! We'd probably best just get one dog. Oh, and I'd love to take up horse-riding again, that was my favourite treat when I was little. Imagine riding a horse on the beach?' Sue's enthusiasm was matching Peter's now, as she was beginning to realise that all the things they were talking about could actually happen. She clasped her hands together and drew in a deep breath, it was overwhelming.

'Come on, said Peter, this calls for "Hits of the 80's"'.

Sue laughed as Peter picked up the remote control and started the CD player. He already had the CD in the deck. This was the music they had listened to when they were young – the last time they were carefree.

'Wanna dance?'

'You bet I do,' Peter replied, putting out a hand and pulling her to her feet. And despite the rigours of the day, Sue found herself dancing, and they both sang out loud, the words of the songs flooding back as if they had listened to them only yesterday.

CHAPTER 4

Gary heard his phone ringing and tried to sit up, dislodging his four sons who were wrestling with him and had him pinned to the floor. 'Come on boys, it might be work ...' he said, before breathlessly answering the call. 'Mills Property Services, Gary speaking.'

'Hi Gary, this is Alan Scott. You came out and did a quote for me recently.'

'Hi, Alan, how are you?' Gary said, trying to remove two-year-old Noah who was clinging onto his leg.

'Just wanted to let you know that I've decided to go with someone else. I know you've left me a few messages, so I thought I'd let you know, save you calling again.'

Gary's stomach tightened, he had been sure that Mr and Mrs Scott were going to hire him, and he was relying on the money from the job. They had seemed so keen, and he'd been back three times to measure and discuss the work they wanted done.

'I'm sorry to hear that Alan, is there anything I can do, knock a bit off the price perhaps? I thought you seemed keen on going ahead?'

'To tell you the truth Gary, I don't believe in beating around the bush, I've asked around and I've had some bad feedback about your work. Well, more your attitude, not turning up when you say you will, going off to do other jobs. I couldn't put up with that ...'

'Oh. Do you mind if I ask who told you that? I've got lots of customers who are happy, I could put you in touch with them,' Gary started to say, but he was interrupted.

'No, sorry, my mind is made up, I just thought it fair to let you know. The other firm starts on Monday. Goodbye.'

Gary heard the phone go dead. Noah jumped against his leg and four-year-old Jack grabbed the other leg. 'Dad, give us a ride,' he said. Gary looked down at his sons, his heart sinking. He was relying on that job to pay his professional indemnity insurance, and to pay the wages for a couple of labourers who had worked on some recent jobs. 'Dad, dad, a ride' insisted Jack, and Noah joined in too, 'ride Dada, ride.' Gary looked down at the excited faces of his sons and was going to do what they asked when his phone rang again.

Snatching it up, he said 'come on boys, I'm busy,' hoping it was Alan Scott with a change of heart.

'Mills Property Services. Gary Mills speaking.'

'This is Matt Mitchell, Ravenswood Avenue, you've just finished my kitchen refit.'

'Hi Matt, how are you?' Gary said, pleased to hear from him. If he was ringing to pay his balance, he could just about make ends meet for another week or two.
'Bloody furious actually Gary. There are so many things wrong with the kitchen that I don't know where to start. I want you round here to put it right as soon as possible. And I'm not paying you another penny until it's all sorted out.'

Gary strained to hear what Matt was saying. His two oldest boys, Jacob and Oliver, were playing a game which involved a lot of shrieking and shouting. And the two youngest were still imploring him to give them a ride, each striving to ask the loudest.

'Sorry Matt, I didn't quite catch that? What seems to be the problem?'

'This is the trouble with you, your mind's never on the job. I want my kitchen sorted out as soon as possible. My wife's in tears over it. '

'I'm sorry Matt, I'm sure it can soon be sorted. I'll call around tonight, and we'll schedule the work in as soon as possible. Is that OK?'

'OK, make it after 7, and we want it done to a proper standard as soon as you can.'

'Yes, I'll definitely be there tonight, sorry about that, see you later.' Gary ended the call, his heart thumping in his chest. He'd left Adam, his labourer, to finish the job, and he had said it was all done. He should have gone and checked himself, but he had another job to finish, and had to get back home because Noah had a doctor's appointment, and he promised Lisa, his wife, he'd come home and take them, save her having to take all four boys on the bus. Never mind, he'd sort it out tonight, it couldn't be that bad.

'Ok boys, who's for a game of hide and seek? Gary asked, trying to look cheerful. And within minutes his boys were scurrying to find a hiding place as Gary hid his eyes and started slowly counting to 100.

CHAPTER 5

With the boys settled in front of the TV, Gary went looking for Lisa. He found her in the kitchen, listening to the radio and ironing a big pile of the boys' clothes. She looked up and smiled when he came in and she turned off the radio. Gary poured himself a glass of water and sat down at the kitchen table.

'You OK babe, you look tired? The boys worn you out playing?'

Gary took a sip of the water and smiled thinly. 'No, I can cope with the boys. Got a few problems at work. You know I mentioned that big job that I'd costed up? Well, the guy has just rung me to say he's going with someone else. And another guy isn't happy with the work that we've done, he's not going to pay until I've sorted it out.'

'You'll sort it out Gary, you always do. You're a good worker.'

'The thing is, money's a bit tight, and I've got quite a few bills to pay. We had tools stolen from the van that have had to be replaced. And the business insurance is due. I've got to pay the labourers for the last jobs that they helped with. We'll have to watch what we're spending Lisa.'

Lisa carried on ironing and pulled a face. 'You know I'm always careful Gary, but the boys grow so quickly, they're always needing new things. But I'll try to not buy anything extra for a while. Just until things are sorted out.'

Gary sighed inwardly. He knew Lisa depended on him to keep things ticking over, but sometimes he felt she didn't really understand the difficulties of running a business. Still, she had lots to do here with the boys and the house, and she put all her efforts into making a lovely home for them all, so he couldn't grumble. But he didn't think she understood how serious their current financial situation was. He decided to try and explain again, they had to spend the bare minimum. He was just opening his mouth to speak when Jacob burst into the kitchen, dressed in his judo kit. 'Are you ready to take me to judo Dad? I've got a test tonight, see if I'm good enough to go for my next belt. I want to be there early and do some practice.' Jacob's face was shining, he loved his judo class.

'Sorry, son, I've got to go and see a customer, sort out some problems with a job. I won't have time to take you to judo.'

Jacob's face fell, and Gary saw tears come into his son's eyes. That made the decision for him. 'What am I talking about, of course I have time to take you. But when we get back I have to go out and see a customer. Is that OK?' Jacob nodded, his good mood restored. Gary could feel Lisa smiling at him and he looked up to catch her gaze. He was lucky to have his family, it was all he ever wanted.

As they drove across town to the judo club, Gary half-listened to Jacob chatting excitedly, and worked out some timings in his head. They should get back home by 7.30pm, 7.45pm at the latest. He could then dash straight off to see the Mitchells. It would take him about half an hour to get to their house. Perhaps a bit less because there wouldn't be much traffic at that time of night. And Matt Mitchell had said after 7pm, so if he got there around 8pm, that wasn't too late. That would work. Feeling relieved, Gary turned his attention back to his son.

*****

'Come on Jacob, got to get going,' Gary said, trying not to sound too impatient. The judo class had overrun by 10 minutes, and now Jacob was talking to his friend in the changing room. Gary wanted to get to the Mitchells' by 8pm at the latest.

Eventually they were back in the van, and on their way home. When they drew up outside their neat terraced house, Gary told Jacob to go straight in, and to tell his Mum that he'd had to go and see a customer. Jacob nodded seriously and repeated the message. As Gary watched his son walk up to the front door, it opened, revealing Lisa standing with her coat on, and Noah in her arms. Oliver and Jack pushed past her and started to run down the path. 'We're ready Dad,' Oliver said.

Gary looked at Lisa, puzzled. She shrugged, 'I promised the boys you'd take us to MacDonald's Gary. They don't have school tomorrow, it's a teacher training day, so it's OK if they're up a bit later.' Gary's heart sank. He hated disappointing his family, but he had to see the Mitchells. And they couldn't afford extras like fast food at the moment.

'Em, Jacob has to get out of his judo kit. Can we just go inside for a minute while he gets changed?' he said to everyone. The boys looked disappointed but turned around obediently as Jacob raced into the house and upstairs to his bedroom. 'Lisa, I have to go and see a customer, tonight. The one I told you about, who's complaining and threatening not to pay.' Gary said in a whisper in Lisa's ear.

'The boys were upset Gary, they think you spend too much time with Jacob. They were saying that he's your favourite. I thought a family treat would help sort it out.' Lisa whispered back. 'Family comes first Gary, that's what we always said.'

Gary sighed. He didn't want his boys to be upset. He'd ring the Mitchells and tell them that he'd be around first thing in the morning. 'Ok then, let's go to MacDonald's. I'm having chicken nuggets!' Gary said out loud, and the boys cheered.

Once they were settled in the restaurant, and all the family had their food, Gary excused himself and said he had to make a quick phone call. He went out to the van, to cut out any background noise, rehearsing what he was going to say to the Mitchells. He scrolled through his phone's contacts and had just found Matt Mitchell's number when his phone screen went blank. The battery was dead. Gary threw the phone down on the passenger seat. What was he going to do now? He had to speak with them tonight, they were angry enough. He could try Lisa's phone, but he hadn't memorised their number, it was stored in his phone. Once they got home he would ring, he could plug his phone straight into the charger. Yes, that's what he would do.

Gary went back to join his family. He felt very worried about the Mitchells, but forcing on a smile, he joined in a game with his boys.

On the way home, Noah started to cry. Normally he was a well-behaved little boy who was always smiling, but when he had a crying fit he really went for it. He roared and howled, and held his breath, and it took ages to calm him down. By the time they got home the noise was practically unbearable. 'He's over-tired,' Lisa explained, and hurried up the stairs with their youngest son. 'Can you get the others ready for bed please?'

Gary couldn't object, the older boys looked upset at Noah's frantic crying, so Gary took them upstairs and diverted them by playing games during bath time, and then reading them a story. He then took turns with Lisa walking backwards and forwards rocking a struggling Noah. Eventually Jacob, Oliver and Jack were all peacefully in bed, and Noah had cried himself into an exhausted sleep. It was now nearly 10pm. Gary wondered if he should phone the Mitchells, but it was late, they could be in bed. He decided to ring first thing tomorrow instead and put the kettle on to make Lisa a cup of tea.

CHAPTER 6

Next morning Gary dropped Lisa and the boys off in town and rang Matt Mitchell straight away. 'Good morning Matt, it's Gary Mills, sorry I couldn't make it last ....'

Matt Mitchell interrupted in a quiet but angry voice. 'Where the hell were you last night? We waited in for you to arrive, you didn't even have the courtesy to ring to say you weren't coming. Well, we aren't wasting our time on you and your crappy firm any more. I'm getting someone else in to finish the job properly. And you're not getting another penny from me. I will be sending you the bill if it costs more than I owe you to put it all right.'

Gary was so shocked he stammered trying to reply, 'I'll put it right, I'm sorry, I can come today.'

'Today? What good is that to me?' spat back Matt. 'My wife and I are both at work, and we have to go home to a kitchen that is half-finished and doesn't work properly. You had your chance to sort it out last night, but you didn't bother turning up. Now I'm very busy, some of us actually care about our work.' The line went dead.

Gary was stunned. It was bad enough losing the Scott's job, but to not get the money he was owed from this job too meant he was seriously out of pocket. The deposit the Mitchells had paid just covered the materials, and he still had to pay the labourer Adam.

After thinking for a few moments, Gary rang Adam, but just got voicemail. Gary left a message, asking Adam to ring him back urgently, but by lunchtime he'd had no reply. Gary tried again, and this time Adam answered. 'Hi Adam, it's Gary. Alright mate? Just

23

checking up what happened at the Mitchells'? Been speaking with him and they're not happy. Were there some problems on the job?'

'The Mitchells'? No, everything was alright, it was all finished when I left. What are they saying is wrong?'

'Well, they're saying lots of things are wrong with the kitchen, and they're talking about bringing in another firm to put it right. They're refusing to pay, and they won't let me in to see the job. Just wanted to get your take on it.'

'Seemed alright to me. They were wanting it done, so I had to rush a bit, so perhaps the finish wasn't 100%. But it was good enough.'

Gary closed his eyes. 'Not good enough for them. Do you think it will take long to bring it up to spec?'

'Shouldn't do,' said Adam, yawning. 'But I think they're making a fuss about nothing.'

'Look Adam, until we get this sorted I'm seriously out of pocket. Is it Ok if I pay you for the work once I've got it from them?'

'I was expecting that money by the weekend Gary. I won't be able to pay my rent if I don't get it, and my landlord is red hot on late payers. I could end up out on my ear.'

Gary thought for a moment, then reluctantly he replied. 'OK, I'll make sure you get what I owe you. But if the job's not up to scratch then you'll have to help me put it right.'

'Depends on when they want the work done. I've got work lined up for other people next week.'

Gary sighed. 'But Adam, if you've not done a good job, then you have to help me put it right.'

'I've done the job you're paying me for, to the best of my ability Gary. If you want some fantastic finish, then you should get skilled tradesmen in. You know I'm just a labourer. I can do you a day or two this week, but I'll need to be paid for my time.'

Gary tried ringing Matt Mitchell again, hoping he would be less angry. But his call went straight to voicemail. Gary didn't leave a message, but instead sent a text. He apologised for not turning up, said he had a family emergency. He added that he was more than happy to put the work right, but as he hadn't had a chance to see what was wrong, he couldn't give any idea of how long it would take. He ended by saying he hoped the Mitchells would give him another chance and apologising again. He hoped it would be enough to make them reconsider.

Putting his phone back in his pocket, Gary headed across town. He had to measure up for some other jobs whilst he was waiting for Matt Mitchell to get back to him.

Gary's stomach rumbled as the smell of fried onions wafted over from the burger van in the car park. Whippet-thin, Gary was always hungry, and Lisa hadn't had a chance to make him any sandwiches this morning, hurrying to get ready for her trip into town with the boys. Gary considered getting a burger, or a sausage sandwich with onions. But then he remembered their financial situation and turned his attention back to the estimates he was working out. He'd measured for two jobs that morning, and had just been into the builder's merchants, pricing up materials. He wanted to get back to the potential customers as quickly as possible. They were both small jobs, but if he could secure them, and get them booked in quickly, that would help a bit. He had no work lined up for the next six weeks. He finished the quotes and looked at the final prices. *If I do all the work myself, don't get in any labourers, then that will be cheaper.* Gary decisively scratched out his original price, put in a lower amount and ringed it in pencil. He rang the first customer, gave him the price and explained that he took the money for materials up front, and then the customer paid the rest when the job was finished.

'I've actually just had someone postpone a job, so I could do it as early as next week if you wanted to go ahead?' Gary felt himself crossing his fingers, like the boys would do when they really wanted something to happen.

'I'll have to discuss it with my wife, but I'll let you know tonight or tomorrow.'

Gary tried to keep the disappointment out of his voice when he said he looked forward to speaking with the customer again then.

The second call was even more disappointing. The customer said they'd decided to put the job off until early the following year and had opted to have a holiday instead. Gary felt his jaw tense. He'd only been there that morning, how come they'd changed their minds already? He suspected they'd agreed to go ahead with another firm already.

Gary logged into his bank account via his phone. Some standing orders and other payments had just come out and it was worse than he thought. He transferred money to Adam for labouring on the Mitchells' job, and got out the envelope containing the other bills he had to pay. A priority was his account at the builders' merchants, or he wouldn't be able to get more supplies. He made another online payment. The next thing that he had to pay was his business insurance. It insured him against anyone being injured on a job, or sub-standard work, and he paid it every year, but he'd never had to claim against it. He just didn't have the money to pay it. Well, no harm putting off renewing it for a few weeks, just until he sorted out this cash-flow problem. Gary put the bill back in the envelope and put the envelope back in the glove box of his van.

Gary jumped as his phone made a noise like a cow mooing. The boys must have been playing with the settings on his phone again. He looked at the screen, he'd received a new text. Hoping it was from Matt Mitchell with a change of heart, he opened the message. It was a photo from Lisa of the boys, sitting in the shopping centre with Gary's Dad, Les. Lisa's text said, "Bumped into your Dad out shopping. He's taking us for a milk shake. Yay! Love you, Lisa and the gang. Xxxx."

Gary looked at the picture. His boys, their eyes so bright and shining, made his Dad look even worse. Les Radley's many years of excessive drinking hadn't improved his looks. His face was prematurely aged, scattered with red veins, and his eyes were blurred and watery. He'd never been married to Gary's Mum, Julie, and he'd seen little of him as a small boy. But when Julie married when Gary was eight, she'd left him with Les, 'for a holiday,' and he'd never seen her again. Gary and Les got along OK, but his drinking was so bad back then that he wasn't fit to look after a small child. Gary often found himself spending time in a children's home or with foster carers. That's where he'd met Lisa.

Lisa's life had been so much worse than his, she never saw her family at all. She knew nothing about her dad, apart from he was 'a black man' which was all her mother told her about him. Her mother had given her up for adoption when she was five, saying she'd 'never wanted a kid.'

Lisa was fostered by a few families over the years, but no-one ever wanted to adopt her or even foster her long-term. She was an awkward kid, shy, silent and solemn, and she wet the bed. But Gary had got to know her and found out she was kind, and funny, and loyal. She grew into a real stunner too with her coffee colour skin and dark eyes and hair. They'd planned on getting married when they were teenagers, vowing to build a family of their own, and to make sticking together a priority, no matter what. They married before Gary even finished his apprenticeship, and Jacob was already on the way. They were lucky.

Gary looked at the photo again. His Dad looked happy to have bumped into his grandsons unexpectedly. He was a good man, apart from the booze. He tried his best, Gary knew that. Gary looked at his boys, and he noticed Oliver sitting apart from his brothers, not smiling and looking downcast. Gary worried about Oliver. Although he never said so to Lisa, he reminded Gary of her when she was a child. He was often anxious, and he was painfully shy outside the house. Gary hoped life wouldn't be difficult for him, and he felt an overwhelming urge to find Lisa and the boys, scoop up Oliver and hug him.

It was late when Gary got home that night. He'd had a couple of small jobs that needed to be finished and had to go back to a previous customer whose sink had started to leak. While he was there Lisa had rung and asked him to pick up some shopping on the way home, so he went to the supermarket on his way back.

Coming back through the town centre, Gary was held up at some temporary traffic lights in the market square. Waiting for the lights to change, Gary looked hungrily into the lit windows of Fratellis, one of the nicest (and most expensive) restaurants in town. Lisa and Gary had saved up to go there for their wedding anniversary and the food and atmosphere had been wonderful. Gary looked again as he caught sight of a familiar figure with a goatee beard just sitting down at a window table. It was Adam, his labourer, out with his new girlfriend. Gary shook his head. *Short for his rent? What a load of bull that was, he wouldn't be eating at Fratellis if he was that skint.* Gary thought about his own empty bank account, about the angry exchange with Matt Mitchell, and vowed to be tougher with anyone he employed in future.

CHAPTER 7

Sue picked up the easel and moved it further into the corner. The light was better there, and she could see into the garden. She stood back, examining the layout, and nodded to herself. *Yes, that was the right place for it.* It was so exciting, setting up her own artist's studio. *Listen to her, calling herself an artist!* It was just a hobby that she'd dabbled in now and again. But now that she had more spare time, she was going to take it more seriously, there had never been enough time before. The orangery at home was the perfect place – there was lots of space and the light was good. She was looking forward to having it all set up as a studio, so that she could come in and paint after work.

Hearing Peter's footsteps behind her, she turned around just in time to see the pretty jar that contained her paint brushes drop from Peter's hand. Sue started forward, but she couldn't stop it from falling onto the floor, breaking into several pieces. Paint brushes clattered onto the floor and started rolling in all directions. Peter stared at the floor and looked horrified.

'Honestly Pete, you're getting to be such a clumsy clot, you're always dropping things …' Sue began, as she got down on her knees to start picking up the pieces of china and the brushes. 'I loved that pot, it was so pretty.' Peter didn't answer, and when Sue looked up, he was looking down at his hand which was twitching uncontrollably. Then he began to rub his arm vigorously as if it was really itchy. 'What's wrong with your hand Pete, it's twitching? Have you trapped a nerve or something?'

Peter finally looked down at her and spoke seriously. 'I'm not sure what it is, it's happened a few times now, and I keep getting this funny feeling in my arms and in my feet. It's like there's something rippling under the skin. As if there are insects crawling under my flesh.'

Sue could see the alarm in his eyes. 'That sounds awful, how long has it been going on? Why didn't you say something?'

'I thought it was just one of those things. It happened once, then not for ages, but now it's been every day for the last couple of weeks. It doesn't last long.'

'It's probably just a muscle spasm or something. Symptom of old age.' Sue smiled at Peter to show she was teasing. 'Might be an idea to see the GP, he will be able to give you a muscle relaxant or something. Not that I want you too relaxed, you're not retired yet!'

Peter smiled. 'It's gone off now, I'm sure it's nothing much. Just a nuisance. If it happens again I'll make an appointment with the quack, see what he can do. Right then, where do you want these canvases?'

CHAPTER 8

It was strange coming home to an empty house. Peter was nearly always home first, except when there was something on after hours at the school, such as parents' evening. The school was only a five-minute drive from the house, whereas Sue had to drive across town to get back from her office. She finished work a lot later than Peter usually. The house was quiet and cold, so Sue turned up the heating, and put on the radio. She hoped that Peter's appointment didn't take long. Last time she'd gone to the GP she had to wait an hour after her appointment time and was then only in for a couple of minutes.

Peter still wasn't back after Sue had been upstairs to freshen up and get changed out of her work clothes. Dinner was already made and just needed to be reheated, so Sue poured herself a glass of wine and went into her studio. Peter said she was obsessed, and she did take any opportunity to spend time painting. There was something about it which absorbed her unlike anything else. With a paintbrush in her hand she felt real peace and enjoyment, and it was addictive.

Sue was working on the corner of a large canvas when she heard the front door close. 'I'm in here Pete, just doing a bit of painting.'

She heard Peter's familiar tread and he came into the orangery and over to the painting, bending to give her a kiss on the cheek. 'It's looking good, I love the colours. You're so patient when you're doing this Sue, you spend ages doing one little bit. It's not like you at all.'

Sue gave Peter a playful shove. 'Are you saying I'm impatient?'

'Well, you're dynamic, shall we say? Artist Sue is a lot more mellow and laid back. It's good.'

Sue smiled and looked back critically at her painting. She painted in an abstract style, flowers mostly, using muted shades with splashes of vibrant pinks and purples for contrast. It was her own style, and she could see it was developing the more she did. Suddenly she remembered why Peter had been late home. 'What did the doctor have to say? Is it a trapped nerve?'

Peter sat down and paused for a moment before replying. 'He's not quite sure. He's referring me to a neurologist.'

'A neurologist?' Sue said, feeling a prickle of alarm. 'What does he suspect?'

'I don't know if he suspects anything. Just thought it was better to get an expert opinion. I think he was baffled really. Nothing to worry about, just routine. He's sent the referral off straight away, and he said the waiting list isn't too long, so I'll be able to get the tests done quickly, get some meds and then I'll be fine. I was wondering if you'd come with me when the appointment comes through? I might be there for a few hours he said, have to wait around at different departments, would be good to have some company.'

Sue looked at Peter and nodded, biting her lip. It wasn't like him to want her to go along, he must be more concerned than he was saying. 'Of course I'll come with you, don't want you having all the fun on your own,' she joked. Their eyes met, and Pete winked at her.

'Thanks sweetheart, knew I could count on you' he said, and smiled, with a worried look in his eyes.

CHAPTER 9

Will this traffic ever move? Sue's car crawled along the dual carriageway, and she felt as if she'd be able to walk home faster. She'd left work slightly earlier than usual, but there seemed to be double the normal rush hour traffic tonight. And she'd particularly wanted to be home in good time. Peter was meeting with the neurologist to get the results of his tests, and she had wanted to have dinner on the go before he got back.

The traffic stopped moving altogether, so Sue tried ringing the house via the hands-free system in her car. She just got the answering machine. Next, she tried Peter's mobile, but it went straight to voicemail. He mustn't be home yet; the appointment must have taken a long time. Sue felt her chest tighten. The tests had seemed to go on for ever, bloods and scans and x-rays. They had spent a whole afternoon at the hospital, going from department to department.

Peter had seemed tired lately, but he hadn't had any more incidents. Hadn't dropped anything or had that strange feeling under his skin. Surely it couldn't be anything serious? He wasn't unduly worried, she knew that. He said he felt fine and had insisted on going for the results on his own. If he'd been worried he'd have wanted her to go too.

But why had the GP not just given him the results? Wasn't that what usually happened? Why did he have to go back and see the consultant?

The traffic eventually started to move and within another 15 minutes Sue was pulling into her own driveway. Peter's car was already there, he had made it back before her. Sue let herself in, and shouted brightly, 'I'm home, where are you?'

Peter replied immediately. 'In here, sitting room.'

Sue entered the sitting room, her coat still on. Peter was sitting in an armchair, a glass of whisky on the table before him. He didn't look up immediately when she came in but raised the glass to his lips, sipped and swallowed. Then he put the glass deliberately on the coffee table and looked up and smiled. 'Hello, have you had a good day?'

'Never mind about my day, how did you get on at the hospital?' Sue said, suddenly feeling alarmed.

'Ah, yes, thought you might want to know about that. Do you want a drink?'

'Do I need one?' Sue replied.

'I think you might.' Peter said, standing and heading over to the drinks cabinet. 'G&T?'

'Yes, no, in a minute, tell me what they said first.' Sue said, suddenly feeling chilly.

Peter poured the drink anyway, and brought it over to Sue, and sat back down in the armchair. He took another drink. 'It's not good news Sue. I've got Motor Neurone Disease. It's a life-limiting condition, I've got 3-10 years, and the symptoms will get much worse. I'll become increasingly disabled by it.'

Sue felt all the energy drain out of her, as if she'd been hit, very hard. 'Are they sure, it can't be a mistake, you've been so well?'

'No doubt about it I'm afraid. Funny, I asked that too. Sue, I'm so sorry, it's just not fair on you. I can't believe this has happened to us again.'

'Oh Peter, don't worry, we'll get through it, we've always coped.' Sue stood up and wrapped her arms around her husband. He put his arms around her, and they stayed that way for a long time.

CHAPTER 10

'Hello, Gary Mills speaking.' Gary's voice sounded strangled as he propped his phone between his chin and his neck. He was answering the phone and sealing a bathroom basin back into place. Gary listened to the caller at the other end, a customer he'd given a quote to the previous day. He found himself agreeing to go and do the job that afternoon, even though it was just a small plumbing job, the sort that barely covered his costs, and which he tried to avoid. Bit like the one he was busy with now. But there wasn't anything else available, and he had to bring in some money, any money, to keep things ticking over.

As he left his customer's house, Gary reviewed the time. He had another two jobs to measure up, and he told the customer that he'd be at the new job by 2pm, and it was on the other side of town. He'd have to skip lunch if he was going to fit everything in. He was hungry and felt a bit light-headed, but he was trying to stay on top of everything, he couldn't risk his reputation by having customers unhappy with him and his work.

It took him a while to find the house that had asked him to call by and quote for some repairs to their porch, meaning he would be cutting it fine to get the other quote done and get to the new customer's house by 2pm. He might just do it. He was just parking outside the customer's house when his phone rang, with the distinctive ring-tone he reserved for Lisa.

'Hi babe, how's things?'

'What time can you get home Gary? The boys and I have a surprise for you.' Lisa sounded excited.

'I'm just measuring up a job Lisa, then I've got another one to do, and then a new customer at 2pm. It's going to be later this afternoon before I can get back.'

'But Gary, it's Saturday, you should be at home with the family. And it's really important.'

'I know babe, but I'm having to do all the work I can now, you know money is tight.'

Lisa sounded disappointed. 'The boys and I have been shopping and we're making a special tea. Any chance you can get home a bit earlier?'

'I'll finish as soon as I can Lisa, I promise. See you soon.'

'OK, please try and get back as soon as you can. Love you.'

'Love you too babe,' Gary said as he hung up.

Gary finally came out of the customer's house, after measuring up the job. The customer had given him a detailed history of the porch, when it was added to the property, what the problem was, what needed to be done. He was a nice man, and Gary listened patiently, all the while wishing he'd just let him measure up and get on with it.

Gary reviewed the time. It was 1pm. He had to go through the town centre to get to the next customer who wanted a quote, and that would be busy on Saturday. If he went directly to the next job, started it early, he could call in to do the second quote on his way back home. That sounded like the best plan, and then he wasn't keeping Lisa and the boys waiting too long. He rang the woman who'd asked for a quote, but just got voicemail. He left a message saying he was doing a rush job and would call later in the afternoon.

Luckily the customer with the plumbing job was at home and didn't mind Gary arriving early. But the job took much longer than Gary had estimated. It was one of those jobs where everything went wrong, and it was nearly 4pm before he left. Gary looked at the money he'd been paid for the job. It was such a small amount compared to the time that it had taken. But that was all he seemed to be able to pick up at the moment.

He was just starting the van when his phone rang again. It was Jacob, asking if he was on his way home. 'Sorry son, the job took longer than I thought. I've just got to call by and see a customer, give her a quote for a job, then I'll be on my way.'

'But Dad, we've been waiting for ages. We've got the tea all ready and everything. Can't you come now? We're sick of waiting.' Jacob's voice was almost pleading.

'OK son, I'm on my way, be back in about 15 minutes.' Gary rang off and immediately rang his remaining customer. She didn't sound pleased that he wasn't coming over that afternoon, saying that she'd stayed in especially. Gary embellished a bit, telling her that he was dealing with an emergency for an old person and he didn't want to leave it unfinished. He promised to call in first thing in the morning to quote for the work.

By the time Gary reached home his stomach was audibly rumbling. He hoped that Lisa and the boys had made lots of sandwiches for the afternoon tea, he was so hungry he could eat them all himself.

He saw the front door open as he got out of the van, and all four of the boys were waiting for him excitedly. He hurried down the path and they pulled him into the house and into the living room. They had moved the table into there from the kitchen and it was set with party food, sandwiches, cakes, ice-cream and jelly. And in the corners of the room there were bunches of pink and blue balloons. There was a banner over the chimney breast saying, "The Mills Family is growing." Gary turned as Lisa came into the room with a tray of drinks. He looked at her puzzled. 'What's all this about?' he said, adding, 'I'm famished, I can't wait for the tea party.'

Lisa smiled and herded up the boys. 'Come on everyone, sit

down, and we'll start tucking in. Dad's hungry.'

They all sat, and Gary started to load his plate with sandwiches and crisps. Oliver and Jack were squirming excitedly in their seats, and looking at Lisa they said, 'can we tell him now Mum? Please?'

Lisa laughed, 'OK boys, after three, just like we practised. One, two, three, WE'RE HAVING ANOTHER BABY!' Lisa and the boys shouted, followed by whooping from the boys, who clapped and bounced around some more.

Gary's appetite immediately disappeared. 'Another baby Lisa, are you sure?'

'Yes, I did two tests this morning, but I suspected anyway. I'm sure. And I think it's going to be a girl this time. And she'll have four wonderful big brothers to watch out for her.' Lisa's eyes were shining, and she just couldn't stop smiling. Lisa adored children and loved everything about being pregnant and having a new baby around the house.

Gary forced out a smile. 'That's wonderful news. No wonder we had to have a special tea to celebrate. Another member of the Mills clan.' He pulled Lisa to him and hugged her, and then all the boys jumped on him and they all hugged each other.

Later, Gary helped Lisa with the washing up, as the boys played and watched TV. Lisa chatted happily, discussing names for the new baby, and wondering if they should try and move to a bigger house before the baby arrived. 'If it is a girl, I'd love to do up a nursery in cream and pink. Lots of unicorns. A real princess bedroom.'

Gary turned around and looked at Lisa. 'We can't afford to move Lisa. And we can't really afford another baby. How did it happen, when you're taking the pill?'

'Well, I thought it was about time we had another one, Noah's two now. So, I might have stopped taking it ….' Lisa said playfully.

'You stopped taking it? Without telling me? Lisa ...' Gary broke off, exasperated.

Lisa looked at him, all the joy drained from her face. 'I thought it would be a welcome surprise. You have looked so down in the dumps lately, I thought it would be the one thing that was guaranteed to cheer you up.'

Gary felt awful. 'It is Lisa, I'm chuffed, really I am. I just want to make sure I can give you all everything that you need, that's all. And business isn't so good. But yeah, about time we had another baby, don't want to lose our touch!'

Lisa flung herself into his arms and Gary held her close and resolved to keep his feelings to himself. He'd find work from somewhere, he had to.

Lisa suddenly pulled away and said, 'we have another surprise for you. You finish drying up then come in the sitting room, we'll be ready for you then.'

When Gary went into the sitting room a few minutes later, the boys were hiding behind the sofa, giggling, and Lisa was sitting on the sofa, and she patted the seat next to her for Gary to sit down. Then she cleared her throat. 'Ladies and gentlemen. On the catwalk tonight we have Noah Mills, a rising young model, wearing a new hoody!'

At that, Noah toddled out from behind the sofa, wearing a bright red hoody. He walked in front of the sofa, spun around, and then opened the coat, showing off the lining which was blue with puppies on it. Gary, Lisa and the other boys clapped, and Noah clapped himself and ran to his Dad to show him the coat. Gary admired it, rubbing the fluffy lining and asking Noah to twirl around to show it off. The hoody still had the label on it and Gary winced when he saw the price, £54. Noah was growing so fast; the hoody would only fit him for a few months. He decided not to say anything, he'd already risked spoiling the day with his reaction to the baby news.

The other three boys did their turn on the 'catwalk' too, showing off their new shoes. Later Lisa explained that she didn't want them feeling left out because of the new baby, so she'd decided to treat them all to something new. Gary smiled and nodded, but mentally added up how much the shopping spree would have cost. That was probably part of next month's rent money.

Later, alone in the bath, Gary sat brooding on the day's events. The baby was on the way now, there was nothing they could do about it, and they'd manage, they'd have to. He'd just have to take on whatever work he could get, do whatever he could to support his family.

CHAPTER 11

Sue stood up and stretched her back, and then stepped back and critically appraised the flowerbed that she'd been rearranging. *Yes, that looks better.* Then she gathered up her tools and headed towards the garden shed. As she walked she ticked off her mental 'to do' list. Shopping was done, and she'd changed the bed linen and cleaned the bathrooms. Gardening was finished, and now she'd start some baking. Then when that was done she'd spend some time in her studio painting. And tonight, they were going out for dinner at that new restaurant where they had live music. She'd have to decide what to wear and make sure it was pressed.

Once she deposited the tools in the shed, she headed back towards the back door, mulling over recipes in her head, trying to decide what she should bake. As she got near to the back door it opened, and Peter poked his head out. 'I was just coming to find you, I've made some coffee.'

'Great, just what I need. I think that border looks a lot better now, don't you?'

'It does Sue, it looks great. You've always had a way with flowers.'

They went into the kitchen together and Sue immediately noticed a wet patch on the floor. 'What happened here?'

Peter looked down, 'Oh, just had a little spill.'

'Anything broken?'

Peter shook his head. 'No, luckily the coffee pot is stainless steel, it bounced. Although it's a bit dented.'

'I'm going to start baking now Pete, so I'll have my coffee 'to go' so I can drink it while I'm working.' Sue said as she washed her hands. She then went towards the larder to start getting out the ingredients for baking.

Peter moved quickly to stand in front of her and said, 'coffee first Sue, come on, sit down, you've been on the go all day.'

Sue shook her head, 'I want to get on, lots to do, and we're going out this evening.'

Peter took her arm gently and led her to the kitchen table. 'Sit. I insist. It'll only take a few minutes to drink your coffee and I've got something important I want to talk about.'

Reluctantly Sue sat down and picked up her coffee cup.

'I've got an appointment with the Head Teacher on Monday. I'm going to talk with him about retirement. I think I'll be able to leave early on health grounds,' Peter began.

Sue took a big gulp of coffee and started to stand, but Peter put out a hand to stop her. 'We have to talk about it sweetheart, it's not going to go away. We must make plans. You can't pretend it's not happening.'

Sue sank back into her chair, suddenly all her energy gone. 'I know Pete, I just don't want to talk about it. I don't want it to be real.'

Peter smiled at her. 'Do you think I don't know that? All this frantic activity. I'd rather it wasn't real myself. But we must face it, make plans. We have to Sue. Discuss it now, and then we'll get on with it.'

Sue sighed resignedly. 'Ok, Pete, shoot.'

'Right, well first, my main fear is going into a nursing home. No matter how bad I get, I really want to stay at home. I know that's going to be hard on you, but we should be able to afford to have carers, full-time if necessary.'

'Ok,' Sue said. 'But surely it'll be a long time before it comes to that?'

'That's the thing, we're not really sure how quickly, or slowly, things will progress. Hopefully it'll be a long time, but we need to think things through for the future. Stairs might become difficult too.'

'What about a stair lift?' Sue suggested, 'Or one of those in-house lifts, they're much smaller now and we have plenty room here.'

'That's a good idea, but as things progress, it might be easier if I don't have to move around too much. I'm a big man, and it'll be hard for carers to lug me around.'

Sue shuddered inwardly. The thought of her big strong husband having to be moved around, and losing all his independence, was just too much. She didn't think she could bear it. 'What were you thinking of then? You staying upstairs all the time? Surely not?'

'Oh God no!' Peter replied. 'I was thinking about the garage. It's huge and we never use it. Could we have it converted into a granny flat? With a bathroom and bedroom? It looks out onto the garden, and I could get into the rest of the downstairs, even if I'm in a wheelchair or on crutches or something. And if we don't need it, well, it will be a good feature for when we eventually sell this house. A good room for guests or teenagers, or aged relatives.'

Sue thought for a moment. 'It is a big space, but it'll cost quite a lot to get it done and make it nice,' she said hesitantly. 'Do we need to have it done straight away?'

'I know, it will be expensive, but the sale of Grace's house is going through now, so we could use some of that money. And I know I don't need it now, but I'd feel happier it being ready in case I ever do. Once it is done it's there if we ever need to use it.'

Sue smiled thinly. 'Yes, you're right, better to be prepared. I'll get some quotes in over the next couple of weeks. The people two houses up had their garage converted into extra living space, and I know they were very happy with it. I could perhaps ask them who they got, and see if they'd recommend them?'

Peter put out his hand and placed it over Sue's. 'I know you don't want to think about things like this Sue. I don't either. But once we have a plan in place we can just get on with enjoying ourselves, and then we'll be ready if I do get worse. The illness isn't going to go away.'

Sue smiled and placed her other hand over his. 'I know, I've just been hoping it was all a nightmare. But don't worry Pete, I'll never let you go into a nursing home. We'll sort it. It's good that we will soon have the money from Mum's house, that'll help pay for anything that you need.'

Peter sat back and visibly relaxed. He was glad they'd had this talk, he knew Sue had been avoiding it. 'OK, he said, what are we baking? Can I help? I'm very good at cake-tasting!'

CHAPTER 12

'Sue, your next client is running a little late. Car trouble apparently. You've got a gap after them, so it shouldn't be too much of a problem. They'll be here in 20 minutes. Is that OK?'

Sue looked up from her desk and smiled at her secretary. 'Yes, that's fine thanks. Could do with a breather, it's been a busy day.'

'Would you like a coffee or anything?'

'No, I'm Ok, I've got some water.'

After her office door closed, Sue pulled out a folder from her desk drawer. Inside were the quotes she'd received for the garage conversion. She laid them out on the desk, but she didn't see them. Instead she was thinking about her conversation with Peter about the future.

He was right of course, they did need to think about it. But all the plans they made, they were all about Peter's future. They, he, hadn't thought about *her* future. The conversion was going to take a sizable chunk of her inheritance, and if they had to pay for carers, then that would probably use up the rest. And *her* retirement plans were on hold indefinitely now too.

And what about afterwards? Sue couldn't bring herself to even think the words 'after Peter dies,' what was she going to do? Suddenly she imagined herself all alone, she'd have no-one. No husband, no family, no children, no friends. She felt a lurch of fear in her stomach. *What would happen to her?* Tears pricked her eyes, but she clenched her jaw and replaced them with feelings of anger and bitterness. *Why did this have to happen to them? Hadn't they had their share of caring and illness? And why did she have to use her inheritance, her nest egg, to pay for something she didn't want?*

Sue looked down at the estimates on her desk. Then she decisively gathered them up, put them back in the folder and pushed it into her bottom drawer. They didn't need the conversion now, they may never need it. She wasn't going to rush into a decision.

CHAPTER 13

The sound of the lawn mower interrupted Sue's thoughts as she stood at her easel. She was still amazed at how absorbed she got when she was painting. She couldn't remember anything else that commanded her attention in the same way, except perhaps when she read an enjoyable book. Painting truly made her happy, although she wasn't always happy with the results. What she had in her head was never the same as what ended up on the canvas. But she was improving, she knew that.

Sue turned to look out into the garden. Peter was always busy now that he was retired. She watched him cutting the lawn, and she could tell it was a real battle for him. He walked so slowly, and frequently the lawnmower handle slipped out of his hand, and he had to bend and start again.

She had said she was going to cut the lawn later, and she knew he was doing it so that she wouldn't have to leave her painting. Every day he did things to try and make her life easier. He'd always been the same, a real tower of strength. As she thought this, her mind went back to that dreadful time at the IVF clinic, when they found out the last of their embryos had failed to implant. It was their last hope for a baby and Sue was convinced she was pregnant this time. And when she wasn't, she thought the disappointment would kill her. As she literally collapsed, her knees buckling under her, Pete caught her and held her tight.

'I'm so sorry, I'm so sorry, I've got you, I've got you,' he repeated, over and over as she sobbed and sobbed. She couldn't have made it through without him.

As Sue watched Peter struggle to turn the mower at the end of the lawn, she was filled with an overwhelming rush of love for him.

Her 'big bear,' he'd always put her first, always supported her, always loved her. Never complained about anything, always made her smile. Sue vowed to herself that she would do the same for him now. His last years, however long he had left, would be as happy and comfortable as they possibly could be. She owed him that at least.

Sue went through to the study and opened her briefcase. She took out the folder containing the quotes for the garage conversion. She found the one that she wanted, a firm called Unique Interiors. They had carried out the work on the house up the road, and their neighbours had said they were very pleased with the job.

Sue opened her laptop and sent Unique Interiors an email, saying she was happy with their quotation and asking them when they could start the work.

CHAPTER 14

Gary put his head on the steering wheel of his van and closed his eyes. He was exhausted. He had already done jobs for three customers this morning and been to see two potential new jobs and given quotes. He had to go back and fix problems with two other jobs this afternoon, do another quote and then he had another job to finish. It all involved a lot of driving backwards and forwards, unloading and loading his tools, and frequent trips to the builders' merchant for supplies.

Noah had been crying all night, and he'd walked the floor with him downstairs, so that Lisa and the boys could sleep. Lisa was tired all the time, and had been suffering badly with morning sickness, so he wanted her to rest when she could. Gary didn't sleep well anyway, he was constantly worried about money. All he was able to find were small jobs that didn't pay much. They were already behind on their rent, and their landlord was starting to make threats.

If only he could get a big job where he could be there all day, and it would bring in a lump sum. That would see them over this rough patch. All this running around from job to job was no good, he used so much on fuel for the van that it ate into the small amount he made from completing the work. He found the only way he could get work was to undercut everyone else and offer to do the job straight away. People didn't want to pay much, but they expected so much. Customers always seemed to be ringing him and asking him to come back, not happy with the level of finish on the job or moaning about something else. What did they expect for what they'd paid?

As Gary was thinking this, his phone started to ring. 'Hello, Mills Property Services, Gary speaking,' he answered, hoping it wasn't another unhappy customer.

'Hi, Mr Mills, this is Kelly from Unique Interiors. You had a meeting with my boss, Mr Greenwood, a while back?'

Gary wracked his brain, Unique Interiors? Ah yes, he remembered, that big building firm that takes on smaller firms to do sub-contracting work. He'd met with them months ago and had hoped he'd get some work from them. It was exciting at the time, but he'd heard nothing from them since. 'Hi Kelly, yes, I remember meeting with Mr Greenwood. How can I help you?'

'Mr Greenwood was wondering if you and your team would be available to carry out some work for us on a sub-contracting basis? It's about four weeks' work and needs to start quickly as the customers are going on holiday and want it done while they're away. Would you be able to help us out?'

'Yes, as it happens I, we, would be able to.' Gary answered excitedly. *Yes! This is what he needed.*

'Excellent, would you be able to pop in and see Mr Greenwood tomorrow at 11.30? Just to talk over the job, look over the plans and schedule? We've already seen your documents, so you don't need to bring anything in. Oh, except your professional indemnity insurance has expired, if you could bring in the renewal certificate, that would be great.'

Gary's heart sank. He didn't have the money to renew his insurance. 'I haven't actually got the renewal certificate yet. I'm going with a new insurer and it's taking them a while to send it through.'

'Well, if you can send me a copy as soon as you have it that should be OK. You are getting the same level of cover?' Kelly asked.

'Yes, absolutely, the same level.'

'Good, we'll see you at 11.30am tomorrow.'

'Yes, see you then. Thanks.'

Gary let out a large intake of breath after he hung up and sat back in his seat. Thank goodness. Perhaps things were looking up after all.

CHAPTER 15

Mark Greenwood's office was one of a suite of offices above the Unique Interiors' showroom. As Gary sat waiting for him to arrive, he looked around and thought he'd like to have an office like this someday. A firm like this. They only took on expensive, large jobs, extensions, conversions, whole house refurbishments. And they built bespoke studies, bedrooms and offices, as well as high-quality kitchens and bathrooms.

Gary stood as Mark Greenwood came in, but the older man waved him down into his seat. He was talking on the phone and he mouthed 'sorry' apologetically to Gary. Gary watched him as he talked. Mark looked to be around 50, perhaps late 40s, but he didn't look in decent shape. He was taller than Gary, probably around six feet, but he was overweight, and this made him look shorter than he really was. He had large expressive green eyes and thinning light brown hair. His complexion was ruddy, and Gary wondered if he spent a lot of time outdoors.

'Sorry about that Gary, thanks for coming in. I'm glad you and your team can help us out, we've got so much work on we don't know what to do with it all.' Mark said, half laughing.

'Andrew Foster will be joining us to brief you on the job. Basically, it's a garage conversion, but a big one, large double garage, nice house. Professional couple. They're going on holiday to Antigua for a little over 3 weeks, and they want the job done when they're away. Bed sitting room, wet room, bi-fold doors onto the garden. We have the plans all drawn up already, and we've ordered the materials and done all the costings. Your guys just have to turn up and do the work.'

Gary felt a prickle of excitement. This was great, he'd been worried that he'd have to buy some of the materials and then claim them back. The door opened, and a tall, powerful-looking man came into the room. He looked as if he had been a rugby player when he was younger, and still looked fit and in good shape. He was carrying a large folder with 'Robinson' written on the outside. Mark introduced him as Andrew Foster, and Gary shook his hand.

'Andrew will be your main point of contact if you have any questions. He'll come out at the end of each week, just see how the job's going, smooth out any issues,' Mark explained. 'Kelly is sorting us out with a sandwich lunch, so we can go through the plans in detail with you, so you know exactly what's expected of you.'

The next hour was spent in detailed conversations. The plans and estimates had been carefully drawn up, showing every aspect of the job. Gary realised he could learn a lot from working with this firm, not only about doing superior quality work, but about operating a business. He paid attention carefully and jumped when his phone rang with Lisa's distinctive ringtone. Mark and Andrew looked up questioningly. 'Sorry, that's my wife, she's pregnant,' Gary began. Mark waved a hand at him impatiently, and Gary stepped out of the office as he answered the phone. 'What is it Lisa? I'm in a meeting. Can I ring you back?'

'I just wanted you to pick up some shopping on your way home. I'm not feeling so good, I've been sick all morning,' Lisa said, sounding flat.

'I'll ring you back as soon as I've finished, I promise,' Gary said, desperate to get back to the meeting. He rang off and went back into Mark's office, apologising for the interruption.

'Not gone into labour has she?' Mark said, in a half-joking voice.

'No, it's just early days yet, still in the morning sickness stage I'm afraid.'

'Good, because we don't want you distracted. Is it your first child?' Mark asked.

'No, it's our fifth.' Mark and Andrew both raised their eyebrows. 'So, don't worry, another pregnancy won't distract me from my work.' Gary adopted a similar jokey tone.

'You don't look old enough to have that many children,' Andrew said.

'Well, we decided to get them out of the way early. We've got four boys, hoping it's a girl this time then we can call it a day.' The two older men smiled, and then turned their attention back to the plans.

Gary was buzzing when he came out of Unique Interiors' offices. The meeting had been great, he'd enjoyed talking about the job with the older, more experienced men. He had been given copies of the plans and work schedules that Andrew had drawn up to take away with him. And he'd been given a set of keys to the house, because the owners would be on holiday before he started the job. And then he'd signed the contract, and the sum he'd get paid was so much more than he expected. It meant he could pay off their debts, pay his insurance and put some to one side for the baby. And Mark said if he did a respectable job there was lots more work available. Things were definitely looking up. He parked his van along the road and phoned Lisa, excitedly telling her all about the meeting and what good news it was. He wrote down what she wanted from the shops and then scrolled through his phone for Adam's number.

'Hi Adam, it's Gary. Alright mate? Listen, I've got a big job on, starting next week. Over three weeks work, and I need a couple of labourers. Are you interested?'

Gary's mood had dropped considerably by the time he got home. He'd tried all the men who usually did labouring for him, and none of them were available to help on the conversion. It was too big a job to do himself. Still, he'd just have to make a start, and look around for someone else to help. Adam had said he had a friend who might be available, so he wasn't going to worry too much yet. He forced himself to smile as he walked up the front path, carrying the shopping that Lisa had asked for.

CHAPTER 16

'Ok boys, let your old Dad have a break, you're wearing me out.'
Gary laughed, and sat down on the park bench. It was a lovely
sunny day, and he had brought the boys to the park to play football
so that Lisa could have a rest. He watched the boys running
around. They were so full of energy, always on the go. He'd been
the same when he was a child.

Gary checked on Noah who had fallen asleep in his buggy.
He'd enjoyed kicking the ball around with his brothers too and had
a good left kick for a toddler. But eventually the fresh air and
running around had tired him out and now he was napping
peacefully. Gary tipped his head back and enjoyed the feel of the
sun on his face. He was taking a couple of days off before he
started the conversion for Unique Interiors, and it was nice to be
free of worry for once. He had work lined up, the boys had just
started their summer school holiday and were having fun. And
Lisa seemed to be a bit better these last few days too. This
pregnancy was different from the others. Lisa seemed tired all the
time and she'd been sick such a lot. With the boys she'd seemed to
have extra energy when she was pregnant and had barely suffered
with morning sickness at all. Lisa saw these changes as a sign that
she was definitely having a girl. They'd never found out the sex of
their babies before, but Gary was sure Lisa would ask when she
had her scan this time. She adored all the boys of course, but she
would love a daughter. She must feel outnumbered sometimes as
the only woman in an all-male household.

There was a slight vibration in Gary's pocket, and then his
phone started to ring. Groaning to himself, Gary looked at the
screen. He hoped it wasn't a customer, he was enjoying his time
off. He was relieved when he saw Les's name on the caller display.
'Hi Dad, how are you doing?' Gary asked.

'Hello Son, I'm fine. Are you all OK?'

'Yes, we're good, just in the park with the boys. Lisa's having a rest at home.'

'Is she keeping alright? New baby growing OK?'

'Yes, everything's fine Dad. I'm starting that big job I was telling you about on Monday. Just having a bit of a break before I get stuck in.'

'That's why I was ringing you Son. I was wondering if you needed any help on the job?'

'Are you looking to make some pocket money Dad?'

Les laughed. 'No, not me, not likely. I was wondering if you could give Danny some work? He's a bit hard up at the moment, and at a loose end.'

Gary was silent for a few moments. Danny was his older half-brother. Les had been married to Danny's mother, but they had split up before he met Gary's mother Julie. Danny lived with his mother mostly as a child, but would visit Les from time to time, so Gary had known him a little bit as he was growing up. The age difference meant they didn't have much in common. He occasionally saw him at family events now that they were adults, but they weren't close. Unfortunately, Danny had inherited their Dad's love of alcohol, so he was a bit unreliable.

'I don't know Dad, it's an important job for me, and Danny doesn't have a trade.'

'I know, poor Danny, he hasn't got his life sorted like you Son. You're lucky with Lisa and your lovely boys, your own business, you're going places. Danny doesn't have anything and he's not good at anything either. He's strong though, and does what he's told, I thought perhaps you could use another labourer?'

Another one? Gary thought ruefully. *I don't have any lined up to help. Perhaps Danny would come in useful after all?* His Dad was right, he had done so much better than Danny. Perhaps he should help his brother out.

'He's not drinking though is he Dad? I need people I can rely on.'

'No, he's on the wagon now, don't worry about that. He'll be ever so grateful.'

'Ok then Dad, tell him he can start on Tuesday,' Gary said, but as he put the phone down, his good mood was marred by a feeling of uneasiness. He hoped his Dad was right about Danny not drinking. He couldn't afford for anything to go wrong on this job.

CHAPTER 17

The house was near the end of a small cul-de-sac in a wide road, lined with trees. All the houses in Willow Drive had unique styles. The only thing they had in common was that they were all large and detached, with big driveways and gardens. Gary found number 8 and pressed the remote control on the key fob. The large timber gates slowly opened to reveal a long, wide, brick driveway, and beyond that a large white house. Gary drove through the gates, pressed the fob again, and the gates silently closed. Gary smiled to himself, the boys would think that was 'magic.' The left-hand side of the drive was lined with a large hedge with green and red leaves, and underneath that a flower bed full of colourful blooms. To the right there was a beautifully manicured lawn, surrounded by more flower beds.

The driveway went straight ahead to the large attached garage, and also curved round to the right, past the front door and around the lawn, and followed around to a similar set of gates at the other side. *In and out gates,* thought Gary. *No reversing around here!* On the outer edge of the 'out' driveway, there were mature trees, totally cutting off the house from its neighbours. All the bordering walls were topped with black wrought-iron fencing, which matched the hinges and handles on the drive gates. Next to the 'in' gates there was a single gate, for visitors on foot.

Gary parked his van in front of the garage and walked around to the front of the house. It really was impressive. Rendered and painted a pristine white, the windows had patterned leaded glass. Above the front door was a magnificent arched window containing a picture in patterned glass. Some sort of nymph carrying a water pitcher. To the left of the front door there was a small round window. Gary guessed this was a cloakroom.

The lock in the sage green timber door opened easily, and Gary stepped into a magnificent hallway. The floor was cream marble, and the hallway was wider and bigger than their sitting room at home. The curved staircase, with a deep beige carpet, was on his left, and then the hallway opened out to provide a seating area. Two cream wing-backed armchairs faced a wide cream fireplace with large glass-fronted gas fire, complete with logs. A gold-framed mirror was hung on the wall above the fireplace, and opposite that there was an abstract canvas in creams and golds. The hallway was half-panelled in cream, with a pale gold paper above.

The kitchen was enormous with solid oak units, a range cooker and a centre island unit with drawers and a built-in wine chiller. One part of the kitchen had floor to ceiling cabinets, including two that were glass-fronted to display expensive-looking matching china and crystal glasses. An archway led through to a dining area which was so large that, despite the table having eight chairs comfortably around it, there was still space to have a game of football too. Gary thought this must be the dining room, but then he found another dining room, more formal with another dining set, including a sideboard. The first one must be part of the kitchen concluded Gary, thinking how it would make a great playroom for the children.

The sitting room had French doors out onto a patio. There were windows at each side of the doors and then another large window at the other end. This meant that sunlight flooded into the room, which was cosy despite being so large. Gary admired the large sofas with curved arms and lots of cushions, and wooden floors with big rugs and an enormous coffee table. One end of the sitting room had built-in bookcases, and beside them, two more formal chairs with a tall coffee table, presumably to make a place to sit and read.

The downstairs accommodation went on further with a huge sun room on the back, which was made into some sort of artists' studio. Then there was another smaller room, with a desk and chair and more bookshelves. A home office or study. Gary imagined himself having a similar room to do his paperwork for the business.

Although he had no reason to go upstairs, curiosity got the better of Gary and he decided to have a look around. He had slipped off his work boots when he'd come in the front door, so he wasn't worried about leaving footprints on the beige stair carpet. At the back of the house he found the master suite. A huge bedroom, with a large wooden bed and bedside cabinets and nothing else. Gary was wondering where they hung their clothes, but he soon found out when he opened the door to a dressing room complete with built in wardrobes and a large dressing table. A further door opened onto an enormous bathroom with a bath, toilet, bidet, twin sinks and a double walk-in shower. The cream, gold and stone theme continued into this room, reflected in the floor and wall tiles. A huge wooden-framed mirror covered most of one wall.

Walking back through the bedroom, Gary noticed that it had a small balcony, that looked over the back garden. He had been so interested in looking around downstairs that he hadn't really noticed the garden, but from here he got a full view of it and he stood for a few minutes, just trying to take it in. The back of the house had a wide patio made from some sort of stone. Garden furniture was strategically arranged at either side. A sitting area on one side, and a dining area at the other. A well-tended lawn was surrounded by flower beds full of shrubs and flowers, of types that Gary had never seen before. The whole garden was a riot of colour. A wooden arch at the bottom of the garden led into a second garden area which appeared to be paved. There was a shed discretely placed in this area, hidden from view by shrubs. The whole garden was surrounded by mature trees and was totally private. Within the flower beds and in the centre of the lawn were elaborate water features made from stone. The one in the centre of the lawn reflected the patterned window in the front of the house, another water nymph. They weren't switched on, but Gary imagined they'd be impressive when they were. They looked like they lit up too. They must have spent a small fortune on the garden alone.

Further investigation revealed 3 more bedrooms on the first floor. Two had en-suite shower rooms and there was another large bathroom complete with a bath and another separate shower cubicle. It really was a stunning property.

As Gary walked around downstairs to have another look, he imagined himself and his family living here. So much space for the children, and that garden! The boys could play all day, make as much noise as they wanted, and not disturb anyone.

He wondered about the people who lived here. He knew they were called Mr and Mrs Robinson, but were there just two of them? There was no sign of any children in the house, no toys around the place, or posters or anything that would indicate teenagers. There were some framed photographs in the sitting room and he studied them closely. The same couple appeared frequently in the photographs. A tall, distinguished looking man, with a smiling, handsome face. And a tall, dark-haired, very slight woman, pretty with glossy hair and flawless skin. Then there were some older couples, probably their parents. This must be the Robinsons, just the two of them with all this space. *They're lucky, must be the sort to have everything handed to them on a plate*, Gary thought. He mentally reviewed the two-bedroomed house that Lisa and he rented. It was too small for them now, would be worse when the baby arrived.

Suddenly Gary felt a renewed sense of resolve. This was what he wanted for his family, he was going to put his all into this work, take on as much as he could, and make enough money for them to buy their own home. He had the skills to take on a wreck and do it up, so they could have lots of space for the children to play. And with that thought, he picked up the keys, pulled on his boots and headed out to the garage to look at the work that was needed.

CHAPTER 18

'Come on Jack, sleep now. You can't stay up any longer, and you're disturbing your brothers,' Gary said firmly, kissing his son on the forehead and turning to go.

It had taken ages to get the boys settled tonight, and Gary was tired. He'd had to be at the job early this morning for the first delivery of materials. He was hoping Danny could have been there for them arriving, but he had an appointment at the addictions' clinic. Gary had done a long day at the Robinsons, and then he'd had another couple of small jobs to fit in. He hadn't intended to take on any more work while he was doing the conversion, but these were people he'd done work for before, and he didn't like to let them down.

He had reviewed their finances today and things were worse than he'd thought. The money from the conversion would clear off their debts, but they'd have to be careful in the meantime. With the boys off on their school holiday Lisa was taking them out every day, and everything seemed to cost such a lot. He'd have to have a word with her, ask her to try and find cheaper things to do, just for now.

Gary winced as his phone rang before he got downstairs. He didn't want to wake the boys, so he snatched it from his pocket and answered immediately. There was sobbing on the other end of the line, then a slurred voice said, 'Son, Son is that you, are you there?'

Gary closed his eyes and leaned against the wall. 'What is it Dad? I've just got the boys to bed.'

'I need your help Son, I'm not well, and I can't get the fire on. I'm shivering. Can you come over?'

Gary could hardly make out what his Dad was saying, his voice was so slurred. He'd obviously been drinking. 'I'm tired Dad, I've been working all day, I don't really want to come out again.'

The sobbing got worse, and then his Dad started to cough too. Gary felt a wave of pity. 'Ok Dad, I'll be over in half an hour. Put your coat on and keep warm.'

His Dad's flat was in a terrible state. Even though it was summer, the flat was freezing cold. Gary suspected that his Dad had been on a bender where he hadn't put any heating on and had left windows open for days. Everywhere was filthy, there were empty beer cans on all the surfaces, and every dish that his Father owned was dirty and piled up in the kitchen, on the floor, on the coffee table. Some still had half-eaten meals on them.

The gas fire came on straight away when Gary lit it. He suspected his Dad had been turning the knob the wrong way, but he didn't say anything. He wrapped the duvet from the bed around his Dad, and then started tidying up while his Dad dozed in the chair. By the time he'd finished doing all the dishes, thrown out the rubbish and run the vacuum around, his Dad was awake and watching him.

'You're looking more like your Mother every day Gary. She was always house-proud. Always cleaning. Used to drive me bonkers.'

'Pity you weren't a bit more house-proud yourself Dad, this place was in a right state, it really was.'

'Nagging too, you get that from your Mother. She was a bonny little thing when I first met her though. Pity she turned into a bitch.'

'Don't talk about Mum like that Dad.'

'Why not? It's true, a right bitch. And she didn't care about you, why are you sticking up for her? Married that other fella and bye-bye Gary, couldn't wait to get shot of you. Left you with me. I looked after you, best I could. She didn't care.'

Gary closed his eyes and tried to control his temper. It was always the same when Les had been drinking, he started calling Julie names, saying how she hadn't cared for Gary. But Gary knew that wasn't true. He only remembered his Mum being loving and kind. Life was just complicated that's all, it must have been her new husband who didn't want Gary, that was the only explanation. He must have stopped her getting in touch.

'Right Dad, I'm going to pop to the shops and get you some groceries, you've got nothing in. Do you have any money?' Gary knew that his Dad would be broke, but he thought he'd better ask, given how little he had in his own bank account.

Les made a show of turning out his pockets, but they were empty apart from a betting slip and a balled-up tissue.

'I'll just get some essentials then, coffee, milk, some tins, bread, butter. I won't be long,' Gary said, picking up his coat and keys.

'If you could just slip in a few cans and perhaps a bottle of vodka ...' Les began.

'No Dad, I'm not wasting good money on booze for you. I'll get you some food and that's all. You shouldn't be drinking.'

'Shouldn't be drinking? It was your whore Mother drove me to it. Going off with another fella and leaving me. And you're just like her, hard-hearted. I don't want the booze, I need it, I need it.' And his Dad started to sob again.

Gary patted his Dad on the shoulder. 'Come on, don't get upset, I'll get some cans. But I can't afford vodka, I'm a bit short until I get paid for this job I'm doing. I'll be back as quick as I can.'

It was nearly midnight by the time Gary got home. Thank goodness for the 24-hour supermarket – at least it had been quiet. But his Dad had wanted to talk when he got back, and Gary found it difficult to get away. The house was quiet when he got in, the boys must be asleep. He went quietly upstairs and peeped into his bedroom. Lisa was fast asleep. He couldn't wake her to talk about money now. Perhaps they'd have time in the morning.

He heard a noise behind him and saw Oliver standing by the bedroom door, rubbing his eyes and looking upset. 'What is it Olly, you should be asleep?' Gary whispered. Oliver looked down at his pyjamas, and Gary noticed the wet patch. 'Oh Olly, never mind, you've just had a little accident.'

'Why does it happen to me Dad? I try not to drink much, and I go to the toilet before I go to bed. It doesn't happen to Jacob or Jack, and even Noah doesn't have to wear a nappy all the time now. Will I have to wear nappies?'

'No Ollie, of course not, it's just one of those things, you'll grow out of it.' Gary pulled his son close. He could see he was really upset. 'Come on, we'll get you cleaned up.'

By the time Gary had changed the sheets, put Oliver into clean pyjamas, and tucked him into bed, it was nearly 1am. He was exhausted, but he couldn't sleep, thinking over what had happened tonight. His Dad hadn't been on a bender for ages. Gary wondered what had triggered it now. And poor Olly, he was such a sensitive soul. Gary hoped that no other children were bullying him. Although that was more likely to happen during term-time. He wondered if he was feeling jealous about there being another baby on the way? He usually just wet the bed when he was worried about something. He was so shy, he often got overshadowed by Jacob and Jack who were so loud and confident. Gary vowed to spend more time with Oliver, see if he could find out what was bothering him.

Lisa moved in her sleep, and Gary put his arm around her, snuggled down and tried to sleep.

CHAPTER 19

Gary tooted the horn again, impatient to get going. He'd agreed to pick Danny up each morning, so they could travel to the Robinsons' job together, but Danny was never ready. *Too much to drink last night*, Gary thought, as he peered through the windscreen to see if there was any movement from Danny's flat. The curtains were still drawn, but as Gary watched, they opened, and Danny waved. *Well, he's up anyway.*

It was another 10 minutes before Danny appeared at the front door, munching on a piece of toast as he came towards the van. Gary's stomach rumbled, he hadn't had time for any breakfast. As they drove across town, Gary went through the list of things that they had to do that day, and Danny nodded absentmindedly as he finished off his toast, then ate a packet of crisps.

'Are you listening Danny?' Gary asked. 'We have to get a move on, we're falling behind with the job, and we only have so long to get it done. If we make a decent job of this one, then there will be lots more work from this firm. I might even be able to offer you a proper job.'

Danny nodded. 'It'll get done Gary, just taking me a while to get into the swing of it. I haven't really done this sort of work before.'

Or any sort of work, Gary thought. But he tried to sound encouraging 'you're doing a good job Danny, and you're being a big help, but we just need to work a bit faster that's all. I should be on site all day today, so we'll get a crack on.'

'But I have to leave at 1.30 today. I have to sign on,' Danny said.

Gary groaned inwardly. He knew Danny would still have to claim benefits because he couldn't pay him until he got paid from Unique Interiors, after the job was finished. But he didn't know he had to go today, and some of the work they were doing now needed two men, it was too heavy for one alone. 'Could I give you a lift to sign on, then we can get straight back?' he suggested.

Danny was shaking his head before Gary finished speaking. 'I have to go for one of those interviews, I've missed some appointments. And as I was over that way, I've agreed to meet up with my mate afterwards. Haven't seen him for ages. I didn't think it would be worth me coming back to the job after I'd finished.'

Gary was irritated but didn't say anything. He'd just have to manage alone. Eventually he said, 'well, we'll just have to do as much as we can this morning.'

Danny was holding up a partition board for Gary to secure, when Gary's phone rang. 'Just a minute mate,' he said, and put the phone to his ear. It was Mrs Ross, a regular customer of his.

'Oh Gary, I'm so glad that I've caught you. My fence has blown down, and I can't let my little dog out in the garden. Do you think you could come around and repair it for me?'

'That's not really the sort of job that I do Mrs Ross, you really need a handyman for that. I've got a lot on at the moment.' Gary replied, trying not to sound impatient.

'Oh, I know dear, but you've done such a lot of work for me, and I don't know anyone else. I'm always worried getting someone new. And I'm not feeling so good, I'm not up to ringing around. I can't get out much now, so need to let Pickles out into the garden, I can't get him for a walk.'

Gary felt sorry for the old lady. She was a good customer, always paying him straight away in cash, and even sending presents for the boys at Christmas. 'I'll try and get around at lunchtime today, see what I can do. Don't you worry.' He put his phone back in his pocket and turned back to the partition board.

Leaving Danny with clear instructions, Gary left Willow Drive at 12 noon and headed over to Mrs Ross's house. The job wasn't big – one of her fence panels had blown down in the wind, the whole fence was badly maintained. Unfortunately, the panel couldn't be re-used as it was rotten, and he noticed another two that were in a similar state. Gary ended up going to buy three new panels, fitting them all, and then coating them up with creosote to protect them from the sun and rain. It took him the best part of the afternoon to get it all done, and he felt anxious as he got back in his van to head back to the Robinsons' house. He hoped Danny had managed to get some more done before he left for his appointment.

Just as he was pulling away, his phone rang again. It was Lisa, so he answered before driving off. 'Hi babe, everything OK?'

'Oh Gary, I'm feeling really sick, I need to go for a lie down. Do you think you could pick Jacob up from his friend's house? He's over there playing.'

Gary was immediately concerned for Lisa. 'Are you OK, it's not like you to be floored by a bit of morning sickness?'

'I'm fine really, just been sick all morning, and I'm really tired. I can't face getting on the bus to go over there.'

'Is there any chance that his friend's parents could bring Jacob back over? I'm really busy with this job.' Gary asked.

Lisa was quiet for a few moments, then said, 'I don't think that will be possible, the Dad is at work, and his Mum has a baby to look after. I wouldn't like to ask.'

Gary sighed. 'No, of course not, text me the address and I'll go. When does he need to be picked up?'

'As soon as possible, he's been there all day and rang earlier to say he was ready to come home.' Lisa replied.

'Ok, I'm on my way.'

By the time Gary had picked Jacob up and taken him home, most of the day had gone. Lisa was lying on the sofa when he got home, she looked tired and pale. 'Oh Gary, I'm so glad you're home, can you watch the boys, so I can go for a lie down please?' she asked. 'They will be ready for their tea, I haven't felt up to cooking today.'

Gary looked at the time. He must do some more work on the conversion today, they were falling way behind. He smiled at Lisa and did a quick calculation in his head. If he made tea for the boys, and something for himself and Lisa, then he could bath Noah and get the older boys into their pyjamas. Lisa could be resting while he did that, and then he could go back to the job. The summer nights are light, so he'd be able to do at least a couple of hours on the job. But when he looked in on Lisa a couple of hours later she was fast asleep and looked so peaceful that he didn't have the heart to wake her. He couldn't leave the boys on their own, so he resolved to stay at home, but get to the job early in the morning. He picked up his phone and sent a text, "*Danny, want to get to job early in the morning, make up for today. Can you be ready at 6.45am? Gary.*"

As Gary was putting his phone onto charge before going to bed, he realised that he hadn't had a reply from Danny. It was only 10.30pm, so he decided to give him a call. The phone connected, and Gary could hear a lot of noise in the background, people talking, glasses clinking, and other noises he recognised as a pub. Danny's voice came on the line, sounding slurred. 'Who's that, you're through to Super Stud,' he said, before starting to giggle helplessly at his own joke.

Gary drummed his fingers on the table, 'Danny, it's me Gary, did you get my text mate?'

'Text, text, did I get your text? Which one, when was that, what?' said Danny, obviously very drunk.

'Doesn't matter Danny, it was just about tomorrow. See you in the morning.' Gary said, and rang off as Danny said something unintelligible.

CHAPTER 20

Although not really expecting him to be ready, Gary called by Danny's flat before 7am the next morning. Instead of tooting the horn and disturbing the neighbours, Gary rang Danny's doorbell. To his surprise the door opened, and Danny was dressed. But Gary's cheerful, 'good morning Dan, you alright?' only received a confused look from a bleary-eyed Danny. Then Gary realised that Danny wasn't in his work clothes, and that he must still be dressed from the night before.

'What you doing here Gary, want to come in for a drink? Lisa let you off the leash for once has she?' Danny asked, swaying slightly. 'I've just got in myself, but plenty of life in the old dog yet,' he said, pointing unsteadily towards himself.

'I've come to pick you up for work Danny, but I can see you're in no fit state.' Gary said shortly. This was just what he needed.

'Work?' replied Danny, sounding confused. 'Oh, WORK, yeah, gotta think about working, working all the time,' Danny started singing.

Gary turned to leave. 'Get yourself sobered up and I'll see you at the job later.' He spoke in an even voice, but his fists were clenched.

At the Robinsons,' Gary took stock of what they'd done so far. He knew they should be much further on by now if they were going to complete the job on time. But still, it was just the end of the first week, they could catch up. Well, they could if Danny showed up, it needed at least two of them. Gary sighed, he wished Adam was available, he was much more skilled and reliable than Danny. Gary hoped Danny wasn't going on a bender, if so, goodness knows how many days they would lose. But he wasn't going to think about that, he just had to get his head down.

Danny turned up around lunchtime, looking fragile and very apologetic. 'I'm sorry Gary, I shouldn't have met up with my mate yesterday. We went to the pub for one, but well, you know how it goes. Were you at the flat this morning? I thought you were, but I wasn't sure if I dreamed it.'

'Yes, I was there, was hoping for an early start this morning, make up for yesterday. But never mind, you're here now.' Gary started, but then his phone rang. He looked impatiently at the screen then swallowed hard when he saw that it was Unique Interiors who was calling. He pressed the answer button and heard Andrew Foster's voice on the line.

'Everything alright Gary?' Danny asked as Gary ended the call. 'You look a bit pale.'

'That was Unique Interiors on the line Dan. Their inspector is coming out at the end of next week to evaluate our progress. We need to be much further on by then. This is my business Dan, I really need this work.' Gary trailed off, not knowing what else to say.

'Well, we'd best get on with it then.' Danny said, 'what shall we do   first?'

CHAPTER 21

Gary felt his stomach clench as the small 'Unique Interiors' van pulled into the Robinsons' driveway at 4pm the following Friday. He was exhausted. Both he and Danny had been working on the conversion for 14 hours a day over the past week, trying to get ready for the inspection.

As the tall, burly figure that was Andrew Foster got out of the van and started to walk towards the house, Gary took a quick look around, catching Danny's eye and smiling thinly. Danny gave a quick 'thumbs up' sign and carried on sweeping the floor.

Andrew Foster was quite a taciturn man, and he said little as he walked around the conversion, occasionally making notes on a folio he was carrying. Eventually, he looked up and asked, 'where are all your team?'

Gary had anticipated this question, so he said, 'I let them finish early as it's Friday and they started earlier – thought it best they were out of the way, so you could have a good look round.' Andrew looked pointedly at Danny, still sweeping in the corner. 'I'm giving Dan a lift home, that's why he's still here, he doesn't drive.'

Andrew nodded briefly, and then looked around again. 'I thought you'd be a bit further on, but what you've done isn't too bad,' he said. 'I've noticed a couple of faults, let me show you.' He then took Gary over to various places around the garage, pointing out about four items which he wasn't happy with. Gary took out a notebook and made sure that Andrew saw he was writing down what he said. When he finished writing, he could feel Andrew's eyes on him, and he looked up to meet his gaze.

'Are you sure you're going to be able to finish this before the Robinsons come back? You are half-way in terms of time, but not half-way in terms of progress. We promised it would be done up to our required standard by the time they got back from their holidays. We are flat out with work, and people are on holiday, so

I can't keep coming around checking up.' Andrew spoke sternly.

'No need to worry Andrew,' Gary said, trying to sound confident. 'If necessary I will bring in a larger team to get it finished. Divert them from other work. We are only a bit behind because there were some delays in delivering the materials. We can easily make up the time.'

Andrew looked at him levelly before answering, 'I drew up the delivery schedule myself, I'm surprised the materials weren't here on time.'

Gary blushed. 'It's not that they weren't here on time, it was just that we hadn't realised that some of the stuff we needed had actually arrived, it was stored in the shed …' he stopped as he really didn't know where he was going with this. All the materials had been there well in advance, and this could probably be checked easily. He didn't know why he'd said that as an excuse, it was stupid.

Andrew stared at him hard for a few moments, then said, 'make sure you check everything off properly when the next delivery arrives. That will be on Monday, here's a list of everything contained in that shipment. Contact me immediately if anything is missing.'

Gary took the list and nodding vigorously, not trusting himself to speak again.

'Ok, Gary, keep up the good work, and ring me if there are any problems at all. We want to help you to do an excellent job. Nice to meet you Dan.' Andrew nodded towards Danny who had finished sweeping and was tidying away tools. 'Have a good weekend both of you.'

Gary shook hands with Andrew and exhaled loudly as he watched the older man get back into his van and drive off. 'Crikey Dan, I think we got away with it.'

Danny sat down on the floor, 'Christ Gary, I'm knackered. I

think I'll sleep all weekend. Don't think I've ever worked so hard in my life.'

Gary laughed, suddenly feeling elated, things were going to be OK after all. 'Good idea Dan, get plenty of rest, we've got a lot to do next week too. But don't worry, I'll see you alright when I get paid for this job. And there'll be plenty more work if you want it. Now, let's lock up and get ourselves home while I've still got the energy to drive.'

CHAPTER 22

Jacob, Jack and Oliver talked excitedly about the film they had just seen, as they waited in the queue at the drive-through at MacDonald's. Gary half-listened to their chatter, but he was wondering how Danny was getting on at the Robinsons' house. Gary knew he shouldn't have taken any time off, but it was the long summer school holiday, and the boys were bored. Lisa was still suffering badly from morning sickness, and so she hadn't been able to take them out and about like she usually did. This morning the boys had rung him to say they were fed up, and to ask if he would take them out. Gary was torn when he heard their voices, but they all pleaded with him so much, that in the end he agreed to come home and take them to the cinema. Noah was too young for the film, so he stayed at home with Lisa, crying bitterly when he saw his brothers going off with their Dad. Gary sighed when he thought of his youngest son, he'd have to make it up to him somehow.

Eventually Gary reached the order window, and requested children's meals for the boys, and a burger for himself. When they sat in the car park eating their food the boys continued to chatter about the film, and Gary found himself smiling at their excitement.

On his way to pick up the boys, Gary had called in to see one of his existing customers, who had asked for a quote for some work. Ironically a few customers had contacted him while he was busy with the conversion. He could have done with the jobs a few weeks earlier when he didn't have much on. Unfortunately, most of the jobs were things that needed to be done urgently, so he couldn't book them in for when the conversion was finished. He had completed the most urgent ones himself this week, because he knew they'd just go elsewhere if he didn't. He didn't want to lose existing customers if he could help it.

As he chewed his burger he wondered again how Danny was getting on. Gary was pleasantly surprised at how hard his half-brother had been working on the conversion. He listened attentively when Gary explained how things should be done, and he took care over the work, and made a decent job. He was a bit slow, but that was because it was all unfamiliar. Gary had left Danny with a list of jobs to complete today, and as he hadn't rung, he assumed he must be getting on OK. Gary felt a twinge of anxiety. He had booked an electrician to come in the morning, so he hoped they were ready for him. Gary would have to pay him for his time anyway, and he knew he was busy. If they had to reschedule, then it could hold them up doing other jobs with the conversion. Gary suddenly lost his appetite and turned around to the boys.

'OK guys, are you all done eating? Got to get you home so I can get back to work.'

There was a collective groan from Jacob, Jack and Oliver. 'Daaad,' said Jacob with an exaggerated whine, 'you're always working, we've never seen you over the holidays, and Mum is just poorly all the time.'

'I know, I know, but I have to get this job done, it's really important. I've left Uncle Danny there on his own. I have to go back and check he's OK.' Gary said.

'I haven't finished my chips yet.' Oliver said, 'I'm still eating.'

'Me too,' said Jack.

'Well, you'll just have to eat as I drive,' Gary said firmly. 'I've been away long enough. And besides, Noah and your Mum will be missing you.'

Lisa looked a bit better when he got home, and Gary was pleased he'd been able to give her a break. Noah wasn't much bother on his own, he liked having his Mum all to himself, so Lisa had been able to rest. He stayed for a quick cup of tea with her while the boys told her all about the film. Just before he left he rang Danny's mobile, but after a few rings it just went to voicemail. *He must be busy*, Gary thought, but he felt slightly uneasy. Danny always had his phone nearby. He hoped everything was alright. Putting his cup in the sink, he kissed Lisa on the cheek, ruffled the older boys on their heads, picked Noah up and swung him around, and eventually made it back to his van, despite the boys' protests.

Traffic was light, so he was able to make it back to Willow Drive quite quickly. When he turned into the drive he saw that the lights were on in the garage, so Danny must be hard at work. Gary felt relieved, he'd been worrying for nothing. Danny must have been working too hard to answer his phone, that was all.

CHAPTER 23

Gary parked up and let himself into the house through the garage door. The lights were on, but there was no sign of Danny, and everything looked exactly the same as when Gary had left earlier in the day.

'Dan, you there?' Gary shouted, suddenly starting to feel alarmed. What if Danny had had an accident? There was no reply. *Perhaps Danny is making a cup of coffee,* Gary thought, and headed through to the kitchen. Still no Danny. Gary stopped and listened, he could hear a funny noise. Gary listened hard and suddenly realised what it was, someone snoring, loudly.

Gary followed the noise down the hallway, and into the Robinsons' sitting room. He slowly opened the door and took in the scene before him. Danny, flat out on one of the sofas, fast asleep, and on the coffee table before him there were four empty wine bottles and an empty tumbler. One of the bottles had fallen over, and the last drops of the blood-red wine were dripping onto the pristine cream and gold rug.

Anger welled up inside Gary and he raced across the room and started to shake Danny roughly. 'Wake up, wake up, what do you think you're doing?' he yelled.

Danny gave a start, opened his eyes and looked up blearily. 'Gary, my old mate, must have just nodded off,' he started, but Gary interrupted him.

'What the hell do you think you're doing? You're here to work, not to drink. And it's dripping on the rug. I knew I shouldn't have trusted you, you're a bloody disgrace.'

Danny grabbed Gary's arm, wiping drool from his mouth with the other hand. He started to cry. 'I'm sorry Gary, I am, but I was just making a cup of tea, and I saw the bottles of wine in the rack in the kitchen. I thought I'd only have one glass, give me some pep, but I must have had more than I thought.'

'You took some of the customers' wine?' Gary said. 'You can't just take stuff from customers. They left us out some tea and coffee and that's all we should have touched. What were you thinking of Dan? And there's no work done, the electrician's coming tomorrow. What the hell am I going to do?' Gary was now shouting hysterically at Danny, as he realised the full implications of the situation.

Danny grasped his arm harder, and his sobs got louder. 'I'm sorry Gary, I didn't mean to, I'm sorry, I'll run my head under the cold tap and get to work now …' he started, tears rolling down his cheeks.

Gary looked down at his brother and saw a younger version of their Dad. His anger left him, and he started to feel sorry for Danny. He should never have left him alone in a house with alcohol. Gary knew he couldn't resist it, he'd been stupid. He patted the hand clutching his arm. 'It's OK Dan, I know you didn't mean it. I'll sort it. Let's get you up from that sofa, see what sort of state you're in.'

After a struggle, they managed to get Danny into a sitting position, and then Gary helped him into the downstairs toilet. Gary got a cloth from the kitchen and tried to clean up the wine stain from the rug. It wouldn't budge. He'd have to ask Lisa what he could use to remove red wine from carpets. Neither of them drank wine, so he had no idea, but Lisa was great at removing the stains that the boys left from playing or dropping food or juice.

Gary picked up the empty wine bottles. He'd have to replace the four that Danny had drunk, he hoped it wasn't too expensive. He took the bottles out to the van and put them in the back. He'd dispose of them at home, and replace the missing ones, that way no-one would know.

When he came back into the house Danny was walking slowly along the hallway towards the garage. 'Shall we get on, work, I could do stuff …' he slurred.

'No way Dan, you're not doing anything except going home and sleeping this off.' Gary said, and he helped his brother out to the van.

It was late by the time Gary got back to the Robinsons' house. He'd taken Danny home, and made sure he'd eaten something before he left. Danny had become increasingly chatty as he woke, and Gary found it difficult to get away.

Gary looked around the conversion and sighed. He had to be ready for the electrician in the morning, so he'd just have to work all night if necessary. He wondered if Danny would have recovered enough to work the next day? He wasn't sure, he suspected he'd have a hell of a hangover. But he couldn't worry about that now, he'd just have to get on with it.

Several hours later, Gary heard footsteps walking up the Robinsons' driveway. He was up a ladder, pulling some wires through the ceiling beams, and couldn't see who it was. It couldn't be the Robinsons home already, he knew that. It was getting dark, a bit late for visitors. There was a rap on the conversion door, and a voice shouted. 'Can you open up please? It's the police.'

Gary immediately felt alarmed. Had something happened to Lisa or the boys, or his Dad? Perhaps it was Danny? He nearly tripped as he rushed to get down the stepladder and raced over to the door. He opened the door to find two uniformed police officers outside. Gary looked at them, his heart thumping.

'Evening Sir,' said one of the officers. 'Is this your house?'

'No,' Gary replied. 'I'm doing some building work when the owners, the Robinsons, are away on holiday.'

'Can we come in Sir?' Gary swung open the door and let them in.

'Can you tell me your name?' the officer asked. Gary confirmed his name and then his address, the name of his firm, and who he was working for.

'You're working a bit late, aren't you?' the officer said suspiciously. 'One of the neighbours was concerned, seeing lights on when the householders are on holiday. That's why they rang us.'

'I'm sorry to have caused any trouble, we had an unexpected delay today, and there's an electrician coming tomorrow, so we needed to be all ready for him. I thought I'd carry on and get it done. We're on a tight schedule.' Gary explained.

Eventually everything was sorted out and the police officers left. Gary sat down on a box, a bit shaken. He'd managed to persuade them not to ring Mark Greenwood at Unique Interiors, explaining that it was his first job for them, and he wanted to make a good impression. The police officers had checked Gary's ID, and his van's registration, and had a good look around the conversion, and into the ground floor of the house. They'd seemed satisfied with his explanation, and had left on friendly terms, telling him not to work too late. Gary grimaced when he thought of that remark. Them turning up had caused a further delay, and he was tired already. But there was nothing to do but keep on working, even if it took all night. He had to have all the wires in place so that the electrician could do his bit and give them the installation certificate, otherwise they'd never be finished on time.

Gary stood up, stretched, and headed back over to the stepladder.

CHAPTER 24

Gary walked around the conversion with a notepad and pen in his hand. He was making a list of what still needed to be done. It was now the end of week three, and they only had another few days to finish the job before the Robinsons came home from their holiday. Gary sighed, there was still so much to do. According to the schedule prepared by Andrew Foster, they should be doing final cosmetic finishes, and cleaning up next week, but the bathroom fittings weren't in place, the kitchen units needed to be assembled and fitted, there was no flooring down, the ceiling still needed to be finished, there was painting to do, and then all the finishing such as sockets, bathroom accessories, and cleaning.

Gary felt an overwhelming feeling of hopelessness, coupled with anxiety when he thought about it. How were they going to get it done? Danny hadn't been well for a couple of days, and although he'd turned up to the job by lunchtime, he worked even more slowly than normal. He didn't say anything, but Gary suspected that Danny was drinking again, and his "illness" was really a hangover. On the third day Gary had been delighted when Danny had contacted him early in the morning, saying he was feel better, and asked for a lift into the job. Gary had managed to avoid leaving the job too, and so in the last three days they had made substantial progress. But they'd lost so much time.

Footsteps behind him roused Gary from his thoughts. He looked around at Danny who was watching him and looking concerned. 'There's still a lot to do, isn't there?' he said.

'You can say that again,' Gary replied. 'The owners are back the middle of next week, we're supposed to be all finished by then. I'm not sure how we can get it all done.'

'I'm not doing anything over the weekend, I don't mind coming in and doing some extra. Make up for the time I missed when I wasn't well.' Danny offered.

To his surprise, Gary felt a prickle in his eyes, as if he was going to cry. 'Dan mate, that would be great. Lisa won't be happy with me, but with a final push, perhaps we can just about make it?' he said, his voice thick with emotion.

Danny broke into a smile. 'We'll give it a good go. Let's hope the neighbours don't report us to the police for working at the weekend though!

Gary smiled back, suddenly feeling a little more optimistic. 'Great, let's call it a day, and I'll pick you up first thing in the morning.'

After taking Danny home, Gary detoured to the supermarket to pick up the groceries for the weekend. He'd offered to go, partly to save Lisa having to carry the shopping, but also because he wouldn't spend as much as she would. Their financial situation was really very serious now. The small jobs that he'd managed to fit in around the work on the conversion had kept them going with day to day expenses, but they didn't have enough to cover their rent, and they had just received a final reminder for their gas bill that morning. He had to get the conversion finished. With the money coming from Unique Interiors, he could perhaps arrange an overdraft at the bank to tide them over until he was paid. In the meantime, the shopping would just have to be the essentials.

Gary reached into the back of the van for some shopping bags, and as he rummaged around something clinked. *Dammit*, he thought, *the empty wine bottles*. He had tried to replace the bottles of wine that Danny had taken from the Robinsons' wine rack, but none of the places that he had tried had stocked that particular brand. He had taken a photograph of the label on his phone – he'd try in the supermarket, see if they had it.

The wines and spirits section of the supermarket was one aisle that Gary and Lisa never visited. Neither of them drank alcohol, except on very special occasions, and then it was usually just cider or lager with lemonade in it. There was so much wine, Gary didn't know where to start. A young man was stocking shelves from a large trolley, so Gary went up to him and asked if they stocked this wine, showing him the photograph on his phone.

The assistant took hold of Gary's phone and studied the label closely. 'Sorry, we don't stock that one, I think it's something special. We have other ones that are very good,' he said.

Gary took his phone back, smiling at the young man. 'It's for a present, has to be that one especially. Thanks anyway, save me looking. Any idea where I might be able to get it?'

The young man shook his head. 'Not sure on that one, Waitrose perhaps, they have a good stock? Or you could try an off-licence or specialist wine place – one of those wine warehouses, but you'd have to buy a case if you went there. It may have come from one of those online wine suppliers.'

As he listened to the young man talking, Gary felt annoyed. *Why did Danny have to drink the wine? If it was something special the Robinsons would notice it was missing. Why couldn't it just have been some supermarket plonk that would be easy to replace?* In the end, he resolved to look in some more shops over the next few days and concentrated on finding the items on Lisa's shopping list. It was in the cleaning products aisle that he remembered about the stain on the Robinsons' rug. He hadn't been back in the sitting room since he found Danny drunk, and he'd forgotten all about it. He resolved to ask Lisa about removing wine stains when he got home, and mentally added 'cleaning the rug' to his 'to do' list.

CHAPTER 25

As the taxi pulled away from the airport, Sue looked out of the window at the rain. Laughing, she turned to Peter and said, 'you were right, it IS raining, good old British weather!'

Peter nodded and said, 'and it's a bit chilly too, we're not used to that.'

They looked at each other and smiled. 'You chose well Pete, Antigua was lovely.' Sue said, sitting back and thinking how relaxed she felt.

'Yes, I think that was one of my better choices. I didn't want to come home, it was so lovely to be warm all the time, and just relax and have fun.'

Sue smiled, and nodded. It had been a wonderful holiday. They hadn't done much sight-seeing but had spent most of their time in the resort, swimming, reading, sleeping, eating. She was starting to get a bit bored as they got into the third week, but it seemed to do Peter good. His symptoms hadn't been so bad, just the occasional tremor and muscle weakness. And it had been good to spend lots of time together and not have any worries for once.

Sue's thoughts were interrupted by Peter saying, 'I'm looking forward to seeing the conversion, see how it's all turned out. I know we've seen the plans, but I still can't imagine what it will look like. It's funny to think it'll be totally transformed from when we left, when it was just a garage. I think I might put a plaque over the door, saying "Man Cave",' he joked.

'Does that mean that no girls are allowed? I'm looking forward to seeing it too. I hope they've made an excellent job of it. They should have, considering how much it's costing.'

'I expect there will be a few things to finish off. Won't be up to your exacting standards! Is it Friday that their quality guy is coming around to make the list of snagging to finish? Andrew, isn't it?'

'Yes, that's right, Andrew Foster. He's coming around on Friday morning, thought that would give us time to have a look around, try everything, see if there is anything that leaks, or doesn't work, or that we don't like. The workmen will be there too, so they'll be able to get straight on with anything that needs done. Hopefully it should just take them the afternoon, so it'll be all done by the weekend.' Sue said.

'Great, we'll be able to go shopping for furniture and stuff over the weekend.' Peter said.

Sue looked at him, frowning, 'do you think we need to furnish it already?'

Peter smiled, 'guess I'm just eager to see it all finished. But I've been feeling so well I may never have to use it.'

Sue laughed, 'that's what I was thinking, you old fraud. We might have to rent it out to students or something.'

Peter joined in her laughter, but then they both fell silent, and looked in opposite directions out of the taxi windows. It would be nice to think that Peter would never need to use the conversion, but they both knew that wouldn't be the case.

CHAPTER 26

As the taxi pulled into their street, Sue felt some of her old tension return. There would be lots to catch up with when she got back to work, she knew that. She was dreading going back. It had been nice to have a long break away, and the holiday had been great, but somehow it just made the thought of returning even harder.

The taxi driver pulled into their driveway but had to stop short as the route to the front door was blocked by a skip. Peter paid the driver and they all got out of the car. The driver retrieved their luggage from the boot, and as he brought the cases round to the front of the taxi he remarked, 'you've got a bit of cleaning up to do there, made a bit of a mess of your driveway. Always the same when you have the builders in, leave you with all the mess.'

Sue felt her jaw tighten as she surveyed the state of the driveway and front garden. The skip was overflowing, and it was obvious that the driveway had been used as a workspace, as there was sawdust, bits of polystyrene and cardboard, and empty containers scattered around, including on the grass. She turned her attention to the conversion itself. The window and door were installed in the front, but they didn't seem to be finished. There was a noticeable gap around the door, and the glass in the window was filthy, with stickers still in place. Sue felt her anger rise. She'd paid for a complete job, including a full clean. The idea was they went away, the work was done, and the conversion was all ready for furnishing and occupation, whenever they needed it.

Peter was also looking around, and he said, 'there doesn't seem to be anyone here, there are no lights on. I thought the building team was supposed to be here to show us how everything worked? It doesn't look as if they are finished.'

'No, it doesn't,' Sue said tightly. 'Come on, let's get in, and have a look from the inside. They might have had to go and pick up some equipment or something.' She picked up one of the suitcases and marched towards the main entrance to the house.

Sue had opened the door and walked into the hallway, before Peter managed to make it along the drive, carrying the rest of the luggage. As Peter entered, she said, 'have you seen this Pete? Footprints all over the hall floor. Why have they been coming in and out this way? What a mess they've left.'

Peter replied, 'and the sitting room door is open. I know I closed it when we left, I always check the doors. Why on earth would they have to go into the sitting room?'

Sue pushed open the sitting room door and went in. She looked around and immediately noticed something red on the new gold rug under the coffee table. She walked over to see what it was. It was a mark of some sort, a stain.

'Have you seen this Pete? It looks like a wine stain. That wasn't there when we left, I would have noticed it. It stands out like a sore thumb.' She said, anger rising in her voice.

'I agree, it definitely wasn't there. I vacuumed in here just before we left for the airport, I would have noticed it. But surely it can't be wine? Do you think they were doing some prep work in here, and it's something they've used in the building work?' Peter suggested.

'But why would they need to work in here? It might be something else, but whatever it is, it shouldn't have been in here. Looks like they've been having a party,' Sue replied. 'Come on, let's have a look at the work they've done.'

Together, Peter and Sue headed for the kitchen. There were footprints all the way along the hall, and into the kitchen, clearly visible on the marble floor. The new doorway into the conversion was in place, and the door and frame had been painted, and looked finished. Sue felt herself relax a little. Peter was just reaching out for the door handle, when Sue thought of something. 'Hang on a minute Pete, I just want to check something.' She moved over to the wine rack and looked at the contents. She had bought a case of Peter's favourite red wine just before they left for their holiday, as they had been down to their last bottle. So that meant there should be 13 bottles in the rack. She knew immediately that there wasn't that many but counted them anyway. Nine bottles. She turned to Peter.

'Someone has been drinking our wine. There are four bottles of red missing.' Sue moved over to the wine cooler. 'I'm not sure about the white, I don't know how much we had.'

Peter shook his head. 'That's unbelievable, isn't it? I'm speechless.'

'Explains the stain on the rug. Come on, let's have a look at the work, see if they managed to fit any in around drinking our booze.'

Together Sue and Peter opened the door into the conversation, groping for the light switch, so they could get a good look around.

'Well, it still looks like a work in progress.' Peter remarked after looking around for a few seconds. 'But I think it'll be nice when it's finished, the space is bigger than I thought.'

Sue gave a brief smile. 'Think you're looking for the silver lining! But yes, you're right, it is a nice space, and there's a great view of the garden from the bi-fold doors.' Sue moved to the big doors and looked out. 'But should there still be wires hanging out? It's supposed to be all finished,' she said, looking up and pointing at the bare wires hanging out of the ceiling. 'Maybe that's where the spotlights are going?'

'I think you're right,' replied Peter. 'Still a lot of plastering to finish and decorating to do. And there is no sink in the kitchen.'

Sue turned around to look at the small kitchen area. 'The units look nice, but they're all finger-marks.' She walked over and opened the cupboard doors. 'And the insides are full of sawdust, and what looks like someone's discarded sandwich wrapping.' She said, speaking tightly. 'There is a hole cut out for the sink, but it's not fitted. I think that must be it over there.' She pointed to a cardboard-clad parcel leaning against the wall. Sue sighed. 'Let's have a look in the wet room.'

Peter opened the door to the wet room, and they peered inside. At first glance, it didn't look too bad. At least it seemed to be complete. Peter groped for the switch and turned on the lights. He heard Sue take a deep intake of breath. Everything was in place, but the finish was awful. The wet room had obviously not been cleaned since it was completed, and all the surfaces were dusty and smeared. There were globules of white sealant on the chrome radiator, on the new vanity unit doors, on the washbasin and on the toilet seat. Peter went up to the shower unit, which seemed to be leaning forward. He put out his hand and touched it, and it sagged forward even more. He turned around to look at Sue, who was standing still, looking stricken. He turned on the shower, there was a gurgling noise and then water started to come out of the shower head, and out of two places in the pipe. The shower unit started to lean forward alarmingly, and Peter quickly turned off the water. He looked down at the water, watching it run away, and he noticed some of it seep down a gap in the edge of the flooring, where it should have been sealed and watertight. He pointed, wordlessly, to it, and Sue followed his gaze.

Sue then moved across to the vanity unit. It was solid oak and had cost a fortune. They'd picked a style that was specially designed for people in wheelchairs, just in case Peter ended up needing to use one. The unit had a high gap in the middle and cupboards at either end. The top of the unit was marble, with a matching basin standing on top. Sue had spent ages picking out the marble, choosing a colour she'd particularly liked. She thought about the care she'd taken, as she looked down at the unit. It was impossible to tell what colour the marble was, as it was covered with a fine layer of white dust. *Plaster or filler or something,* she thought. She turned on the tap and water ran into the basin. *Well, that worked,* she thought. As soon as she turned off the tap, she heard a dripping noise. Looking around she noticed water dripping through the bottom of the unit and onto the floor.

'This doesn't work properly either.' Sue said, turning to Peter, who was examining the tiling on the wall opposite the shower.

'This tiling is dreadful. I could have done better myself. Some of it's not grouted, and the tiles don't line up. Look here, you can see what I mean.' Peter pointed to the wall. Sue crossed over and stood beside him.

'Christ, what a mess it all is. This isn't just incomplete, it's shoddy workmanship. I'm going to make a cup of tea and then ring Unique Interiors and see what they're playing at. Come on Pete, let's get out of this place, it's making me feel depressed.'

They both turned and walked back into the kitchen. As Sue went over to the kettle, Peter went over to the kitchen table and sat down. When Sue brought over the tray of tea things, she was struck at how pale Peter looked, despite his tan.

'You ok, you look a bit tired?'

'Yes, I'm Ok,' Peter replied, 'just a bit disappointed I guess.'

As he spoke Peter involuntarily looked down at his hand, and Sue noticed for the first time that he was suffering from a bad spasm. She felt her heart sink, he'd been so well the last few days that she'd begun to believe that his illness wasn't progressing. But seeing him like this made all the anxiety and concern rush back. *Probably the stress of the shambles in the conversion*, Sue thought, again feeling angry at the unfairness of everything.

CHAPTER 27

Gary had just turned into Willow Drive when he saw a taxi pulling out of the Robinsons' drive. Damn, I wanted to be there when they got back. I hope Danny is doing a good job of explaining the plan to finish off the outstanding work. As he was thinking this, Gary noticed a familiar figure walking along the pavement. It was Danny. He must have been for lunch. As Gary slowed to speak to Danny, he realised that his half-brother was swaying slightly. He must have been drinking again. Thank goodness I found him before he got back to the house.

As Gary pulled up alongside Danny he wound down the van window, and said, 'Dan, it's me, where have you been? The Robinsons must be back, I've just seen a taxi come out.'

Danny smiled broadly. 'Hiya Gary. How did you and Lisa get on at the hospital? I've just been out for a bit of lunch. Didn't think they'd be back already. We better get along and show them round.' His words were slurred, and he swayed as his stood talking.

Gary swore under his breath. He should have been at the conversion this morning, made sure everything was tidied up. But Lisa had an ante-natal appointment, and he couldn't let her go alone, even if they'd found someone to look after the boys. He'd given Danny a list of jobs to do so that the conversion would look tidy for the Robinsons coming back. Of course, the appointment had taken much longer than he thought, and Lisa looked tired out, so he'd taken her for some shopping on the way back, save her going out later.

'Get in the van,' he said curtly. 'It was a liquid lunch I see. Did you get all the jobs done?'

'Well, I never actually got there ….' Danny started to say.

'What?' Gary said, incredulous. 'It's the afternoon, where have you been Dan?'

'I called into that café along my road for a bit of breakfast, had nothing in the house. Bumped into a mate of mine, got chatting, and he had a dead cert., so I went to the bookies with him. Then it was getting on for lunchtime, so I thought I'd have some lunch and then crack on,' Danny said, chuckling to himself. 'He's a right laugh my mate, had me in stitches all morning …'

'But Dan, I told you how important it was to get the place tidied up before the Robinsons got back,' Gary started, but he stopped when he could see that Danny wasn't listening. 'Come on, I'll take you home, you can sleep it off.'

Gary dropped Danny at home as quickly as possible, and then headed back to Willow Drive. He'd go in, be friendly, explain to them that there was still some work to do, and get straight on with it. *They might be OK about it*, he thought. *The garage will look so different from what it was when they left, they won't notice the details. It'll be fine.*

Sue was just clearing away the tea tray when she heard a noise from the conversion, and then there was a knock on the kitchen door, and a voice called out. 'Hello, Mr and Mrs Robinson, are you there? It's the builder.'

Sue was just crossing to the door when it opened, and a thin young man walked straight into the kitchen. Peter was walking across from the table, and the young man held out his hand to him.

'Hi, Mr Robinson, Gary Mills, I'm working for Unique Interiors, I'm in charge of your conversion. By you spoil your wife, don't you? Fab house like this, long holiday in the sun. She's a lucky woman.'

Grinning, he turned towards Sue. 'I hope you realise how lucky you are?'

Sue ignored his outstretched hand. *Lucky? She thought. Who is this idiot? What does he know about us?* She could feel a rage rising inside her, and she spoke tightly, through clenched teeth.

'We have inspected the work and we are very unhappy with what we've seen. The quality of the finish is appalling. I was just going to ring Andrew Foster at Unique Interiors and complain.'

Gary continued smiling, but he could feel his heart thumping, and suddenly he felt hot. 'There are still a few bits that need to be finished, and then we'll clean it up and then it'll look as right as rain, you'll see. Should have stayed on holiday for another day or two,' he said, trying to placate Sue, whose eyes were flashing in an alarming manner. 'No need to phone Andrew, I'll get it sorted for you.'

'Where are the rest of the workmen?' Sue asked. 'Are you just working on your own? We were told there would be a full team of skilled tradesmen completing the job. And we paid for a full conversion, decorating and cleaning. It's obviously a long way off that, there is more than a day or two's work still to do.' She looked directly at Gary as she said this.

'Don't you worry about it, I know what I'm doing, I have my own building firm. I can see you like things nice, and in another few days you'll be so pleased with the work you'll be inviting me around for Sunday lunch.' Gary said, trying to sound reassuring. He found this woman a bit scary, she was glowering at him. As he spoke her eyes opened wider and she looked ready to explode. She was just about to speak when her husband spoke for the first time.

'We have tried the shower, it's hanging off the wall, and it leaks. The wash basin leaks, and the tiling is sub-standard. We have also noticed footprints in our hallway and sitting room. Why have you or your workmen been in there? There was no need. Some of our wine is missing, and there is a wine stain on our rug. I don't know what's been going on here, but it's not the level of service that we expected. I agree with my wife, we should speak with Andrew Foster about this, see how we can resolve the matter.'

Sue nodded vigorously. 'Yes, I'm going to ring Andrew now, he needs to know the situation here.'

Gary started to feel angry. What was the matter with this

woman, she wouldn't give him a chance? 'But I'm here now, and I'm going to get to work. Honestly, I'll have it sorted in no time, and some more of my team will be here tomorrow. No need to trouble Andrew.' Then, trying to calm down, he said, 'you're probably just tired from the journey, why don't you go and put your feet up, and I'll get on? You'll hardly know that I'm here.'

Sue had walked over to the bench to pick up her mobile phone. Holding it in her hand she turned back towards the young man. She felt heat rise in her body, and her fists clenched. *How dare he speak to her in such a patronising way? Who the hell did he think he was, incompetent little oik?*

'I am ringing Andrew Foster, and I don't want you to touch another thing. You've done enough damage. In fact, I don't want you in my house, I want you to leave now.' Sue said, her jaw tight.

Gary began to speak, 'but I've got to finish …' but Sue stopped him, speaking in a raised voice.

'Get out of my house, now. Or I am phoning the police.'

'Yes, I really think you should go.' Peter said, more calmly. 'Please leave.'

'We can sort this out.' Gary started to say, but seeing the fury in Sue's eyes, he turned and walked back into the conversion. He heard footsteps behind him and turned to see both the Robinsons following him. *Don't they trust me to leave?*

As they reached his van, he decided to try again. 'Look, I'm sorry, we seem to have got off on the wrong foot. If you can just see it from my point of view, I'm being paid to do this job, and I just want to finish it. Can't you just let me get on, and not get Andrew involved?'

'See it from your point of view?' Sue raged. 'What about our point of view? We are the injured party here.'

'I don't know why you're making such a fuss. You're no worse off, you've got the rest of your house to live in while I finish the job. It's not as if you need any more space just for the two of you.' Gary said, hoping he could appeal to reason. But this just seemed to make things worse.

'Get into your van and get off our property.' Sue said. Trying to think of something to say to resolve the situation, Gary slid open the side door of his van, and put his tool bag inside. As it dropped into the rear foot well, there was an unmistakably clink of bottles. Sue rushed forward and peered into the van.

'Our wine.' She said triumphantly. 'I knew you'd taken it. Drinking on the job, no wonder it's such a mess. And you're driving around under the influence of alcohol, you could kill someone. You're nothing but a criminal. A drunk and a criminal.' Sue looked at the phone in her hand, pointed it towards the van and took a few photographs of the empty bottles. 'That's my proof. Just in case you dump the empties.' And then she turned and marched back towards the house.

Gary closed his eyes in horror. *Why didn't I replace the wine? Dammit Dan, why did you have to drink it?* He noticed that Mr Robinson hadn't followed his wife, and he was looking at him more sympathetically.

'Addiction is a terrible thing. You need to get help before it ruins your life. You should go and see your GP, he'll be able to refer you for some help.'

'I hardly ever drink,' Gary started to say. But how could he explain it to this kind-faced man, in a way that would seem alright? He just nodded and went around to the driver's side of the van, got in, and slowly drove away.

When Peter returned to the house, Sue was speaking to someone on the phone. As he took a seat at the kitchen table, he half-listened to his wife's conversation. He couldn't remember ever seeing her so angry. She must be on the phone to someone at Unique Interiors, as she was outlining what they'd found when they got home. Peter thought about the young man who'd just left. He didn't seem to be drunk, but he obviously couldn't help himself, stealing and drinking wine from a house he was working in. Peter sighed. *Some people really know how to screw up their lives,* he thought and turned to Sue as she ended her call.

CHAPTER 28

Sue was waiting at the door of the conversion next morning, when Andrew Foster from Unique Interiors arrived for his 10am appointment, as agreed on the telephone the previous day. Sue had been up since 6am, no longer able to sleep, after a restless night where her rage at the state of the conversion had grown since the previous day. She kept thinking about Gary Mills' sarcastically smiling face, 'you're lucky,' that's what he'd said. Lucky was the last word Sue would have chosen to describe herself.

'Come in,' she said curtly, at Andrew's offered greeting, and she led him straight into the conversion, and started pointing out the faults. Andrew followed Sue around, silently making notes on a clipboard that he'd brought with him. When they finished the tour of the work, Sue asked if he'd like a coffee. Andrew said that he would, so she led him into the kitchen, where Peter was sitting at the table, reading his newspaper.

Andrew and Peter chatted about the news while Sue made coffee and brought it over on a tray to the table. After the coffee was poured and distributed, Sue and Peter looked expectantly at Andrew, who eventually commented on the work.

'First of all, I want to apologise. This isn't the standard of work that we promised, or that I expected to see. Mills Property Services is a new sub-contractor for us. We did carry out due diligence before employing Mr Mills and his team, but it seems as if he hasn't upheld his part of the bargain.'

Sue couldn't help herself any longer, she started to speak. 'We didn't realise that you used sub-contractors, we thought that you employed your own workers. We are very disappointed, both with the work, and the attitude of that Gary Mills person when we arrived back. He was rude and unpleasant.'

Andrew shook his head, 'I'm sorry to hear that, he always seemed pleasant when I spoke with him, I can only assume he was feeling a bit ashamed of the work, and that came over in his manner. We will, of course, expect him to finish the job and make good all the faults, with the utmost urgency, even if he has to bring in extra workers to get it done,' Andrew started, but Sue interrupted.

'I refuse to have that man back in my house, I want someone else to do the work.'

Andrew shook his head. 'We expect Mills Property Services to put the work right, it's their responsibility, they have signed a contract with us. I assure you that I will oversee the work personally, to make sure it's up to standard. We don't have any other teams available at the moment.'

Sue could feel her head starting to thump, and her face felt flushed. She was trying to calm herself before speaking, when Peter spoke instead.

'I'm sorry but I have to agree with my wife. I don't think it's fair to ask us to have Mr Mills back in our house. You see, not only is the work substandard, but we have evidence that he has a drink problem. And unfortunately, he has been helping himself to our wine when he should have been working. We really couldn't trust someone like that to do a decent job.'

Sue sighed, she was glad that Peter had brought that up. She didn't trust herself to discuss it without shouting. Andrew Foster looked shocked.

'That's a very serious accusation. What makes you think that?'

Sue stood up and walked over to the wine rack. 'I bought a whole case of wine the day before we left for our holiday. It's Peter's favourite, we were down to one bottle, so as I was in town, I picked up a case. That's how I know there were 13 bottles, and there were only 9 when we got back.' She turned the rack slightly so that Andrew could see it. Then she picked up her mobile phone and walked back over to the table.

'And we saw empty bottles, with the same distinctive label, in

Gary Mills' van.' Sue scrolled through her phone as she sat down. She found the photograph and handed it over to Andrew.

Andrew studied the photograph carefully, and Peter said, 'and it's obvious that someone has been in our hallway and sitting room, there are dusty footprints on the floor, and a wine stain on the rug. That definitely wasn't there before we left for our holidays. Come on, I'll show you, we deliberately didn't wash the floor before you came.'

Led by Peter, they all walked through into the hallway, where Peter pointed out the footprints, and then into the sitting room, where Sue went over to the rug and gestured to the stain. 'This is a new rug, I'm not sure how we'll get that mark out, it will probably have to be specially cleaned.' She indicated to Andrew to take a seat on one of the sofas.

Calmer now, she said levelly, 'I can't tell you how disappointed we are at this business. I'm not a woman who likes to beat about the bush Andrew. I'm very tempted to sue your company for breach of contract. And we are considering a criminal action for theft of property. It might only be a few bottles of wine, but the thought that workmen were going through our house when we were away, well it just makes me shudder. Goodness knows if they've taken anything else, we can't be sure yet. We employed your firm because you have a good reputation, and we thought you'd have safeguards in place.'

Andrew's attitude seemed to change once he heard this statement, and he replied decisively. 'I agree Mrs Robinson, Mr Robinson. This is appalling and I'm as disgusted as you are. I will find one of our own in-house teams to put the work right, and as quickly as possible. As for the criminal action, well, that's up to you of course. I'm shocked, it looks as if Mr Mills was hiding a drink problem from us by the sounds of things.'

'Yes, I agree,' Peter said. 'I'm afraid it must be a severe problem if he has to steal from his customers' houses. He needs help, and I have some sympathy for him, but that doesn't help us with our conversion.'

Sue glared at Peter. She had no sympathy for Gary Mills and his drink problem. Everyone has problems, but they still behave decently. Gary Mills was obviously an addict who didn't know how to behave, drunk or sober.

Andrew left shortly afterwards, after taking some photographs of the house and the conversion. He repeated his promise that he would personally see the work was finished and to the required standard. 'Mills Property Services will not be working for us again, I assure you of that. We like to encourage smaller firms, but not at a risk to customer satisfaction, or our reputation. I can only apologise again.'

As they closed the door, Peter turned to Sue and said, 'you're not really going to the police, are you?'

'I should do,' she replied, 'he is a criminal. How dare he think he can steal from us, poking around our kitchen, lying on our sofa, getting drunk when we're paying good money for work to be done. He's stolen from us twice, once with the wine, and once for drinking when he's being paid to work. But the police have enough to do, I won't waste their time over this. But I don't want other people to fall prey to that man and his bogus firm.'

Peter smiled and patted her arm, 'good, I'm glad you're not taking it further. It would just be stress we don't need. Listen, I'm going to have a nap if that's OK, didn't sleep so good last night, and I think the journey is catching up with me.'

As Peter started climbing the stairs up to the bedroom Sue noticed how slowly he was walking, and he grasped onto the bannister as if it was a lifeline. For the first time, Sue noticed a tremor in his leg as he lifted it onto the next stair, and she suddenly felt a lurch of fear. The illness was progressing. He had seemed so well when they were on holiday. *Probably all the stress since we got back*, she thought angrily, again seeing Gary Mill's smiling face saying, 'you're lucky.'

CHAPTER 29

Thump, thump, thump. How can they be making so much noise?
Sue thought irritably. Shouldn't they be plastering, painting and
cleaning? They can do all of that without making a noise. Coming
home to work this afternoon had been a mistake. The team from
Unique Interiors had been working all week, and Peter said they
were making substantial progress. Sue hadn't been back into the
conversion, telling herself there was plenty time to see it when it
was all done. She shuddered slightly when she thought of it, it had
been so dusty and dirty and horrible when she saw it last. For once
on a Friday she had no clients in the afternoon, so an afternoon of
paperwork at home had seemed tempting. More relaxing than the
office she'd thought, and she'd miss the rush hour traffic coming
home. She'd assumed the workmen would be painting quietly in
the conversion and hadn't anticipated so much noise.

Sue felt her teeth grinding together. This should have all been
done while they were on holiday. Peter was tired out each evening
when she came in from work, it must be listening to that noise all
day that was doing it. It was all that Mills creature's fault. Not able
to concentrate on her work, Sue pulled her laptop towards her and
typed 'Mills Property' into the search engine. Eventually she found
a one-page website that seemed to be the one she was looking for.
There were some links from the website to a Facebook page, and
to some trade directories where you could add reviews and give
feedback.

Sue clicked onto the Facebook page first, and jumped back
slightly as the thin, smiling face of Gary Mills burst onto the screen.
She looked at him with hatred, remembering him saying, 'I hope
you realise how lucky you are.' She clicked 'next,' and there was a
family photograph of Mills, and a pretty woman with dark curly
hair and beautiful dark skin. Surrounding them were a gaggle of
four smiling children. Sue looked at them more closely, this must
be his family. All boys she noted, looking at them one by one. The
oldest one was very like his mother, with the same dark skin and
big brown eyes. His hair was also dark, but straight, like his
Father's. Then there was a toddler, an adorable little boy with

chubby legs, blonde hair and the same big brown eyes as his eldest brother. The boy next to him looked a real imp, grinning cheekily into the camera. He shared the same brown eyes as his mother and brothers, but looked more like his Father, with a thin face and mousy hair. The final boy looked a bit shy, he was biting his lip and peeping up at the camera. This one had his Father's hazel eyes, and was much fairer-skinned than his brothers, with dark blonde hair.

There was a caption under the photograph. *My beautiful wife Lisa and our four boys, Jacob, Oliver, Jack and Noah. Busy cooking up baby number five!*

Five children, Sue thought. *How old were Mills and his wife? In their twenties, no older. And they had five children already. They must be able to just pop them out at the drop of a hat*, Sue thought bitterly. It had never happened for Peter and her, despite all the treatments that they'd tried. *But sodding Gary Mills had four, soon to be five, just like that.* Seeing his family just made Sue even more furious. *He probably drives around drunk with his pregnant wife and his sons in his van. And having all those children must be expensive, no wonder he resorts to stealing his alcohol if he can get away with it. What an idiot he is*, she concluded. Sue felt an overwhelming need to get back at Gary Mills for the way he had spoken to her. She clicked back to his website. Yes, there was a guestbook, that would be a good starting place.

Half an hour later Sue had submitted scathing reviews to Mills Property Service's website and Facebook page. She'd taken her time drafting the email. She didn't want people to think she was some old battle-axe with nothing to really complain about. She carefully listed the faults that they'd found with the conversion, concluding that she was only posting as she didn't want anyone else to experience the same disappointment and inconvenience. She also said that someone else was having to put the work right for them.

Sue realised that Mills could easily remove these posts, even before anyone saw them, so she clicked through to the trade websites linked from his website. He couldn't remove feedback posted on these, so she submitted similar reviews on each website, with a title for her posts of 'Avoid at all costs, zero stars.' Each time she pressed 'submit' she felt a bit better. Sue wished there was some way she could post photographs, show people just how shoddy the work was. Peter had taken a lot of photographs before the Unique Interiors' team had arrived. So that he could look at the 'before and after' he'd said.

A couple of hours later, Peter came to find Sue, who was hammering away at her laptop, looking totally absorbed. 'Will you be much longer sweetheart? he asked, making her jump slightly.

'No, I'm just about done. Come here and I'll show you what I've been working on.' Sue said, looking more animated than he'd seen her for ages.

Peter went over to the desk and sat down beside Sue, who turned the laptop around slightly, so they could both see.

'I've been developing a website,' Sue said, 'it's to name and shame cowboy builders in the local area. I've bought a domain name and set up a few pages to get it started.'

Peter looked at Sue in surprise. 'I thought you had work to do, when did you have time to do this?'

'I couldn't concentrate on work with all the noise from the builders, so I decided to do this instead. I don't want other people to suffer like we have.' Sue said, looking serious.

'Are you sure that's why you've done it?' Peter asked. 'Is it not about getting back at Gary Mills, I know you blame him for everything.'

'I am mad at him, yes, and of course he's going to feature on the site. But how many other people have had to put up with situations like this? It's so stressful Pete, and some people won't be as assertive as us and what will they end up with? Imagine if we'd hired that Mills guy directly, we would have really struggled to get the work done. No, I feel someone has to do this,' Sue said, nodding decisively.

Peter looked concerned, and Sue said, 'what, have you got an issue with it?'

'Well, not really, but I was just wondering if it was legal?' Peter said slowly.

'I thought of that too,' Sue replied. 'But I'm backing up what I'm saying with photographs, so it's not as if I'm saying anything that isn't true. I'll have to monitor anything that goes on the website of course. I'm going to promote it locally so that people can add their own stories.'

'But isn't that why they have those trade websites, or business review sites?' Peter asked.

'I've been on them this afternoon, and you can't upload photographs or anything. That's what made me think of doing this. I think it's something that's long overdue actually.' Sue sounded determined.

'Ok,' Peter said, 'you've obviously given it a lot of thought, but it just seems to be a lot more work for you that's all. But I do like your website design, when did you learn to do that?'

'Oh, we went on a course from work on how to use WordPress. I use it to update my partners' blog each week. I used a template, so it was a lot easier than it looks,' Sue answered, sounding distracted. 'I'll just have to think about where I can publicise the site,' she went on, speaking more to herself than Peter.

'It's getting on a bit now,' Peter said, changing the subject. 'Should I ring for a take-away, I don't feel like cooking, do you?'

'Hmmm,' muttered Sue, 'whatever you like, not Chinese though, don't fancy beansprouts.' And she started moving the mouse, not removing her eyes from the screen.

CHAPTER 30

Gary looked into the rear-view mirror of the van, to straighten his tie and check that his hair was tidy, and he noticed a film of sweat on his forehead. *I look pale*, he thought, *probably lack of sleep*. He had just driven into the car park of Unique Interiors and parked up. Mark Greenwood's PA, Kelly, had rung him to make the appointment. He'd tried to engage her in conversation, to try to find out what was going to happen, but all she would say was that it was to discuss the Robinson job. Gary looked down at his hands, they were actually shaking. He rummaged in the glove-box of the van for a mint, his mouth was so dry, and his stomach was making ominous gurgling noises. He hoped he wouldn't vomit.

Luckily, he didn't have to sit in the reception area for long, as he was becoming increasingly agitated with each passing moment. The receptionist had smiled politely, but not engaged him in conversation, just rung through to Kelly to say he'd arrived. He heard footsteps come along the corridor and Kelly appeared, smiled tightly, and said, 'they're ready for you now, follow me please.'

As they walked along the corridor, Gary thought anxiously, *they, who was they? Will the Robinsons be there?* But when Kelly showed him into the office, it only contained Mark Greenwood and Andrew Foster. Both men nodded at Gary and Mark asked him to take a seat. Mark got straight to the point.

'I guess you know why we've invited you in Gary? We've had a serious complaint from the Robinsons about the work that you did.' Gary opened his mouth to speak, but Mark appeared not to see and carried on talking.

'Andrew has been out to view the work and he agrees with Mr and Mrs Robinson, the work is sub-standard, and not of the quality we expect from our sub-contractors. We have some photographs.'

Then followed the most humiliating ten minutes of Gary's life so far, as photograph after photograph was laid on the desk between them and discussed. Seeing each little fault in a large glossy photograph seemed to make it worse than the reality, and Gary found himself unable to speak as Mark and Andrew pointed out exactly what was wrong in each case. By the time they had finished, Gary was rubbing his sweating hands on his trouser legs and looking down at the floor. He could feel his face burning and for a horrible moment he thought he might cry. Eventually the photographs stopped, and Andrew spoke for the first time.

'I pointed out some of these issues when I came for the first inspection. You assured me you and your team were onto it. What happened?' He sounded as if he genuinely wanted to know.

'I had some problems with the team,' Gary mumbled, 'sickness and so on. We got behind and then rushed to get caught up.'

When Andrew replied, his voice was louder, his words clipped. 'I told you to contact me if you had any problems. If you were down on labour, then we might have been able to help. Instead you've just made us look like a bunch of cowboys. The Robinsons are, quite rightly, furious.'

Mark then joined in, and when Gary looked towards him, he saw that he had another photograph in his hand, but it was turned down, towards the desk, so Gary couldn't see what it was. 'They have also raised concerns over another matter. There were several bottles of wine missing from their kitchen, and a wine stain on a rug in their sitting room. What do you have to say about that?'

Gary couldn't speak, he just shook his head numbly. *Could he drop Danny in it?* But then he'd have to explain why he didn't sack him. *Best to say nothing*, he decided.

Mark laid the photograph face up on the desk. It was an enlarged picture of the back foot well of Gary's van, clearly showing the empty wine bottles. Gary stared at it in horror, that Robinson bitch had taken it when he was leaving, he hadn't realised it would be so clear. He couldn't deny it, he knew that, so again he said nothing.

'Do you deny that's your van?' Mark asked, sounding exasperated. Again, Gary just shook his head.

'So, you stole from a customer's house, drank on the job, spilled wine on their very expensive rug, and just left the empties in your van for the world to see? Do you really think that's acceptable behaviour?' Mark's voice was louder now, he was nearly shouting.

Gary still couldn't get any words out, and just continued to look down at the floor.

'Do you have nothing to say for yourself?' Mark was shouting now. 'What's the matter, didn't have time for a touch of Dutch courage before you came in?'

Eventually Gary managed to squeeze out a few words. 'I'm so sorry, I'll put it right, I'll go there now and start work straight away. Please give me another chance, I didn't mean ...'

He looked up when he heard a snort. Andrew Foster was laughing, but not in a very pleasant way. Mark just looked thunderous, his brows furrowed, and his face flushed with anger.

'Mr and Mrs Robinson have categorically said they don't want you anywhere near their property again. And quite frankly, I don't blame them. We've had to pull one of our teams off another job to finish the work for them, and to re-do things like the tiling which wasn't up to standard.'

'I'm sorry,' Gary mumbled again, he wanted to explain, but what could he say? *I couldn't afford labourers, there was only me and my alcoholic half-brother. Oh yeah, that would really bring out some sympathy.* His shoulders slumped, he felt totally defeated.

'Ok, then Gary, this is the situation.' Mark said, sounding a little calmer. 'We will put the work right, but as you didn't complete your contract, you won't be entitled to any payment.'

Gary interrupted, finding his voice at last. 'I won't be paid for all the time I spent working there? And what about my labourer, I mean labourers? I have to pay them. I must be entitled to something?'

'No, you're not,' Andrew butted in, sounding pleased. 'If you review the contract that you signed, the work must be completed as per the specification, and to the required standards before you get paid. You signed the contract, you should have checked it before you defaulted on the work. If you had contacted me then I could have helped, but you didn't.'

Gary really felt he was going to faint. No money at all? What was he going to do? But there was worse still to come. Mark resumed talking. 'To put the work right, we are having to replace some materials that we've already paid for. We've had to chip off those expensive stone tiles in the wet room for starters. We couldn't reuse them, so we've had to order more. Same with the flooring. You will be billed for the replacements. And we are having to pay overtime to our staff to finish the remedial work, so we will bill you for the cost over and above our initial estimate.'

'But I can't afford that,' Gary said, his voice rising almost to a whine. 'Not if you're not going to pay me for the work I've done.'

'Well hopefully your professional indemnity insurance will cover most of it.' Mark said, 'but we will be billing you. We offered you an opportunity here, and we're not going to end up out of pocket because of your incompetence.'

'Oh, and by the way,' Andrew joined in, 'the Robinsons are thinking about a criminal action in relation to you taking the wine. That's up to them of course.'

Gary stared at Andrew, his eyes wide in shock. 'A criminal action? Over a few bottles of wine?'

'Well, why not? It's theft, and it's the principle of the thing, isn't it?' Andrew replied, looked at Gary with disgust. 'Should have thought about that before you sat boozing when you should have been working.'

'Needless to say, we won't be asking you to do any more work for us,' Mark said coldly. 'Plenty more firms who won't cause us any trouble and be grateful for the work.'

Gary hung his head again, he felt physically drained, as if he'd been run over, or beaten up, or ran three marathons, one immediately after another.

'I think we're done here,' Mark said finally. 'Our finance team will be in touch.'

Gary managed to drag himself to his feet. He felt he should say something, but he just didn't know what. He kept his eyes down to the floor, nodded, and then headed back to the reception area.

Back in the van, he drove away as quickly as he could. He just wanted to be away from this place, from the shame and disappointment, and shock. As he drove through the town, he could feel tears running down his face, and his hands still shook as he grasped the wheel.

Eventually he realised he was near the river, and he pulled into a picnic area car park. There he gave way to his tears, put his head down on the steering wheel and sobbed in a way he'd never done before. Every time he tried to stop he thought about the look of contempt on Andrew Foster's face, and about how angry Mark Greenwood had been. Then he thought about Lisa, and how she had her heart set on a princess nursery for their new baby. *How the hell am I going to tell her?* And this thought brought on yet another burst of crying.

Eventually the tears subsided, but he couldn't stop replaying the conversation in his mind, again and again. The photographs seemed to get larger and larger whenever he recalled them. Had that Robinson bitch taken them? She'd taken the one of the wine bottles, so maybe she'd gone around taking a whole load of photographs, making maximum trouble. Suddenly Gary remembered what Andrew had said about criminal action. Gary thought about the Robinsons' beautiful house, and all their expensive stuff. They were going to the police about a few bottles of wine? 'Bitch, bitch, bitch!' Gary said under his breath, thumping the steering wheel. It had to be her, he'd seemed a decent sort of a bloke. *Why had Danny drunk the wine? We would have finished the job if he hadn't been drinking. Well, I'll not be able to pay him now, serves him right. But I'll not be able to pay anything else either.* And with that thought, Gary's tears flowed again.

CHAPTER 31

It was late when Gary got home, and Lisa was in the middle of getting the boys ready for bed. 'Oh, at last,' Lisa said, distractedly. 'Did you end up going over to finish off that job after your meeting?'

Gary shook his head, and said, 'I'll tell you all about it later. Let's get this lot sorted first.' After he finished with the bath and bedtime routine, including reading a story, he was starting to feel a little bit better. He could smell something cooking downstairs and his stomach growled. He hadn't eaten all day.

When he went downstairs Lisa was placing a plate of food on the kitchen table and had made him a cup of tea. He sat down and began to eat hungrily. Lisa chatted about the day, what the boys had been up to, and how they'd bumped into one of Jacob's friends from his judo class when they were out in town. Eventually Gary pushed the plate away, feeling much better than he had all day. Lisa picked up his plate and said, 'are you going to tell me what happened?'

Gary took a gulp of his tea and looked over at her. 'It's not good babe, the meeting didn't go well. They aren't going to pay me for the work that we did, and they are going to have to re-do some of the work, like the tiling, and they're going to bill me for the replacements.'

Lisa was silent for a few moments while she thought this over. 'But can they do that?' she asked eventually. 'You've done so much work, surely they have to pay you for that?'

'That's what I asked too,' Gary replied, 'but I signed a contract and there are clauses in it about the work having to be up to a certain standard, and about the job being completed. I don't think there is anything I can do about it. Oh, and I forgot, if the labour costs more than their original estimate, they are going to bill me for that too.'

'But why can't you go and put the work right? Then there won't be any additional labour. Can't you just pay for the replacement tiles or whatever, and finish the job?' Lisa asked, sounding exasperated.

'The couple who own the house, well, the wife anyway, doesn't want me back on her property,' Gary said uncomfortably. He hadn't told Lisa about Danny taking and drinking the wine. He'd only said that Danny hadn't been well and that's how they'd fallen behind on the job.

'That seems a bit extreme,' Lisa said. 'Can't the firm insist that you go back? Doesn't seem fair that you don't get a chance to put it right.'

'No, I asked, there is no way that's going to happen. I don't know what we're going to do Lisa, I was relying on that money. And the bills we'll get from them, well, I haven't paid my indemnity insurance, couldn't afford it, so I'll have to find the money for that, it won't be covered. I've no idea how much it will be, the tiles looked expensive,' Gary said, feeling despair start to overwhelm him again.

Lisa sighed deeply. 'I don't know why you wanted your own business Gary, I've never understood it. At least when you worked for someone else we had regular money coming in, and you didn't have all this hassle.'

'But I'd always just make the same money working for someone else,' Gary said. 'I thought having my own business, I'd be able to build it up, make more. And have the freedom to spend more time with you and the boys.'

'Well it doesn't work out that way, does it? You're always working, the boys have hardly seen you over the summer holidays. It's not fair on them, and for what?'

Gary wrapped his arms around himself and huddled up. He was hoping that Lisa would understand, and that she'd support him. Help him to work through this. 'The meeting was awful Lisa.

It's been a horrible day, they weren't very nice.'

'Where have you been all day Gary? Did you have some more jobs on?' Lisa asked, ignoring his remark about the meeting.

'I've just been driving around, thinking. I was really upset.' Gary said, looking at her, hoping she'd see how bad he felt.

'What, driving around, with the boys here driving me nuts? Why didn't you come home and take them out, give me a break? That's so selfish of you Gary, honestly, I can't believe it.' Lisa sounded angry.

'But I needed to think about it, it's such a big deal Lisa. I don't know how we're going to pay our bills.' Gary willed her to understand.

'And did you come up with any bright ideas while you've been driving around all day, wasting petrol?' Lisa asked sarcastically.

'No.' Gary mumbled, 'I didn't.'

'I think you should look for a job,' Lisa said firmly. 'And in the meantime, you'd better get in touch with all your past customers, see if any of them want any work done. I'm off to bed, I'm tired out, looking after the boys on my own all day, while you were driving around, *thinking*.' She rose to her feet while she said this and headed out of the kitchen.

Gary sat for a while in the kitchen, holding his tea mug in his hand. The tea was cold, but he sipped at it absently. Lisa didn't seem to understand what it meant and how difficult their finances were. *But what can she do about it? It's up to me to sort it out.* Gary slumped in his chair. Everything just felt so difficult and hopeless. He didn't know where to start putting it right. Lisa's words kept coming back to him. *Did she really not want him to have his own business?* He always thought that she was proud of him striking out on his own. His role model was George, the owner of the company that he'd worked in since he qualified as a plumber, following his apprenticeship. George and his wife Sally had the type of life that

Lisa and he had always imagined. They had a comfortable home that they owned outright, in a nice part of the town. They went on holiday twice a year and spent occasional luxurious weekends in country hotels. They both had a decent car. And best of all, their three children had grown up responsible and happy, and were doing well in their chosen careers. Their son was a doctor, their elder daughter a dentist. And their younger daughter, Jennifer, excelled in languages and she did some sort of interpreting job for MI6. Gary smiled for the first time that day as he remembered George telling him that. All the guys in the team had joked about Jennifer becoming a spy like Ian Fleming's 007. They started calling her 'Jenny Bond.' George had laughed along with them, but he was so proud of all his kids, and rightly so.

Working for George had been good for Gary. George's firm did all sorts of building work, so Gary had picked up lots more skills to supplement plumbing. The firm had a great reputation, and never needed to look far for work. As he got older, George didn't do any of the manual work himself, but instead oversaw estimates, design, ordering materials, dealing with customers, giving advice to the team, and making sure all the work was completed to a good standard. Sally did the paperwork, including all the invoicing, taxes, payroll and book-keeping. Because they both worked in the business, they jointly understood the pressures, and worked together to build it up. It gave them a strong bond. Gary had secretly hoped that when Noah went to school Lisa could learn some business skills and work with him. But of course, there would be the new baby now, so that wouldn't happen for years.

George's business wasn't as flashy as Unique Interiors, but it was a professional, solid firm that did excellent work. It had been a shock when George told them he'd decided to retire and was selling the business. The new owners already had a building firm, in a neighbouring town, and bought George's business to expand. They didn't need more plumbers, so Gary was able to take redundancy, and with the small amount that he got, he decided to go it alone. George had been a tremendous help to him when he started up 18 months ago. And some of George's existing customers had given Gary work when he was setting up, which had got Mills Property Services off to a great start.

But after 6 months, George and Sally had sold up and moved to a villa in Spain, and now Gary only heard from them at Christmas, via a letter and Christmas card. For the first time, Gary was pleased George had moved away. He'd hate him to see what a mess he'd made of everything. He recalled some of the things that George had told him. 'Remember Gary, the customer is always right. Always apologise, even if you've done nothing wrong. Say that you're sorry they're feeling that way. Once you've apologised it's easier to negotiate and sort things out.' And, 'even if it's just a small job, treat it like it's the biggest, most important job you've ever done. That way you'll build up a good reputation. Never, ever, let customers down. If you're going to be late, ring and apologise. But try and turn up when you say you will, and be respectful, take your shoes off, even if you're just going to measure for a job. You're in their home.'

Gary felt a little bit guilty, he hadn't always followed this advice. But then again, George had never had to deal with Susan Robinson. This was all her fault, the vindictive bitch. If she'd let him put the job right, then he would have been paid, and he wouldn't be sitting here alone now, feeling like crap. *I don't know how, but one day lady, you'll get your comeuppance, I'll see to that*, he vowed to himself. And with that thought he headed off to bed.

CHAPTER 32

The next morning, Gary woke early, and the house was quiet. Lisa was sleeping peacefully beside him, and the boys were still in their room. He took advantage of the stillness to plan for the day. He was feeling slightly more positive, and thought he'd concentrate on trying to get some work in quickly, see if he could head off financial disaster. His plan was to spend some time ringing around his past customers, say that he'd had a cancellation, so if they wanted any work done, he'd be able to fit them in quickly, and offer a discount. He couldn't afford any advertising, but perhaps he could do some fliers and take them around a few shops? He'd take the boys with him, get them out from under Lisa's feet for a while. They could stop off at the playground on the way.

But the first job he had to do was going to see Danny, and tell him the unwelcome news about Unique Interiors, and explain that he wasn't going to get paid. He'd do that this morning, no point delaying it any longer.

After breakfast, Gary explained his plan to Lisa, who smiled at him, and said it would be good for him to spend some time with the boys. Telling the boys to be good until he got back, Gary got into the van and headed over to Danny's flat. It was still early, so he was sure he'd find him at home.

Danny took a while to answer the door, and opened it dressed in boxer shorts and a t-shirt. His looked sleepy and crumpled, and Gary guessed he must have woken him.

'Morning Dan,' Gary said as cheerfully as he could. 'Did I get you out of bed? Sorry mate, got a lot on and thought I'd pop around early. OK if I come in for a few minutes?'

Danny smiled back and opened the door wider, nodding at Gary to come in. The flat smelled stuffy, of sweat and stale beer. The place was a mess, and Gary thought of his own comfortable and tidy home, and silently thanked Lisa for being so house-proud.

'Do you want a coffee?' Danny asked as they moved into the living room, but Gary shook his head.

'No, you're alright Dan, thanks. I've promised to take the boys to the playground, so I can't stay long.'

Danny looked a bit disappointed, and Gary wondered if he sometimes got a bit lonely, living here by himself? Gary thought he must make more of an effort to see Danny, perhaps invite him around for Sunday lunch. He had grown to know him better over the weeks they'd been working together, and he'd liked him, despite the problems.

Gary sat on the sofa, and Danny sat down in the armchair, and looked at Gary expectantly. Gary took a deep breath and went straight into what he'd come to say.

'I met with Unique Interiors yesterday. The news isn't good Danny, they aren't going to pay us for the work they did. Something in the contract, the work has to be completed to the client's satisfaction and up to their, Unique Interiors, standards. The work we did wasn't, so they won't pay up. And the customers won't let us go back to finish it, so they've got one of their own teams doing it. They're going to bill me for the replacement materials too.' Gary felt his mood sink again as he re-told the story. He could feel Danny's eyes on him.

'That doesn't seem right, all that work we did. You'd think they'd have to pay you something.' Danny said.

'Yes, I know, that's what I thought. But it's all in the contract. I probably didn't read it clearly enough, I just looked at the key bits, timescales, scope of works, fees.' Gary replied.

Danny sat thinking for a few moments, and then said, 'well you don't have to pay me everything you owe me all at once, just give me a bit to tide me over, and give me the rest later.'

Gary felt uncomfortable, Danny obviously didn't understand

what he was trying to say. 'I'm sorry Dan, I won't be able to give you anything. I haven't got any money, I was relying on this money to pay our rent and other bills, and I'm going to get a bill from them for the replacement materials. I'm seriously out of pocket.'

Danny stood up suddenly. 'You're not paying me for all that work that I did? Oh no, I'm not having that. You owe me, I broke my balls on that job, even came in over the weekend.'

Gary suddenly felt a little intimidated with Danny standing over him, while he sat on the low sofa. He tried to keep calm and replied, 'I'm sorry, I really am, and if I had any money I would share it with you. But don't you realise how serious this is for me? Oh, and I forgot, apparently the customers, Mr and Mrs Robinson, they might be going to the police over the stolen wine. The wine that you drank.' Gary said pointedly.

He immediately regretting saying this, as Danny flushed angrily and seemed to increase in size.

'Oh, now we're getting to it aren't we, you little cunt? It's all Danny's fault because he had a few glasses of wine. Trying to put all the blame on me because I like to drink and get out of paying what you owe. I wasn't born yesterday, you're not getting away with that.' Danny raged, spittle flying out of his mouth as he spat the words out.

'Whoa, whoa,' Gary said, trying to calm the situation. 'I'm not making any of this up. They had photos Dan, of the empty wine bottles in my van, and they're mad about the stain on the rug. I don't know if the police will do anything about it, but they knew how many bottles there were, and they're blaming me for drinking it. I didn't say it was you. But that's one of the reasons they won't let us go back to finish the job.'

But rather than calm Danny, this seemed to make him even more angry. 'You've taken the blame? Oh, of course smarmy little Gary will take the blame for his hopeless older brother, but he's not going to pay what he owes him. I know what you're like, going around so nicey nicey all the time, Gary the happy family man, Gary the good son, Gary helping out his poor drunken brother by giving him some work. You needed me because no-one else would work with you, that's the truth of it. I worked hard, and I expect to be paid.'

'And I will pay you, when I can, but I've got no money, you can't get blood out of a stone.' Gary said, starting to feel exasperated. He didn't know how to explain this any more clearly.

'No, you can't get blood out of a stone, but I can get blood out of you.' Danny said, and he leapt forward and punched Gary on the nose.

The pain seared through Gary's face like he'd been stabbed with a red-hot knife, and when he raised his hand to his face it came away covered in blood. Stunned, he jumped to his feet.

'What the hell are you doing? That's not going to solve anything. You messed up the job for me Danny, you've got to take some responsibility. I can't pay you, and that's that.' Gary turned to leave, but Danny blocked his way. When Gary tried to side-step him, Danny kept turning his body, blocking his path, and sneering at him in a threatening way. Suddenly Gary saw red, and he balled his fist and aimed a punch at Danny. He caught him on the side of the head, and with a look of surprise, Danny fell backwards into the armchair.

'I'll pay you when I can,' Gary said, and quickly left the flat.

Back in the van, Gary examined his nose in the rear-view mirror. It didn't seem to be broken, but it was still bleeding, and very red and starting to swell. His hands were shaking, he thought Danny would have shown some shame or remorse for his role in the whole sorry situation, he hadn't anticipated his anger. He couldn't believe he'd hit back at Danny. He was beginning to feel quite proud of himself. Hitting Danny had given him a bit of a rush, but now Gary's hands were shaking, he'd never had a physical fight before. He heard a door open in the street, and fearing it was Danny coming out for round two, Gary quickly started the van and drove away.

By the time he got home his nose had stopped bleeding, but his face and head were throbbing. The rush had gone, and he was beginning to feel bad about the whole situation. He hoped that Danny wasn't in debt, that he hadn't borrowed from a loan shark or something, thinking he was coming into some money. His reaction had seemed extreme, so perhaps he had. He sighed and went into the house.

As soon as he opened the front door, Lisa rushed out of the kitchen, looking pale and worried. 'Oh Gary, thank goodness you're back,' she said, not seeming to notice his swollen and bruised face. 'I've just had the landlord around, he says he's going to start eviction proceedings if we don't pay the rent by the end of the week. He was so nasty Gary, it was awful, and in front of the boys too.'

Gary pulled her into a hug. 'I'm sorry I wasn't here babe. He definitely said the end of the week? Do you think he might have been bluffing to get us scared?'

'No, he wasn't bluffing,' Lisa replied, her voice muffled from being buried in Gary's shoulder. 'He was serious. You know how hard it is to rent anywhere around here, he said he's got people waiting for houses like this.'

Lisa pulled out of Gary's embrace and looked into his face. 'Oh Gary, what are we going to do? We'll end up on the streets at this rate.'

'Shush, it won't come to that. Come on, I'll make some tea and we'll discuss it.' Gary said, trying to reassure her. But inwardly he was agreeing with her assessment of the situation.

As Gary put the kettle on, Lisa sat at the table and wiped at her eyes. She looked pale and shaken and couldn't stop the tears escaping almost continuously.

'Where are the boys?' Gary asked as he waited for the kettle to boil.

'Jacob's friend James rang; his Mum has taken Jacob and Jack to the swimming pool with them. Noah's having a nap in his bed, and Oliver's in the boys' room, reading.' Lisa replied distractedly. 'Oh Gary, what are we going to do? she repeated, looking at him. Then she said, 'what's happened to your face?'

Gary brought over two mugs of tea and sat at the kitchen table opposite her. 'Yes, well, I've had a bit of an experience too, it was Danny, he wasn't happy that I couldn't pay him. He punched me.'

'What? He punched you, that's terrible.' Lisa said, looking horrified.

'He was mad that he wasn't getting paid, but I tried to explain our situation. He didn't seem to see that most of it was his fault.' Gary began, then stopped, remembering that Lisa didn't know about the wine.

'What do you mean, it was his fault?' Lisa asked immediately.

Gary sighed. He might as well tell her the truth. 'I was off doing another job, and while I was away, Danny drank four bottles of the customers' wine. He spilled some of it on the rug in their sitting room and it stained it. I was going to replace the wine, but I couldn't find the same one. The customers are making a fuss about it, threatening going to the police. They think I drank it. That's why they won't let me go back and finish the job.' He said all this quickly and then looked at Lisa to make sure she'd taken it in. She was staring at him with her eyes wide and her mouth set in a tight line.

'Well, did you tell that Andrew guy what really happened? That it wasn't you who drank the wine?' she asked.

'No, I didn't, how could I explain it Lisa? They'd want to know why I hadn't sacked him, they thought I had a whole team of men.'

'But you should have sacked him, you should have thrown him off the job and told him never to come back. No wonder the customers are mad, they've got every right to be. They're paying for a decent job and the workers are drinking their wine and spilling it on their carpet. I'd be furious too,' she said angrily.

'But I needed him to get the job finished Lisa, I didn't have anyone else to do it.' Gary replied, a bit shocked that Lisa was siding with the Robinsons. 'And my Dad asked me to give Danny a chance, said he was at a loose end.'

'Yes, and your Dad also said that Danny was on the wagon,' Lisa said, sounding exasperated. 'I don't know why you trust either of them, they're both drunks and liars. All they do is let you down and cause trouble. And now you've let us down.' She was shouting now. 'You shouldn't have taken on this job if you didn't have men to do it, it was stupid to rely on your useless, drunken relatives. What the hell are we supposed to do? You should have thought about your real family, me and the boys.' Lisa had stopped crying now, and was glaring at him, red-faced.

'That's not fair Lisa, I *was* thinking about you and the boys. If it had worked out we'd be set up.' Gary said, and he could hear his voice quavering. 'It was a fantastic opportunity.'

'Yes, such a good opportunity that you risked it by employing your useless, stupid, drunken brother. You're a pushover Gary, why can't you stand up to your Dad? He just takes advantage of you. And Danny's obviously just the same,' Lisa screamed. 'And now we're going to be out on the streets because of it.'

'I did stand up to Danny.' Gary said, 'I punched him back.'

Lisa looked at him, shocked. 'That's your idea of standing up to someone, physical violence? What a good example to your sons. How does that resolve anything? You're a wimp Gary, a useless, weak wimp. You've let us all down.' And with that she walked out of the kitchen and into the sitting room.

Gary stood to go after her but stopped himself. What could he say to her? She was right, he was useless, and he had let them down. But he was angry about what she'd said about his Dad and

Danny. They were his family, he had to try and help them if he could. Gary sighed. Lisa didn't have any family apart from him and the boys, so she probably didn't understand what it was like.

Lisa still hadn't reappeared when Gary had finished his tea, so he decided to leave her alone and give her time to calm down. They rarely rowed, and he guessed she would be as shaken as he was. It had been a hard morning. Gary thought about the landlord, perhaps if he could give him something, even part of what they owed, then he would change his mind? Gary reviewed his bank account on his phone. It would be a small amount, but it would be worth a try. He *had* to get some more work in. He needed to do something, so he decided to continue with the plan he'd made earlier, make some flyers to distribute around local shops, then ring around his existing customers to see if anyone wanted anything done.

Gary went quietly upstairs and peeped into the boys' room to check on Oliver. He was lying on his stomach on his bed, with his book in front of him. 'Hi Olly, did you not fancy going swimming with Jacob and Jack?' Gary asked. Oliver shook his head vehemently,

'No, I wanted to read my book. There was a nasty man came, he was mean to Mum, I didn't want to leave her on her own. She was crying,' Oliver said solemnly, his eyes brimming with tears. Gary went and sat on the edge of his bed and patted him on the back.

'I know Olly, Mum told me about it, it's OK, I'll deal with him now.'

'I heard you and Mum shouting at each other too. Why do people have to shout?' Oliver asked, a tear escaping and rolling down his cheek. Gary wiped the tear away with his finger and carried on rubbing the little boy's back.

'We were just a bit upset about the man, and a few other things. Everything's OK now, don't you worry,' Gary said, trying to sound reassuring. Poor little Olly, he was so sensitive.

'Are you sure?' Oliver asked, in a wobbly voice.

'Yes, sure, I promise.' Gary said. 'I'm going to make some adverts on the computer, do you want to come out later and help me deliver them?'

Oliver nodded his head. 'Just the two of us?' he asked, sounding hopeful.

'Well, we might have to take Noah, because he hasn't been swimming either. Will that be OK?'

Oliver looked up, thinking for a few moments. 'Yes, that's OK, he'd probably like it.'

'Ok, then, that's a deal. You read your book, and I'll get on the computer and make my adverts. We'll go after lunch.' Gary ruffled his son's hair, and then went quietly into the other bedroom. Noah was still fast asleep in his cot bed, so Gary tiptoed over to the little office area that he had set up in the corner of the bedroom. It was only an old chest of drawers with his laptop and a printer on it, but it worked OK for the small amount of paperwork that he had to do.

Gary opened the word processor and started to draft a flyer. He wasn't that good with words and couldn't think what to put. He remembered that he had some good text on his website that the copywriter had written for him when he'd had the site designed, so he logged into the web admin page instead. He noticed the icon that said he had a new comment on his guestbook, awaiting moderation. He clicked on it, hoping it was a customer enquiry that would lead to some work.

Two minutes later, Gary was still staring at the comment. It wasn't a request for work, or even someone trying to sell him something. Instead it was a scathing review from 'Mrs S Robinson,' reporting on the terrible experience she'd had with Mills Property Services, and how she felt she had to post this review so that other people didn't suffer the same distress as she had. Gary read the review again, and then pressed the 'spam' button to delete it. Thank goodness comments didn't appear automatically, he wouldn't want any other potential customers to see what she'd written.

Suddenly a thought struck Gary. There were other places where she could leave a comment. The trade associations that he subscribed to, and other review sites. Clumsily he operated the touch-pad on his laptop and clicked on the links that he had on his website. On each site, there was a similar review from Mrs S Robinson, and these ones he couldn't remove. Gary slammed down the laptop lid, he couldn't bear to look at it any longer. His face flushed, and his chest restricted, meaning his breathing was ragged. *Oh God, what am I going to do?* Taking a deep breath, he tried to think it through. *Do people really look at these sites? Some people perhaps, but not everyone. Trouble is, I haven't got that many positive reviews, I've never asked customers to leave feedback. It's not going to give a good impression.*

Ten minutes later Gary heard Lisa walk slowly up the stairs and go into the bathroom. He wanted to tell her about the bad reviews, but he didn't want to worry her any more, or cause another row. But he hoped she would come in to see him, so that they could make things up. He hated it when they rowed. Gary heard Lisa chatting to Oliver, and when he heard her say, 'see you later then,' he turned towards the door, sure she would come in here next. But instead, he heard her footsteps going back downstairs.

CHAPTER 33

'Hi, thanks for coming in Sue – it is ok if I call you Sue?' Iain asked, reaching out to shake hands, as he carried on talking without stopping for an answer. Sue had listened to Iain Gilbert's show on the local radio station many times, and he obviously talked as much in real life as he did on air. 'So glad you could come in, I think this is such a key issue. I mentioned it at a dinner party the other night, and everyone there had a horror story. Either something they'd experienced themselves, or an elderly parent or neighbour who'd had a similar problem. Now just a few ground rules if you don't mind. We want to talk about the site, and why you set it up, but don't mention any firms by name – we don't want any lawsuits on our hands!' Iain said, smiling broadly whilst shrugging his shoulders. As he talked they were walking through the radio station. Sue had been quite interested in seeing what went on behind the scenes, but what with trying to keep up with Iain's chat and his loping walk, she didn't really see much.

She never envisaged that setting up a website to 'name and shame' Mills Property Services would result in her taking part in a radio show. The site had taken off quickly. She had put a link to it in her partners' newsletter, which went to all her firm's customers, and the other companies that they worked with. She'd been able to include it via a 'keeping your money safe' blog post. It had then been picked up by a firm of solicitors that they worked with and had gone out to *their* customers and wider network, and it had gone on from there. Every day there were new posts appearing, and Sue found herself moderating posts every evening after work. It was time-consuming, and Sue was beginning to regret starting it. And now the local radio station had picked it up and was making 'cowboy builders' the topic for today's phone-in.

They had reached the studio now, and Sue found herself being introduced to several people whose names and titles she instantly forgot, it was all such a whirl. She was instructed to sit opposite Iain by an efficient-looking young woman in a sweatshirt and jeans. She clicked a microphone to Sue's jacket, and asked Sue to speak so that she could conduct a sound check.

'We are live in 5, 4, 3, 2, 1,' someone said, and the familiar 'Issues with Iain' jingle started to play. Suddenly Sue felt butterflies in her stomach and her hands started to sweat. She hoped she didn't make a mess of this. Iain did an introduction to the subject which seemed to go on for ever, and then it was Sue's turn. Iain turned out to be a great interviewer, something Sue hadn't appreciated as a mere listener to his show. He smiled reassuringly at her while she spoke, nodded encouragement, and prompted her if she rambled off track a bit. Sue explained a little about her experience, and about why she'd set up the website, and the interest and response it had provoked. It was over in a flash, and they were onto the live phone-in section. Firstly, an old lady called, and asked for advice on choosing a good builder. Sue and Iain both helped respond with some tips. Then Iain said, 'our next caller is Matt Mitchell, who has had a similar experience to Sue's. Welcome Matt, what would you like to say?'

A deep voice came on the line. 'Hello Iain, hello Sue, yes that's right, I have had a similar experience, in fact almost identical because the firm who did my kitchen was the same firm that did Sue's conversion. How Mills Property services can continue to operate I don't know, it's a disgrace.'

Iain cut in, 'if we can just avoid naming particular firms, thanks Matt. Can you briefly tell us what happened in your case?'

Matt then went on to describe succinctly how a labourer was left to finish off the kitchen refit in their house, and the finish wasn't good at all. 'We rang the owner of the firm and asked him to come around and put it right. He said he would come that evening, but he didn't turn up or even ring to let us know. My wife was in tears, we'd saved up all year for a new kitchen. When he eventually rang the next morning, I told him not to come back and I got another firm in to put it right. It ended up costing me more money, but it was worth it in the end. I only paid for materials up front, so I was able to withhold the payment for labour, and I was glad I did. I'd advise other people to do the same.'

There was time for another 4 callers, and then the show moved onto another topic. One of the team came over and unclipped Sue's microphone and beckoned her to follow them. Iain smiled broadly, gave a 'thumbs up' sign, and waved as Sue left.

The woman who showed her out gushed about how well it had gone. 'Well, apart from that guy naming the firm, whoops, we told all the callers not to do that. That's the danger of live radio. Let's hope Mr Mills wasn't listening.'

I hope he is listening, thought Sue, as she walked back through to the reception area. *He should understand how people feel about him and the poor service he provides.*

Once she was back in her car, Sue switched her phone on and noticed a voicemail. It was Peter, congratulating her on her performance on the radio. He said that he'd taped it so that she could listen to it when she got home. Sue smiled, it was nice to think that Peter had been there, cheering her on. She felt pleased with how it had gone too, and she smiled as she put the car in gear and headed back to the office.

CHAPTER 34

Sue smoothed the duvet cover and plumped up the pillows then stood back to look at the bed. She'd done her best with the striped blue and white duvet, nautical-themed scatter cushions and dark blue throw, but it still looked like a hospital bed. Sue sighed. They had used the services of an Occupational Therapist to find out exactly what sort of equipment would work best for Peter, and she had recommended this bed. It plugged into an electric socket and vibrated silently, designed to prevent pressure sores and aid circulation for people who spent a long time lying down.

Peter's condition had deteriorated far more rapidly than either of them had imagined. Over the past few weeks the tremors had got considerably worse, and he struggled to make it upstairs. He had stumbled several times, and it was just sheer luck that he hadn't fallen. He also struggled to get dressed, his fingers couldn't cope with buttons, and he had looked aghast at Sue's suggestion that he abandon his shirts and trousers and wear a track suit instead.

'Why not just put me in pyjamas permanently and have done with it? I may be decrepit, but I can at least look smart.'

Mornings had become fraught affairs, with Sue getting up even earlier than usual, and making sure that Peter was showered, dressed, and downstairs before she left for work. It took him so long to do things that she struggled to remain patient, all the time worrying about the rush hour traffic, and the meetings and paperwork desperate for attention in the office. Eventually Peter had said that he thought it was time for them to bring in professional carers. Sue had resisted at first, partly because she wanted to look after Peter herself, but also because by admitting they needed help, she also had to admit that Peter was getting much worse, and she didn't want to face that. Eventually though, she agreed to have help in the mornings. Once she'd made that concession, agreeing that it was time for Peter to move into the conversion seemed easier somehow.

That had been a few weeks ago, and on the advice of the

Occupational Therapist, they had furnished the conversion with appropriate equipment. But it wasn't all vibrating beds, and lifting chairs, there were decorative touches too which made the place look more homely. Peter had decided on a nautical theme, so they had picked blue and white, with touches of red in the accessories. Pictures depicted jolly seaside scenes with beach huts, and boats with brightly-coloured sails. And Sue had bought Peter a special wooden sign, which read 'Welcome aboard the HMS Man-cave,' which had made him laugh and hug her close.

Sue looked around appraisingly. It looked quite cosy now it was all done. The small kitchen area was light and clean, with a row of striped blue and white mugs hanging from a rack under one of the wall cabinets. There was a bright red glass worktop saver, and a red kettle and coffee machine. The kitchen wasn't really needed, as their own kitchen was next-door, but Sue liked the idea of the carers, strangers in their home, using this kitchen, rather than venturing into the main part of the house. The back wall of the 'man-cave' was taken up mostly by huge bi-fold doors which looked out onto the garden. There were two armchairs in front of the doors, positioned so that you looked outside when you sat in them. There was a tall coffee table in the middle of the chairs. Sue had envisaged a smart sofa in that spot, but the chairs were more practical. They were high, so made it easy for Peter to get up and sit down, but with the push of a button they raised up slowly, lifting you into a standing position. Sue had chosen a cornflower blue fabric, and with red and white striped cushions they didn't look too bad. A small round dining table and two high dining chairs completed the kitchen area.

The vibrating bed was at the opposite end, with chests of drawers at each side. On the facing wall, they'd hung a huge TV so that Peter could lie in bed and watch films and sport if he wanted. To divide the room, they had installed a set of shelves, placed at a right angle to the wall, and these were filled with some of Peter's books. Underneath the TV, there was a small desk with an iPad at one end and a home pod at the other. This had been Peter's idea, after he'd read about it in a magazine. If you spoke certain words it sprang into life, and would answer questions, search the internet, tell you the time or weather forecast, or even tell jokes. They had gone beyond the basic specification, and had a technology firm install special lights, a replacement thermostat and some clever curtain tracks. This meant that Peter could talk to the pod and ask it to turn the lights and heating on and off, open and close the curtains, turn on the TV, play music, or more often, play his latest audio book. Peter was evangelical about the merits of audiobooks, and he listened to several a week. Neither of them acknowledged that this was because he found it so difficult to hold a physical book.

The door opened, and Peter shuffled in. He was having a particularly difficult day today, and he was using the walking frame that the Occupational Therapist had provided. For ages it stood in the hallway, untouched, but one day, when he'd stumbled twice just walking across the sitting room, he had retrieved it and he used it on days like today, when his symptoms seemed particularly severe. Sue turned to him and smiled. 'Man-cave all shipshape and ready for inspection Captain.'

Peter looked around slowly. 'It's really great Sue, thanks so much. I'll be frightened to use it in case I mess it up.'

Sue suddenly felt tears prick her eyes, and she turned and vigorously plumped a cushion again. 'Bet you can't wait to get in here, you can do everything lying on your bed. If you can just work out a way for the pod to make you a whisky and soda, you'll have everything you need.' She tried to sound light-hearted, but really her heart was sinking. She didn't want Peter to be so ill that he had to move in here. Determined to keep busy, she said, 'right then, what shall I put in these drawers?'

Peter sat down at the dining table and thought for a moment or two. 'I guess I'll need pyjamas, underwear, socks, and my clothes for the next day. Medication? Just the things the carers need to get me ready in the morning.'

'Ok, I'll nip upstairs and get all that stuff. I've put your things in the bathroom, do you want to arrange them how you like them? I've just put them on the counter top.'

'Will do.' Peter replied, as Sue hurried out and headed towards the staircase.

Once they got everything put away, the rest of the day was a typical Saturday. They went out for lunch, and then did some shopping, and when they got back they had tea in the kitchen. Later, after a light supper, they sat together in the sitting room, watching a film. *Maybe it's not too bad after all,* Sue thought, as they laughed at the film. *It'll just make the mornings easier.* After the film they sat chatting for a while until eventually Peter stretched and said, 'bed for me I think, I'm tired out.'

It was strange to come out of the sitting room and turn towards the kitchen, rather than towards the stairs, and Sue could feel a knot in her stomach as they entered the conversion. Peter must have sensed her mood, as he tried his best to be cheerful, chatting to the pod, and making lights come on and off, and the curtains open and close several times. Sue smiled, despite herself, and adopted a similarly playful mood as she helped him get ready for bed. She pretended his sweater was stuck as she pulled it over his head and sang the strip tease song as she undid his shirt and trousers. She sat on the edge of the bed while Peter went off into his bathroom, and then helped him into bed, placing the walking frame close by, in case he needed it in the night.

'Sleep tight, don't enjoy the vibration too much,' she said, with a wink. And with a goodnight kiss, she hurried out of the conversion and upstairs to bed. It was once she was in bed, and the light was off that she allowed the tears to come. Nothing was ever going to be the same again. Part of her wanted to run downstairs and seek comfort from Peter. But that wouldn't change the situation, he would still have this awful condition. And Sue cried again, until she eventually fell asleep.

Downstairs, Peter turned off his audiobook and lay listening to the creaks and groans of an unfamiliar room. He was thinking about Sue and wondered if she was asleep? He was worried about her. She kept busy all the time, to the point of exhaustion sometimes. This campaign against that young builder chap was over the top, he knew that. And all the hours she spent on that website she'd set up. He knew it was all to distract her from the reality of the situation, which was that she'd end up looking after him, like she'd looked after their parents. It wasn't fair. One of the things he'd liked about Sue was her impulsiveness and ability to get things done. But when she'd nursed their parents she'd shown another side to her character. Kind and patient, nothing was too much trouble. He was seeing that side of her again now. But when he looked into her eyes she looked terrified, and close to tears most of the time. And he was going to get worse, it was happening so quickly. He made an effort when Sue was at home, but it exhausted him, and when she was at work he rested all the time, so that he'd have as much energy as possible when she came back.

Peter thought about suicide. It really would be the kindest thing. He was going to die from this condition, he'd accepted that. But what sort of state would he be in by the time it happened? And how would it affect Sue to watch him deteriorate and end up helpless? He didn't want her to remember him like that. But he loved her so much, he didn't want to leave her quite yet, not when they could still talk and have some fun together. He relished days like today, when they were together all the time. He thought back over the day, at them laughing together at the film, and sampling each other's lunch choices. *No, not yet*, he thought, *I'm not ready yet.*

But what about when I am ready? Will I have the physical capability to do anything about it? I don't want to live if I can't do anything for myself, Peter mused. Then he thought back to when his Father was in hospital after his second stroke. Labouring for every breath, unable to talk, his face slack on one side, and hardly able to move. He had beckoned with one finger for Peter to come close and using every ounce of effort he could muster he had mumbled, 'help me son, I'm ready to go, don't let me suffer like this.'

And Peter had helped him. He took off his oxygen mask, and when his Dad stopped breathing, he replaced it and called the nurse. No-one suspected anything, his Dad hadn't been expected to survive as long as he had. He'd never told anyone about it, not even Sue. He had intended to tell her, but he'd started the conversation by introducing the topic of euthanasia, and to his surprise Sue had expressed very strong feelings about how it was wrong, and the start of a slippery slope leading to people being 'put down' like animals. Peter had been surprised by her attitude. She had seen her Father suffer terribly with terminal cancer, and then his Father, badly affected by first one stroke, and then a second. He hadn't pursued it further. But now he wished he had. The time would come when he would choose to die, he was sure of that. But who would help him if he couldn't do it himself? Would Sue relent to prevent him suffering? But was it fair to ask? What if he was gone, and she got into trouble for helping him? Could he really expose her to something like that?

And with these troubling thoughts swirling in his head, Peter passed a night of fitful sleep.

CHAPTER 35

As Gary walked back into the house from the van, he became aware for the first time that day of how cold the temperature was outside. As he walked into their empty house, it felt even colder. He was sure that they had packed everything, but he wanted to make one last check.

Walking through the empty rooms, Gary couldn't help remembering the happy times they'd had in this house as a family. They had rented it since they first got married, moving in a few weeks before the wedding, and being so excited about decorating and choosing furniture and furnishings. They saved up for the things they needed, so every additional item was celebrated and enjoyed. Gary smiled when he remembered them getting a new sofa, and both Lisa and he sat on the floor and looked at it, rather than be the first to sit on it.

Shortly after the wedding they had brought Jacob home from the hospital. Although they had decorated the nursery in lemon and white, it was a long time before they could bear to leave him in there on his own, and they had moved his crib into their room. At night they often sat up, holding hands and just looking at their son sleeping.

In the next few years, they'd brought home all their sons, first little Olly, then Jack, the sweetest-natured of all their babies, always smiling. And finally, baby Noah, with his thick head of blonde hair. Their new baby wouldn't be coming here from the hospital though. None of them would be coming back any more.

Gary finished looking around downstairs, and slowly went upstairs, his mind flooded with memories. So many firsts. First home, first child, each of their son's individual milestones, first word, first step. Every one of them was pictured in one of these rooms. He went into the master bedroom, looking large now that all the furniture had been moved out and put into storage. He looked in the built-in cupboard. Nothing left in there, Lisa had left everything neat, tidy and clean. The landlord may have evicted them, but Lisa still had her pride and was determined to leave the place spotless. There was a new couple moving in tomorrow. Lisa and Gary had met them when they'd come around to view. It was their first place together and they looked so happy and excited. Suddenly Gary felt old, worn out from the weight of responsibility. And yet he and Lisa were probably younger than the couple who were moving in.

The only room left to check was the boys' bedroom. Gary walked in and was shocked at how large it looked without all the toys and clothes that usually filled every space. He ran his hand over the cabin beds that he'd built into the room the previous year. Top bunks for the older two boys, and bottom bunks for the younger two. Noah hadn't even slept in his, he still slept in his cot bed in their room. Gary had spent ages designing and building the beds, and one weekend Lisa had taken the boys out for a day and he'd assembled all the pieces that he'd previously made out in the shed. The boys had been so excited when they'd come home and seen their new beds. Jacob and Oliver had immediately climbed up the steps into their bunks, and Jack had tried out both bottom bunks before settling on the one nearest the window. They had all been so happy that day.

Over the last couple of weeks Gary had removed the spaceship frieze from the room and touched up the walls with paint. He'd been going to dismantle the beds, but the landlord had said to leave them in place, he wasn't sure why. Suddenly Gary felt his eyes swim with tears. He had let his family down badly, he knew that. But they hadn't been able to hold onto the house, falling further and further behind with the rent. So now most of their furniture was going to storage, and they were moving into a small flat in a dubious area of town. He didn't want his boys growing up there, but they'd had no choice. With their only income coming from benefits, and no bond to put down, it had been impossible to get something in a decent area. The local housing office had put them on a waiting list and given them details of landlords who accepted families on benefits. Viewing what was on offer had been a real eye-opener. Gary didn't realise there was such run-down property in this town. They'd been lucky with this house, in a nice quiet street, with parking and a garden for the boys to play in. He hadn't realised that until recently, when it was too late to appreciate what they had.

The business had closed too. He hadn't heard the item on local radio, but his Dad had, and he'd rung him to tell him about it the same day. He needn't have bothered, because the story was picked up by the local newspaper too. Lisa came home from the shops with a copy, after noticing the story on the front page when she was browsing the news. The story didn't mention his firm by name, but mentioned the 'name and shame' website, so it was easy to find out who they were talking about. Then it was picked up on the internet, with him being labelled 'heartless' and 'disrespectful,' while Sue Robinson was described as 'articulate,' and 'sincere.'

He didn't stand a chance, no-one would employ him after that. Unique Interiors had contacted him and said that he shouldn't comment. They had legal representation, but they were barely mentioned in the story, all the blame was put onto him. Then some reporter tracked down Danny, and he gave an interview. In it he said he'd helped Gary out with the job but had frequently been left on his own while Gary went away to do other work or take his family out. Danny explained that he wasn't trained and was just supposed to be labouring, but he'd been left to do skilled work that he wasn't qualified to carry out. The reporter had asked Danny about the wine, but Danny had refused to comment on that, so people just assumed Sue Robinson's version was correct. Then Adam, the labourer he'd previously employed, also jumped on the bandwagon, and said that his experience had been similar to Danny's, and that he'd refused to work for Gary after the Mitchell job. Danny and Gary hadn't spoken with each other since their fight over payment. Their Dad had said that Danny was 'very disappointed' in the way Gary had treated him. By that time Gary was too defeated to explain the full story to his Dad, so he'd said nothing.

Taking a final look around, Gary wiped away his tears and stepped out of the front door for the last time. The boys were staying with his Dad and Lisa was at their new flat, doing some cleaning before the van arrived with the items they were taking with them. It had left about half an hour ago, so should be arriving around now. Gary had better get a move on, he needed to be there to help Lisa unpack. He removed the van key and then pushed the house keys back through the front door. He looked down at the single key in his hand. That would be going later today too. He'd had to sell the van, to someone he used to work with. He'd been very good and said they could hold onto it until they moved. Gary was taking it over this evening, and that was everything gone.

Gary sat in the van for a few moments before driving away. He couldn't remember ever feeling so low. Not even when his Mum had gone away and left him when he was only eight, and he worried that it was something that he'd done. Even when his Dad had gone on a bender and Gary had been taken to a children's home for the first time, scared and frightened for his future. Even those two experiences hadn't been as bad as this. He'd wanted to create a perfect family, but all he'd done was let them down. Blackness and misery engulfed him as he started the van and drove slowly away.

CHAPTER 36

As Gary turned into their new street, he noticed a gang of teenagers standing on the corner, drinking cider out of cans. They were laughing and joking and pushing each other, and Gary didn't fancy Lisa having to walk past them daily.

The removal van was still parked in the street and Gary pulled in behind it. He looked up at his new home. It looked even worse than he remembered. It was a large Victorian villa, which probably was quite grand at one time. But, like the others in the street, it had been split into flats and bedsits, and people didn't usually stay long enough to take any pride in their surroundings. The window-frames were beginning to rot, and although they had once been painted dark blue, most of the paint had now chipped off or been worn away by wind, rain and sun.

The small front garden had some wiry grass in places. There was an old kitchen cupboard in one part of the garden, apparently placed there and left to rot. Four extra-large wheelie bins stood to one side of the front door, one with the lid open, so that rubbish was spilling onto the ground. The path up the middle of the garden was cracked and stained.

God, this place is horrible, Gary thought, and his mood lowered even further. Steeling himself, he got out of the van, locked it, and went into the house. The front door was propped open, he supposed the removal men must have done that, and so he walked straight into the hallway. The floor was covered with some sort of linoleum, but goodness knows when it had last been washed. Dirt was ingrained into the cracks. There were a couple of bicycles chained to old-fashioned radiator further down the hallway, and on the left-hand side there were several metal post boxes attached to the wall. The hallway smelled damp, and of stale cooking, and some underlying smell that Gary tried not to think about.

Their flat was on the first floor, so he started to walk upstairs. The stairs were plain wood, painted a yellowing white, without carpet. Gary hoped they wouldn't be too slippery, and had visions of Lisa, now heavily pregnant, slipping and falling down the whole flight. Gary shuddered. The door to their flat was at the top of the first flight, on the right. The door was painted dark green, and like everything else in the house, was chipped and worn. They had been getting desperate when they'd found this place, they had been turned down for so many. The local housing department had been sympathetic, especially when they said how young their children were, and because of Lisa's current pregnancy.

'We just don't have anything,' the harassed-looking housing officer had said kindly. 'I'll put you on our priority list, but as you aren't actually homeless at present, you won't be given the highest status. Once your landlord has actually evicted you then you will move up the list. Then we have some emergency bed and breakfast accommodation that we can put you in. But there is a huge demand for it.'

Gary and Lisa had been shocked. They had no idea that there was such a homeless problem in this area, or that there were families who didn't have a place to live. Wrongly, they had assumed it was only single people who were homeless, and that there was help in place for people with children.

'Don't you have any family you can stay with for a while?' The housing officer had asked. Gary and Lisa had looked at each other. The thought of them all squeezing into his Dad's one-bedroom flat was ridiculous, even if he'd take them in. But, now that he contemplated this new place, his Dad's flat was beginning to look more attractive by the minute.

'No, I've only got my Dad, and he rents a small one-bedroomed flat. There wouldn't be any room for us.' Gary replied, and the woman turned her gaze to Lisa.

'No, I don't have any relatives, I grew up in care.' Lisa mumbled. She hated to talk about her childhood. The woman looked even more sympathetic and carried on talking.

'Landlords around here really can pick and choose their tenants. Property prices are so high that there is a huge demand for rental properties, so they can demand large bonds, several months' rent in advance, and can be choosy about who they rent to. They are much more likely to take families where there is a wage coming in.' She turned to Gary. 'How long is it since you've had a job?'

'Not long at all.' Gary replied. 'I had my own business, but I had a few people who didn't pay, and it ended up going under. Because of that we owe money to a few people.'

'Not those easy loan companies I hope?' The housing officer asked. And when Gary shook his head, she smiled. 'We see people get into such a lot of trouble with those loans, the interest rates are exorbitant. People borrow a couple of hundred to tide them over and end up owing thousands.'

'We went to the Citizen's Advice Bureau,' Gary explained. 'They sorted out a repayment plan for us, and we sold everything that we could to pay off what we owed, and to leave a little bit for moving. But we fell behind with the rent when I had no money coming in from the business. I kept hoping it would turn around.'

'What sort of business was it?'

'Property services, building, conversions, kitchens, bathrooms, that sort of thing.' Gary replied.

'Oh, I'm surprised you weren't inundated with work, I can never find anyone to do jobs around my house.' The woman joked, and Gary felt himself blush. She must have noticed, because she said, 'but it's hard keeping a business going, lots of new businesses don't work out, at least you gave it a go. Hopefully you might be able to find a job soon, with your skills?'

Gary nodded, but it wasn't so easy. Who wanted to employ someone with his reputation?

The housing officer looked at her watch and became more business-like, their appointment must have been taking too long. 'I can give you a list of landlords who will accept people on benefits. All you can do is ring around, see if anyone has any vacancies.'

Lisa had taken hold of the list, which was quite short, and when they'd got home they had started ringing around. Even the landlords who had vacancies seemed reluctant to even let them look around once they said how many children they had. Lisa had assumed her advanced pregnancy would elicit some sympathy, but instead it turned out to be another barrier. In the end, they viewed some rooms in a shared house, where they'd have to share a bathroom with another family. And a two-bedroomed flat which would have been fine except it was up three flights of narrow stairs. It would have been too tricky to carry a baby and a buggy up there, and the landlord was adamant that the pram couldn't be left downstairs. Another flat sounded promising as it was self-contained, with its own front door. But when they arrived to view it, several of the other flats in the block had their windows boarded up, and the outside of the building was covered in graffiti. They didn't even get out of the van, the place just looked fit for demolition. A flat in the next street to this one had been taken by the time they'd got there, on the same day as they'd rung about it. So, when they viewed this one, and the landlord said they could move in for a modest deposit, they had snapped it up. Gary's Dad had loaned them the deposit, and now that Gary had sold his van, he was able to pay him back, as well as pay the removal men.

Once inside the flat, what was immediately obvious to Gary was that they had brought too much stuff with them. The two removal men were shifting items around at Lisa's instruction, but they had wildly overestimated what they could fit in.

Half an hour later, some of their belongings had been put back in the removal van. The two removal men seemed to take pity on Lisa and Gary, making Lisa sit down regularly to rest, and joking around with Gary, trying to keep his spirits up. Gary and Lisa felt so defeated that they couldn't decide anything, so the men moved furniture into logical places, and made suggestions about how they could make the place liveable. In the end, they took away the sofa that they'd brought from their old house. There was a sofa-bed already in the flat, so they'd just have to make do with that. They also took away some drawers which were meant for the boys' room, several boxes of toys, and some boxes of kitchen equipment.

146

Gary and Lisa had already rented a storage unit, so these items could join the rest of the stuff in there, safe for the day they would be able to unpack it again. *I wonder if we'll ever have a place big enough to unpack it?* Gary mused to himself, disheartened by the entire day.

Once all the furniture was in place, Gary followed the removal men to the storage depot. He thanked them for their help and paid them the money he owed. Luckily his ex-colleague had agreed to pay him in advance for the van, so he had some cash. There was little left after he'd paid the removers, even though they refused to take anything extra for the additional journey to the storage unit.

Before going back to the flat, Gary took the van to its new home. As he walked away he felt his fists clench. *Why did this have to happen to us?* he thought, feeling helpless and frustrated.

It took him a while to walk back to the flat, and Lisa looked exhausted when he got back, she mustn't have stopped all day. She'd gone to the flat early, wanting to clean it thoroughly before all their belongings arrived. And she'd obviously been working non-stop while he'd been away, putting things away.

Gary looked around their new home. There was one main room, which had a small kitchen area at the right-hand side. There was a two-ring hob and a small oven, a fridge, and a couple of base units and wall cupboards. There was no room for a dishwasher or washing machine. They could wash dishes by hand, but they'd have to go to the launderette to wash and dry their clothes. As there was no storage at all, they had brought their wardrobes, and placed them opposite the kitchen area, to hold their clothes, shoes and other items, such as the iron and ironing board. On the left there was the sofa bed, which would double up as Gary and Lisa's bed. Behind that, Lisa had placed a row of storage boxes for the boys' toys and books. There was no fireplace, so the sofa faced the TV, which was on a stand against the wall. They had placed a large storage box in front of the sofa, to double as a coffee table and to store the duvet, pillows and bed-linen during the day. In the middle of the room, opposite the door, they had placed their small kitchen table and six folding chairs, so they could at least sit and eat. This would also give the boys somewhere to read, draw or play board games.

In the middle of the wall on the left, there was a door into the only bedroom. This was a narrow, long room, which was just wide enough to hold the double bed from the main bedroom at home. This was where the boys would sleep, two of them at the top of the bed, and two of them at the bottom. There was a small built-in cupboard with shelves inside, and Lisa had placed neatly-folded piles of the boys' clothes on the shelves. From the bedroom, there was a door into a tiny bathroom, which held a corner shower cubicle, a toilet, and a corner washbasin on the wall. It wasn't ideal, as during the night he and Lisa would disturb the boys if they needed the bathroom. *Better than sharing with another family*, Gary concluded.

There were still several boxes to unpack, so Gary made Lisa sit down, and asked her to direct him to where she wanted the contents of the boxes stored. It didn't take long to put everything away, and then Gary folded the empty boxes and took them down to the bins outside. Now that everything was put away the place looked tidy but cramped. Gary made some tea and they sat on the sofa and looked around, neither of them speaking.

Eventually Lisa broke the silence. 'At least the landlord had the place painted, like he promised.'

Gary hadn't noticed, but now he looked around appraisingly. Yes, Lisa was right, the walls did look cleaner. Something caught his eye and he got up to examine the light switch. 'Don't know who he got to do it, they've painted over the light switch,' he observed. 'Oh, and over the sockets too. Must never have heard of masking tape.' He smiled at Lisa, but she looked too tired to smile back. Gary didn't mention the mould he'd noticed near the skirting boards, already starting to show through the freshly-applied paint.

'Must go to the loo,' Lisa said, struggling to her feet. 'Baby's pressing on my bladder.'

She walked into the bedroom, and a couple of minutes later,

Gary heard a weird banging noise as the cistern flushed and then refilled. Lisa came back into the living room, looking shocked. 'Did you hear that dreadful racket? That was the loo flushing. The boys will never sleep through that.' She sat down at the kitchen table and put her head in her hands.

'Hey love, it'll be OK, we'll get used to it.' Gary said, distressed and wanting to comfort her. He went over and started rubbing her back. Lisa flashed him a look, her eyes full of tears.

'Don't say that, we don't ever want to get used to this, we've always got to focus on something better. This is not the place to bring up a family, where are the boys going to play? Where are we going to put the new baby? There isn't even any space for her crib. Don't you dare think of this as permanent, or even long-term, not ever, not for a second.' Lisa raged at him, anger flashing in her eyes alongside her tears.

Gary sat down, as if she'd slapped him. She was right, this was no place for children. *How could I have done this to my family?* he thought, as shame caused him to flush in response to Lisa's words.

CHAPTER 37

'Daddy, No-no cold,' Noah said, rubbing his little hands together and looking up at Gary from his buggy.

'Not No-no, No-ah,' Gary said, smiling. 'Tell you what, why don't I take you out of that buggy, and we'll run a race? See how fast you can run.' Noah smiled and started wriggling to get out of his pushchair.

It *was* cold, a frosty December day, and when Gary checked the time he realised it was nearly 10am. Gary had walked the older boys to school, then came back a long circuitous route via the river-bank and the park. He said these morning walks were to give Noah plenty of fresh air, but mainly it was because Gary hated being in the flat. There was always noise from the other flats and studios, with people constantly running up and down the stairs. He found it difficult to relax, day or night. And there was no space, nowhere to get a breather. *It's funny the things you miss*, Gary thought. *I'd give anything for a long soak in the bath.*

He undid Noah's harness, and placed him on his feet, and after a count of three they started running through the park as quickly as Noah's little legs would carry him.

When they arrived back, Noah's cheeks were red from running and the cold. Lisa was sitting at the kitchen table and she looked up when they came in. 'Hello, you two,' she said cheerfully, 'you've been a long time.'

'Yes, we came back along the river, and through the park. We had a couple of races and Noah beat me both times. I must be getting old.' Gary replied, ruffling Noah's blonde hair.

'No-no ran fast,' Noah told his Mummy, and she picked him up and listened to his chatter. Gary put the kettle on for a cup of coffee and looked over to where Lisa was sitting. On the table in front of her was her sewing box, and a pile of the boys' clothes.

'Are you doing some repairs? he asked.

Lisa looked down at the pile of clothes and fabric in front of her and picked up an item from the pile. 'No, I'm redesigning some of the stuff that Noah has grown out of, making it into clothes for the new baby.' She held-up a half-finished baby pinafore, made from a patchwork of Noah's old dungarees. 'These dungarees have been through all four boys, and they were wearing at the knees, so I thought I'd recycle them. What do you think?'

Gary turned away from her to make the coffee. He was always near to tears these days, and he didn't want her to see his eyes filling up now. *What sort of husband and father am I? Can't even afford new clothes for our baby.*

He wiped his face roughly with a piece of kitchen paper. 'My nose is running with the cold and all that running,' he explained, trying to sound cheerful. 'The baby's definitely a girl then?' He said, smiling at Lisa and taking her a cup of coffee. They had chosen not to find out the sex of the baby when they'd had their scan.

'This pregnancy is so different, I'm sure it's going to be a girl.' Lisa replied, and she looked happier and more excited than she had for a long time. 'And girls mean pretty dresses.'

'Good job she's got a talented mum then,' Gary replied, unable to keep the bitterness out of his voice. 'I didn't know you could make things from scratch, I only thought you could do buttons and mend holes, that sort of thing?' He said, trying to sound a bit more positive.

'One of the foster families I lived with for a few months had a lovely Grandmother who used to work as a seamstress. She made all her own clothes, and she showed me how to cut out patterns and do different stitches. When we have space for a sewing machine I'd like to take it up a bit more seriously.' Lisa replied, turning back to the little dress.

Gary was surprised. He thought he knew everything about Lisa, but this was something she hadn't mentioned before. He put some juice in Noah's beaker, and took it over to where he was playing on the floor in front of the sofa.

'No-no cold,' Noah said when he handed him the drink. Gary looked down at his son and felt his hands and face. He was freezing. It was cold in the flat, and they had no way of boosting the heat. He noticed that Lisa was wearing a large cardigan on top of her jeans and jumper. She was looking at Noah, with a concerned look on her face.

'I know,' said Gary, 'let's play some jumping games, that'll warm you up.' Ten minutes later, Noah collapsed giggling on the sofa, looking considerably warmer, and Gary winked at Lisa as he collapsed next to him saying, 'Daddy's tired out, must have a rest.'

Lisa headed off to the bedroom, saying she'd get an additional jumper to keep Noah warm, so Gary answered when there was a knock on the door. It was their landlord, a tall man in his early sixties, called Reuben Rust.

'You settling in Ok?' He asked gruffly.

'Yes, thanks,' Gary replied, 'although the cistern makes a terrible noise, it wakes the boys up at night. It really needs replaced.'

'It's about the boys I've come,' Reuben said, ignoring Gary's remarks about the cistern. 'I've had complaints about them making a noise, and I could hear squealing and noises when I was coming up the stairs. I can't have that, don't want the other tenants complaining.'

'We were just playing,' Gary said defensively. 'It's so cold in here that I was jumping up and down with our youngest to warm him up. It was only for 10 minutes or so.'

'Take this as a first warning and keep the noise down. I wasn't sure about taking you with all them kids, and another on the way. Plenty more people want this flat,' Reuben said, in a very unpleasant way. Then without acknowledging anything that Gary had said, he turned and started walking down the stairs.

Gary went back inside, feeling a bit shaken. They had nowhere to go if they lost this place. He looked at Lisa, who looked upset. 'I hate that man,' she said. 'He always seems to be hanging around when I go out or come in. He gives me the creeps.'

'He does live on the ground floor, he's bound to be down there sometimes.' Gary replied, feeling uneasy.

'Is he ever hanging around when you go in and out?' Lisa asked, and when Gary shook his head, she said, 'see, I told you, creepy. Was he complaining about the boys?'

'Yes, he said that people have mentioned the noise to him, made a complaint. We'll have to try and keep them quiet Lisa, we can't risk losing this place, even if it is grim. Not until we're back on our feet.'

Lisa sat down dejectedly. 'They're young boys Gary, how can we keep them quiet? They're just playing. It would be different if they had a garden, like ...' She stopped herself saying, 'like in our old house.'

'I know, I know.' Gary said, 'but we'll have to try. Anyway, I'd better get off to the Job Centre, see if my dream job has come in today.'

Gary went to the Job Centre every day, willing to take any job that would bring in more money than the benefits they received. For the first time in his life he was in debt too, something they had always avoided at all costs. He owed money to their old landlord, to the utilities company who supplied their old house, and a huge amount to Unique Interiors. Gary hated to think about how long it would take to pay it all back. With the help of the Citizen's Advice Bureau he had arranged to pay a nominal sum to each of them, to be renegotiated when he started work again. He once worked out that if he continued to pay the insignificant amounts he was currently paying, then he'd never be debt-free in his whole lifetime, and he wasn't even 30 yet. If he could make decent money, a job with overtime perhaps, then once they moved somewhere better, he could start chipping away at the debt.

He had managed to secure a few interviews, but they always seemed to go wrong when interviewers asked him about his previous employment. He always started to blush and stammer, and prospective employers seemed to think he had something to hide. His advisor at the Department of Work and Pensions had given him a dressing down last time he'd gone to sign on. She suggested that he took a course in interview skills. Perhaps he would, at least it would get him away from the flat for a while.

There wasn't anything new at the Job Centre, so he got the man helping him to provide proof that he'd been in, so he could show his advisor next time he went to claim his benefits. Then he headed to the supermarket, to pick up some essentials that they needed. He and Lisa had pooled their cash before he left home, and when he had bought the things on his list he had exactly £2.50 left. That had to see them through until Friday and it was only Tuesday. *Let's hope there are no emergencies,* Gary thought as he started to walk slowly back to the flat.

Gary dropped off the shopping and then strapped Noah into his buggy and headed off to the school to pick up his other sons. Because he was older, Jacob finished school later than Oliver and Jack, so he took the younger boys to the playground beside Jacob's school while they were waiting.

'It's freezing Dad,' Oliver said, visibly shivering. 'Can't we wait in MacDonald's?' he added, sounding hopeful. 'Yes, MacDonald's,' Jack echoed.

'No boys, Jacob will be out soon, and your Mum's getting the tea ready. If you're cold run around a bit, that'll help.' Gary replied, but he felt awful. The temperature was dropping, and he was making them hang around outside in the cold.

Eventually Jacob came racing out of school, and over to join them. He looked excited, and immediately launched into an explanation for his good mood. 'It's the judo club Christmas party tonight Dad, they have it early because there are other things going on nearer Christmas. It's going to be great, we're having a class first, then a demonstration from a real professional, he's been in the Olympics,' Jacob said, sounding awe-struck. 'And then we're having a party with cakes and hot dogs.'

Gary's heart sank. Judo was right on the other side of town from where they lived now. He couldn't expect Jacob to walk that far and back again, so they'd have to go in the bus. He wondered how much the return fare was. *More than £2.50, I'm sure of that,* Gary thought, desperately trying to think if they had any more cash anywhere. But then there was the cost of the class, and would there be a contribution towards the party?

'Jacob, did you get a letter about the party or anything? I can't remember you mentioning it before.'

Jacob thought for a moment, 'I think it might be in with my judo kit,' he concluded, his eyes shining with anticipation.

Gary didn't say anything more about it, but when they got home, whilst the boys were telling Lisa what they'd been up to at school, he looked in the wardrobe, found Jacob's kit bag, and rummaged inside. The letter was there, and it told Gary what he'd expected; there was a £5 contribution towards the party.

As the boys sat down and started tucking into their food, Gary went over to Lisa who was over by the sink. 'How much is the bus fare to get to judo and back, do you know?' He whispered so that the boys wouldn't hear.

'£3.80 return,' Lisa replied.

Gary looked at her. 'It's £5.00 for the party, and then there is the cost of the class, that's another £4.50. I've only got £2.50 left after the shopping. Do we have any other cash anywhere?'

Lisa shook her head, 'no, not a penny. And we'll have to pay the annual fees before the end of December. That's both the club and the judo association, it comes to nearly £40 for the year. And if he carries on going, then he's going to need a bigger suit, he's outgrown that one.' Gary and Lisa looked at each other, neither wanting to be the one who made the decision. Eventually, Lisa spoke. 'You better tell him he can't go then.'

Gary waited until the boys had finished eating, and then Jacob started talking about the party again, so Gary interrupted him. 'I'm sorry son, you won't be able to go to the party tonight. In fact, you can't go to judo for a while, we just can't afford it now that I haven't got a job.'

Jacob stared at Gary in disbelief. 'Can't go? But I've been looking forward to it for ages. All my friends are going.'

'I know it's hard Jake, and I'm sorry, if we could find the money then I'd be happy to take you. But it's not only the cost of the party, there's bus fare, and the cost of the class. We just can't afford it now. You can go back to judo when I get a job.'

Jacob's face reddened, and his lip started to tremble. 'You're mean, I hate you, we never have any fun anymore. And I hate living here, it's a dump, I want to go home.' And with a sob, he turned and ran into the bedroom and slammed the door.

Gary hesitated, wondering if he should go after him, but then Noah, upset because his brother was upset, began to wail loudly. Lisa picked Noah up and started to talk quietly to him and Gary looked at Oliver and Jack, who were watching him, looking apprehensive.

'Jacob really wants to go to the party,' Oliver said, his voice quavering. 'He talks about it all the time when we go to bed. I don't mind not having MacDonald's or sweets, or anything, if he can go.' Jack nodded his agreement.

Gary said, 'Oh Olly, it's not that simple …' But then he trailed off, they were children, how could he expect them to understand?

CHAPTER 38

Shopping takes ages these days, Gary thought as he stood in the frozen foods aisle of the supermarket, weighing up the large bag of frozen vegetables in one hand and a tub of ice-cream in the other. The vegetables would just about fit in the ice-box of their fridge, which was empty at the moment. On the other hand, Lisa had been craving ice-cream. Gary looked at the other items in his bag, did a mental calculation and reluctantly put the ice-cream back. *It's too cold for ice-cream anyway,* he thought, trying to convince himself that he was doing the right thing.

They had so little storage in the flat that they couldn't keep supplies of food in, so Gary walked to the shops nearly every day. He usually came in the evening, and had designed a weekly itinerary, so that he could pick up the reduced and cut-price items each day. One supermarket had the best offers on a Monday, another one on a Wednesday, so he rotated around them, buying what they needed for the next day's meals. He calculated the cost as he was going around, that way he made sure he didn't overspend. This was one of the more expensive supermarkets, but they often had the bigger reductions. The boys had asked for some sweets, but he hadn't been lucky bargain-hunting today, so he wasn't going to be able to afford much. He eventually managed to get a few bags of fun-sized sweets for £1.00, and hoped they'd be happy with those.

After he had paid and was making his way out of the shop, he found his way blocked by a middle-aged woman who had stopped with her heavily-laden trolley and was fishing in her handbag for something. She didn't seem to notice Gary trying to get around her, and eventually she fished out a mobile phone, and said, 'Hi Pete, is everything OK, I've just come out of the supermarket?' Gary froze. He'd recognise that voice anywhere, it was bloody Sue Robinson, he was sure of it. He wouldn't have recognised her, bundled up in a winter coat, as he'd only met her once. But he remembered her voice, as he'd replayed what she'd said to him so many times in his head. 'Get out of my house, now. Or I am phoning the police.' And, 'get into your van and get off my property.'

Gary hung back as she finished her call and put away the phone. He loitered in the entrance to the supermarket and watched her push the heavy trolley across the car park. He didn't know why he was watching her. A part of him wanted to confront her, but what would he say? But he couldn't tear himself away from her, the source of so much misery for him and his family.

Sue stopped beside a shiny dark silver car, parked underneath one of the large lampposts in the car park. Gary looked at the registration plate, it must be brand new, that registration mark had only come out in September, a couple of months ago. He watched her put her many bags of shopping into the boot, lock the car, and then start to wheel the trolley away. But instead of leaving it in the trolley park, she walked past it, and headed towards the wine warehouse at the other side of the car park.

Gary felt his breathing grow shallower, and his fists clenched around his shopping bags. *That must be where the bitch buys her cases of wine*, he fumed. *The wine she accused me of drinking.* Gary looked back at her car, it looked expensive. Walking between the cars, he moved a little closer. He was right, a BMW X5. Goodness know how much that cost. And all that shopping, just for the two of them. It was more than they could afford in a month, and there were six of them.

Gary could feel his heart thumping, and his breathing got heavier. His jaw ached where he was clenching it. He felt like screaming, 'see her, she ruined my life, for no other reason than she's a vindictive cow.' She'd probably never done without anything her whole life.

Shielding himself with other parked cars, Gary drew nearer to the shining BMW. Moving both shopping bags to one hand, he fished out his keys with the other hand, and keeping his hand low, he dragged two keys slowly along the pristine paintwork of Sue Robinson's car. The noise of the metal grating was like the sweetest symphony, it was the sound of revenge. Gary walked from front to back, scratching with the keys as he walked, unhurriedly. Then, keeping his keys concealed in his hand, he sauntered off in the direction of the car park exit. He forced himself to walk slowly down the ramp. As soon as he rounded the corner onto the main street, he started to run, not out of fear, but out of pure exhilaration at what he'd done. Blood was pumping through his veins, and he was laughing out loud. *I'll get you, you bitch*, he thought, *you'll not get all your own way*. And he headed home, feeling happier than he had for a long time.

CHAPTER 39

Sue lugged the case of wine into the shopping trolley and navigated her way out of the shop. Luckily there was someone on their way in, and they held the door open for her. They still had several bottles in the rack at home, but she thought she'd stock up now, make sure they had plenty to see them over Christmas, which seemed to be coming along alarmingly fast.

As she headed back over the car park, Sue ticked off all the things she still had to do this evening. It had been a busy day at work, but when she got home, she realised that they were seriously short of essentials in the food cupboards and fridge, and she needed to shop. Peter hadn't wanted her to go out again. He got bored and lonely home alone during the day, she knew that, but he had felt too tired to come shopping with her. She had rushed around the supermarket, throwing things in randomly. Not her usual way at all, she liked to make a list and take her time, shopping in a relaxed way. She had bought a lot, she knew that, but felt that stacking up as much as she could would mean that she could just pop into the M&S food store near her office for the next few weeks.

Unfortunately buying a lot of shopping meant it would take a while to put it all away. Sue resolved to get organised for home delivery in future. It would be much easier. When she got home she'd need to make some supper, iron some clothes for tomorrow, do some tidying up and she had some papers to prepare for a meeting in the morning. Sue sighed, she was feeling tired already and would prefer to just sit down with a glass of wine and the TV.

Sue stopped half-way across the car park and looked around in panic. *Where's my car?* she thought, before remembering that she'd sold her little red Audi. She located their new car, swearing it was looking at her sternly. She really couldn't get used to it. They had decided to sell both their cars and buy one bigger one. Something that Peter could get into and out of easily. This had seemed ideal in the showroom, but in day to day use Sue found it a bit of a trial. It was a bit too powerful, often leaping ahead at junctions faster than Sue anticipated. It was too big to park easily too, and had a pillar just in the wrong place, it blocked Sue's view when she was coming out of junctions. And it was all so sophisticated with computers and cameras that came on when she reversed or tried to park. It always seemed to be barking orders at her. *German efficiency?* 'German bully-boy tactics!' she muttered under her breath as she walked up to the car.

It took her a few minutes to heave the case of wine into the boot of the car. Breathing heavily, she took the trolley back to the parking bay, and then returned, glad that she was done and about to go home. As she walked up to the driver's door, she noticed a mark on the metal. Despite the lamppost near her parking space, visibility was poor, so she rubbed at the mark, thinking it must be mud. It felt rough under her fingers. She opened the car door so that the interior light came on and illuminated the side of the car. She put her hand to her mouth in shock when she saw the side of the car. All the way along there were gouges in the pristine metal. Ragged, jagged scratches, starting at the boot and going all the way along one side.

Sue sat for a few moments in the car, thinking about what she should do. *Should she report the scratches to the police?* She supposed she needed to, for the insurance. She knew paintwork repairs were expensive, so they may have to claim. *Perhaps the supermarket would have CCTV, and that might show who had damaged the car?* Tomorrow she'd have to phone the BMW dealer and arrange for the car to go in for repair. *I wonder if they'll give me a courtesy car while it's in the paint shop?* Sue wondered, thinking how inconvenient it would be if they didn't. Suddenly despair flooded over her. *Just one more bloody thing to sort out*, she thought. Sue felt tears of anger and self-pity fill her eyes. *Why do bad things keep happening to me?* she thought as she rubbed her face and tried to decide what to do next.

CHAPTER 40

Gary found himself whistling as he walked back from the dropping the boys off at school the next morning. Noah was asleep in his buggy, so Gary didn't keep up his usual chatter, and instead thought about the previous evening. He thought about the satisfying grating noise as he'd pulled the keys down the side of that bitch's car, cutting into the pristine silver paintwork. Her actions had made his whole life spiral out of control, and now he was taking some of that control back. She was messing with the wrong family.

Even the sight of their new street didn't darken his mood, and after he pushed Noah, in his buggy, through the front door, he opened the post box for their flat and retrieved a few items from inside. *Mostly fast food menus by the looks of things,* he thought, scanning them quickly. There was one that looked a bit more official, through the window in the envelope he could say his name and address neatly typed. Feeling a little stab of apprehension, Gary tore open the envelope and read the contents. His good mood evaporated immediately.

Noah was still sleeping, so he lifted him and the buggy and carried him up the stairs to their flat. Lisa was still in her pyjamas, and she looked up sleepily when he came in.

'Caught me napping,' she said, struggling to her feet. 'Oh, and Noah too, by the look of it. Might as well just leave him in the buggy until he wakes up. Are you still in your good mood?' She asked Gary, smiling.

'No, not really, I was, until I opened this,' he said, handing Lisa the letter he'd just received. She sat down again on the sofa and read it over a couple of times. 'But I don't understand,' Lisa said, looking puzzled. 'The Citizen's Advice Bureau sorted it all out, and we've been paying the instalments, how can they be threatening to sue us?'

Gary took the letter off Lisa, and looked at it again, not really believing what he was reading. It was from Unique Interiors' lawyers, and the letter said that if he didn't pay more off the amount owed, then they were going to take him to court for non payment.

'I don't know love, I don't understand it either.'

Gary and Lisa looked at each other helplessly. Eventually Lisa pulled herself up and said, 'right, we need a plan. First, best talk to someone at the CAB, they might be able to suggest something. It could just be a mistake, or routine or something. We can't panic just yet.'

Gary considered Lisa's words. He hoped she was right, and it sounded like a good plan. 'Ok, I'll head off there now then, that seems the best thing to do. Get it sorted as quickly as possible. Will you be Ok here on your own with Noah?'

'I think I'll just about cope,' Lisa said, 'you go and get this sorted out. I'm sure it'll turn out to be a mistake.'

Gary snatched up the letter, kissed her lightly, and hurried out of the door. As he walked towards town to the Citizen's Advice Bureau offices, he hardly felt the cold. Things were horrible, living in the flat, and he had no idea how they'd cope when the new baby arrived, but they *were* just about coping. They couldn't cope with any more worry or afford to pay anything else. *God, I hate being in debt*, Gary thought, feeling his jaw clench. *But I can prove how much … how little money we have, surely that will help?* Gary started to walk more quickly, he just wanted this sorted out.

When he got to the CAB offices, the waiting room was already full. He gave his name at the reception and explained that they'd helped him before.

'You might have to wait a long time; all these people have appointments,' the woman on the reception desk said. 'Would you like to make an appointment for another day instead?'

Gary shook his head, 'no, thanks, it's a bit important, I don't mind waiting.' But he did mind, after two hours, he was bored, and increasingly anxious about the letter. He was also hungry and thirsty. Eventually his name was called, and he went into the office and sat down, facing a middle-aged woman with blonde hair and a wide smile.

'Now then, Mr Mills, I'm Judy, how can I help you?'

'I have been here a few times before and you, well, one of your colleagues, helped me to arrange a payment plan for some money I owe. My wife and I have four children, and a baby on the way, and I'm out of work. We've been paying the instalments, but we've had this letter this morning. We don't know what it means.' Gary explained, handing over the letter.

Judy read the letter carefully and frown lines appeared on her brow. 'Hmm, yes, I see, it's upsetting to get a letter like this. I will just get your case up on the computer.' She started tapping away at the keys, then smiled reassuringly at Gary. 'Computer's running a bit slow today, bit like me.'

After what seemed like half an hour, she sat upright and turned to the screen, 'ah yes, here we are, I'll just read through the ...' but before she finished speaking there was a bang, the office lights went out and the computer screen went dead. 'Oh, must be a power cut,' Judy said. 'Excuse me a moment, I'll just find out what's happening.'

Gary could have screamed with frustration. Were they ever going to get this sorted out? He got up and started to pace around the small office – three steps one way, three steps back the other way. He could hear muffled voices on the other side of the door as Judy and the receptionist discussed the sudden lack of power. He had just sat again when the door opened behind him and Judy came back in.

'I'm sorry, Mr Mills, Gary ... the power has gone off in the whole block. We have rung the electricity company but there is just a recorded message saying they are aware of the fault and trying to resolve it. Without access to your notes, I won't be able to do anything else today on your case.'

Gary closed his eyes momentarily, why did this have to happen now, to him? 'Yes, of course,' he said. 'Would I be able to leave the letter with you and come back tomorrow?'

'We aren't open tomorrow,' Judy replied, 'funding cuts I'm afraid. Why don't you see Margaret on reception and she'll book you an appointment? Luckily, we still do that the old-fashioned way, so she can put you in the diary.'

Gary stood up to go, suddenly feeling incredibly weary. He nodded at Judy, who hurried over to the desk and picked up his letter. 'Best if you take that with you and bring it back when you have your appointment.' Gary took the letter and shoved it into his coat pocket without looking at it again.

The next available appointment was three days away, but Gary could see from the diary that the bureau was busy. He asked Margaret if she could ring him if they had a cancellation beforehand, and she said that she would, but Gary didn't think that was really going to happen. He left the office and started to head back home. He was hungry and thirsty, he hadn't had any breakfast, but instead of hurrying home, his footsteps grew slower. He couldn't face going back to the flat yet. He imagined Lisa looking at him hopefully as he walked in the door, assuming that he'd managed to sort out the letter, and waiting to hear good news. But he had nothing to tell her except the promise of more days of waiting and worrying.

I don't need to go home yet, I can go for a bit of a walk, just say I was at the bureau all this time. And with that thought, instead of turning left, which led back to the flat, he turned right and headed out of town. As Gary walked, his mind buzzed with the events of the last few months. He saw him and Danny, working so hard to finish the conversion, and Sue Robinson screaming at him to get out of her house. Peter Robinson, feigning concern and suggesting that Gary gets help for his 'addiction.' Andrew Foster at Unique Interiors, looking triumphant when Mark Greenwood told him that he'd never work for them again. The pained look of disappointment on

Jacob's face when he couldn't go to judo. Gary's head thumped as it all swirled round, and he realised that he was practically running as adrenaline and anger surged through his body. A picture of him thumping Danny came into his head and his fists clenched, he wanted to punch someone now, punch and punch until all the bitterness was out of his system. He drew to a halt and looked around him. At first, he was disorientated, but then he realised he was on the road which led to the Robinsons' cul-de-sac. He didn't know if he'd set out to come here, and he didn't care if he had or not. Now he was here he wanted to teach her another lesson, let her experience some of the pain he'd felt over the past few months.

Keeping his head down, he turned into Willow Drive and walked quickly up to number 8. It was impossible to see in past the large gates, so he quietly opened the access gate adjacent to the double entry gates. He stepped in quickly and shut the gate behind him. The house was quiet, there didn't seem to be any lights on to brighten it against the winter gloom. There were curtains now in the window of the converted garage, and they were firmly closed. Gary walked over to the edge of the driveway and stared at the house. Now he was here, he wasn't sure what he was going to do. He looked up at the pristine façade of the house, but he had nothing with him that could attack the perfect white paint. He decided to go around the side of the house and into the back garden, where he'd be hidden from prying eyes.

Gary stood at the side of the house and peeped around the corner into the back garden. Despite it being winter it still looked lovely, many of the thousands of plants were still in bloom or had sprouted multi-coloured decorative leaves. The house and garden were even bigger than he'd remembered. He thought about their damp and cramped flat, with no room for the boys to play. A picture of Lisa came into his mind. Uncomfortable already owing to her huge baby bump, she struggled to get comfortable on the sofa bed, which took up all their living space when they unfolded it every night. And the Robinsons had all of this for themselves and they'd taken away what little they had. Gary felt bile rise from his empty stomach, and his heart started to thump. He had to do something, get back at her somehow. His eyes scanned around the garden and alighted on the decorative stone fountain which acted as a centrepiece for the whole garden.

Keeping low, Gary scuttled along the back of the house. The curtains on the bi-fold doors at the back of the conversion were also closed. A quick peep in the kitchen and sitting room windows revealed dark, empty rooms. *They must both be at work,* Gary thought. He picked up a heavy edging stone from the side of the lawn and ran over to the fountain. He held the stone in two hands, swung back and then flung it against the fountain. There was an almighty crack, and a large chip appeared in the arm of the stone water carrier. Gary swung the stone back again and hit the fountain harder. Again, and again he hit the stone against the fountain, causing bits of stone to fly off all over. Then he took hold of it near the bottom and with all his strength, started rocking his whole body against it, again and again, until he could feel it moving under his weight. He grasped both arms around it in a strange sort of embrace, and pushed and pushed, rocking backwards and forwards, anchoring himself against the ground with his feet. Suddenly the fountain moved, and he just managed to get his footing as it tipped forward. It was leaning over but hadn't quite left the ground, so he alternatively kicked and shoved it, putting all his weight in the movements. After another few minutes there was a creak and a cloud of dust, and Gary felt himself being sprayed with water. He ran backwards as the fountain fell slowly onto the lawn and bounced, releasing dust and slivers of stone. From underneath, where the fountain was plumbed into the water supply, water began to spray upwards, slowly at first, but then increasing in volume, so that it started to soak the grass round about.

Gary looked at the wreckage and a surge of power rushed through his body. *That's what I do to people who hurt me and mine,* he thought, and started laughing to himself as he looked at the mess that he'd made. He suddenly realised he was cold despite all the physical exertion and he looked down at his jeans. They were soaked where the water had sprayed on him. He was covered in dust and bits of stone, and as he wiped at the dust patches, he noticed dark red streaks appearing on the fabric. His hands were bleeding, he hadn't even noticed. He examined them closely, some of the cuts looked quite deep.

I'll have to think up a good story to explain this mess when I get home, Gary though, smiling to himself. But despite the wet, the cold and the cuts on his hands, Gary felt better than he had done for months. Standing upright, he took a last look at the damage he'd caused, then turned and left the garden.

CHAPTER 41

For the first time since he became a father, Gary was not the first one up on Christmas morning. Usually he couldn't wait to see the boys' faces when they opened their presents, but this year he felt ashamed that he hadn't been able to buy them new toys. He and Lisa had spent ages scouring charity shops, trying to find just the right gifts for the boys. Noah and Jack were easy to buy for, but Jacob and Oliver had written letters to Father Christmas with very specific requests, and they hadn't been able to find any of the toys that they had asked for. Jacob had been a bit quiet and withdrawn since he'd stopped going to judo, and Gary had really hoped they'd be able to find the transformer robot that he wanted. But it was one of the 'must have' toys for Christmas this year, and they were difficult to get even if you paid full-price, and despite extensive searching, there were none available second-hand.

Lisa looked up groggily, rubbing her eyes. 'Merry Christmas babe,' she said, smiling. 'Aren't the boys up yet?'

'I don't think it's going to be long,' Gary replied, 'I've heard some giggling in there.'

'Come on then, let's get the sofa folded away, and then they'll have space to open their presents.' Lisa struggled to her feet, her swollen belly making her movements awkward.

'I'll do it,' Gary replied. 'You put the kettle on, I'm choking for a cup of tea.'

Gary folded up the sofa and put away the bedclothes as quietly as he could. He wanted to clear some space before the boys came out. Plus, he was trying to put off the moment as long as he could. He was just putting the cushions back on the sofa when the door to the boys' bedroom opened and Jacob's face peeped around the door, quickly followed by Jack, and then Oliver. There was a scuffling noise and Noah's face appeared, peeping through his brothers' legs.

'Happy Christmas,' Gary cried, putting as much enthusiasm as he could into the words.

The boys looked a bit apprehensive. 'Has he been?' Jacob said solemnly. 'Did Santa know that we've moved to a new house?'

'Of course, Mum and I wrote and told him, don't worry about that. He's been, and you must all have been good boys this year because there are presents for all of you.'

Jacob's shoulders visibly sagged with relief, and the other boys started to cheer and jump up and down with excitement.

'Ssshh,' Gary said, thinking about the landlord and his threats over too much noise. 'Don't get too excited, other people might still be sleeping.'

The boys bounded into the living room, looking over to the small Christmas tree that they had also found in a charity shop – they'd always had a real one before. Lisa had placed all the presents under the tree before she and Gary went to bed last night. The boys went running over, but Gary stopped them from grabbing the presents.

'How about wishing your Mum a Merry Christmas?' The boys ran to Lisa, hugging her and shouting, 'Merry Christmas Mummy.' Lisa hugged the boys to her closely, closing her eyes and enjoying the moment.

'Come on Dad, you be Santa Claus,' she said, 'hand out the presents.' She carried a tray over to the sofa, with cups of tea for her and Gary, and juice for the boys, along with a plate of biscuits.

Gary went over to the tree and picked up the first parcel. He made a big show of reading the label, and then pronounced, 'this one is for Oliver,' handing it over to his second son. One by one he handed out the presents, and they all watched as the recipient opened each gift and examined the contents.

Eventually he handed over the last present and the boys sat on the floor, surrounded by discarded wrapping paper and various games, books and toys.

'That's them all,' Gary said, 'didn't you all do well?'

Oliver looked up at him, biting his lip and looking worried. 'Is everything Ok, Olly?' Gary asked.

'Did you and Mummy not get any presents?' Oliver asked, his lip trembling.

'They must have been naughty.' Jack shouted, sounding excited.

Gary looked at Lisa helplessly, he didn't know what to say. He and Lisa had decided not to spend money on each other this year, but how could he explain that to four boys who still believed in Santa Claus?

Lisa replied for him. 'Santa has such a lot of people to make presents for, so this year, we wrote to him and said that we didn't want anything. We are getting our new baby very soon, so no other present could be as good as that.'

Oliver smiled at Lisa's explanation, and then looked at his pile of presents. He picked out a selection box full of chocolate and came over to Lisa and Gary. 'You have this, I've got lots of other things.'

Gary saw Lisa's eyes fill with tears, and love for his funny, sensitive little boy welled up inside him. 'That's lovely Olly mate, it really is, but why don't we just take one thing out of it, and you keep the rest? Santa wanted you to have it.'

Oliver nodded, and Lisa and Gary made a big thing out of deliberating over which of the chocolate bars to choose. They ate them carefully with their mugs of tea and declared that it was the most delicious chocolate that they'd ever had.

As Gary was putting the empty cups on the tray, he looked down at the boys. Oliver, Jack and Noah were playing happily with their new toys and chatting with each other. Jacob had stacked his gifts into a neat pile and was flicking half-heartedly through one of the books that they'd bought him.

'Everything OK Jake?' Gary asked.

Jacob nodded, but Gary could see that his eyes were brimming with tears. He went over to his eldest son and crouched down beside him. 'What is it Jake?' he asked, concerned.

'Santa forget to bring my transformer robot,' Jacob mumbled. 'James has got one, and it's just brilliant. We've made up a game we were going to play when I got mine.' Gary closed his eyes. James was Jacob's best friend at school, and Jacob often went around to his house to play.

Gary had no idea what to say to make things better, so he just pulled the little boy close to him. Gary could feel Jacob's silent sobs as he hugged him, and then Jacob pulled away, stood up and went back into the bedroom. Gary got up to follow up, but he felt Lisa's hand on his arm. 'Just give him a few minutes,' she said.

Gary nodded, and busied himself with washing and drying the mugs. He had a heavy feeling in the pit of his stomach and his heart was thumping. He could remember what it was like when he was a child, and all the other kids got the thing that you wanted most. It felt like the end of the world. It had happened to Gary many times when his Dad was drinking and hadn't had any money left for presents. He had vowed it would never happen to his children, but it had. And it was all his fault. He suddenly realised that Jack was trying to get his attention. He turned around, and saw that Jack and Oliver were sitting at the table, with colouring and puzzle books and coloured pencils in front of them.

'Dad, someone has already filled in some of the pictures in my book.' Jack said, holding up the book to show some half-coloured pictures. He looked puzzled and a bit annoyed.

Gary looked back, feeling helpless. They had checked everything to see that they weren't too worn, how could they have missed this? Gary didn't know what to say, but luckily Lisa replied for him.

'Must have been Santa's naughty elves. They must have done some colouring during their tea break. Better not make too much fuss about it, or they might get into trouble.'

Jack seemed happy with this explanation, and went back to colouring in.

'Ok boys, we'd better have some breakfast, then get your clothes on. We have to get to Grandad's early so that we have plenty of time to cook the turkey.'

The boys all cheered at this and started moving their books and pencils off the table, to make room for bowls of cereal instead. Lisa went into the bedroom, and came out with Jacob, who was looking a bit happier, and was dressed in jeans and a new jumper that had been one of his Christmas presents.

'I'm looking forward to seeing Grandad,' he said. 'But I'm glad Mum's cooking, Grandad's food is terrible.'

Gary laughed, 'you're right there. He can even burn a jam sandwich!' And all the boys laughed.

Gary was looking forward to spending Christmas day with his Dad too. They had called in to see him when they were out Christmas shopping, and Lisa was saying how difficult it was going to be to cook Christmas dinner at their flat, because they didn't have a proper kitchen. And his Dad had suggested they went to his flat instead, and that they could all pitch in to prepare the dinner. It was a great solution because his Dad's flat had a separate kitchen with a full-sized cooker and plenty of storage space. There was more space all round, and as his upstairs neighbour was away for Christmas, it wouldn't matter if the boys made a noise. Suddenly Gary couldn't wait to get there, away from this dismal, cramped room.

It seemed to take forever for them to have breakfast and get dressed. The boys were excited and couldn't concentrate. And then they started watching a Christmas film on TV and wanted to see the end of it before they left. Gary had been sitting with his coat on for 10 minutes when his phone rang. He picked it up and looked at the screen. It was his Dad.

'Merry Christmas Dad,' he said cheerfully, as he answered the call. 'We are just about ready, we'll be setting off in about 5-10 minutes.'

'That's why I'm ringing son,' his Dad replied. 'There's a bit of a problem. Danny's just turned up, he's got nowhere else to go for Christmas day, and he wants to spend it with me. I can't turn him away, it's Christmas.'

Gary swallowed, he hadn't seen or spoken with Danny since they'd had their fight. 'That's Ok Dad, there's enough food for an army. It will be nice for us all to be together for Christmas.'

'But he doesn't want to see you Gary. He's never got over you not paying him for all that work he did. I'm sorry son, but you've got Lisa and the boys. He doesn't have anyone but me. I think it's best if you just stay at home. I'll pop over tomorrow to see you for half an hour, I've got some bits and pieces for the boys.'

Gary became aware of Lisa and the boys looking at him, and so he just said, 'OK, Dad, I understand. Take care.' And he ended the call. Gary sighed then stood up and started pulling off his coat.

'Change of plan. Grandad's ... not well. We won't be able to go over today. We'll just have to have Christmas here instead.'

Lisa looked at him, puzzled, and then she frowned. 'I'm not sure how we'll manage with this kitchen ...' she started to say, but Gary said crossly, 'well, we'll just have to won't we, we don't have any choice.'

In bed that night, Gary lay awake, thinking over the day. *I think that was the most crap Christmas I've ever had*, he thought. *Even worse than when Dad was drinking and forgot it was Christmas. And Christmas day in the children's home was usually quite good fun.*

After his Dad's call, the day had deteriorated badly. The boys were disappointed at not going to their Grandad's house, and the novelty of their presents soon wore off, and they got restless with eating too many sweets. It was raining and bitterly cold, so there was no chance of taking them to the park to run off some energy, and they started to squabble amongst themselves. Half-way through the morning their landlord Reuben knocked on the door, complaining about the noise, and Gary struggled not to punch him as he repeated his threats about eviction.

Lisa tried her best to make a tasty Christmas dinner, but with the small oven and only two electric rings, it was very difficult to get it all done, and they ended up with a plate of dry turkey and under-cooked vegetables. The crackers for the table, the pudding and all the extras they had bought were already at his Dad's house, taken there in advance because they had no storage here. The boys left most of their dinner, and Lisa was so stressed and tired from cooking in the cramped kitchen that she could barely eat. Later the boys said they were hungry and asked if they could go to MacDonald's instead. Gary replied that they should have eaten their dinner if they were hungry, and when the boys replied that it was 'worse than Grandad's cooking,' Lisa had started to cry and gone into the bedroom and lain down on the bed.

Gary shuffled in bed, trying to get comfortable. Something in the bed was sticking into him. He started to itch, the room was cold, but the air was thick with cooking smells. He thought about his Dad and Danny, imagined them spending the day together in his Dad's flat. *Getting drunk together*, he thought, resentment rising up. When it had come to a straight choice between him and Danny, his Dad had chosen Danny. *Now that I'm a failure, he's the favourite son again, but no need to make Lisa and the boys suffer any more than they have already.* As Gary lay awake he thought over the last few months. Of Danny, lying drunk on the Robinsons' sofa, and of Sue Robinson immediately assuming it was him, Gary, that was a drunk.

Gary turned on his side, trying to get comfortable. He

imagined the sort of Christmas the Robinsons would have, with all that space in their beautiful home. Perhaps they went out for lunch, to a posh hotel, or fancy restaurant? They'd drink some of that expensive wine, hadn't he seen her buying a whole case of it? That was probably for Christmas. He wondered how much they spent on presents for each other? Their presents wouldn't have come from charity shops. Did they invite their family around, perhaps the older couples he'd seen in the photographs in their house? A nice, jolly, refined family Christmas, and they wouldn't be thinking about him and his family, about the damage they had caused. If only they'd let him go back and finish the job, his life, his family's lives, they'd all be different.

Gary thought about the damage he'd done to their car, and their fountain, and he felt himself relax. At least he'd done something, he'd fought back. He might not be able to change what had happened, but at least he'd made them suffer a little bit too.

CHAPTER 42

Sue woke much later than usual on Christmas day. The rain was making the skies dark outside, and as she hadn't switched on her alarm, like she did on a work day, she'd slept through until nearly 9am. Sue stretched, and smiled when she remembered it was Christmas day. Not that they had much to celebrate, but she was still determined to make it as happy as she could. *In case it's Peter's last*, she thought, before she could help herself. She sighed, *why did every thought and feeling she had come back to Peter's illness?* Yes, there was no denying that he was deteriorating, but he still enjoyed life, they still enjoyed each other's company, and they might do so for quite a few years yet. So, no point being miserable, better enjoy every moment, she said, repeating the pep talk she gave herself most mornings.

When she showered, she remembered that there were no carers coming in today. She had told them they didn't need to whilst she was off work for the Christmas break, she had time to help Peter get ready. The carers were very good, kind and professional, but it was still nice not to have strangers in your home, so Sue was glad about that. She tried to think about more things that she could be glad about. She'd have time for painting this afternoon, when Peter had his afternoon nap. She didn't seem to have much time for it these days, so that was a treat. She was planning a lovely lunch, and she'd ordered everything already prepared from M&S, so everything just had to be placed into the oven, such an effortless way to cook. Then she thought about the parcels under the Christmas tree in the hallway. Peter hadn't been able to go out shopping, as he usually did, but he'd ordered things online, and had received several packages in the post. She wondered what he'd bought her and felt a little thrill of anticipation. She hoped he'd like what she'd bought him. Books, and an aged malt whisky. An expensive warm dressing gown, new slippers, and an electric diffuser for his room, which squirted essential oils into the air. And she'd had one of her paintings framed and ready to hang up somewhere in the 'man cave.' It was a seascape that Peter had particularly admired, and it fitted with the nautical theme. Suddenly she was filled with desire to get downstairs and see Peter, hold him close and wish him a Merry Christmas.

Sue did her hair and make-up quickly, and slipped into casual trousers, and a Christmas jumper with a reindeer on it. She'd bought this on a whim, thinking it would make Peter smile.

The conversion was still in darkness when she entered it. *Peter must be having a lie in too,* Sue thought, as she called out, 'Merry Christmas Pete, wakey, wakey.' There was no answer. Sue hurried over to the bed, where Peter was lying on his back. She leaned over him and planted a kiss on his cheek. That didn't wake him, so she shook his shoulder gently, not wanting to give him a fright. That didn't work either, so she shook him a bit more vigorously, and started to pull the covers back. Still nothing. 'Open curtains' she commanded, and Peter's gadget leapt into life, and the curtains started to slowly open. Peter looked very pale and clammy, and although he started to move his head, he still looked asleep. Feeling alarmed, Sue took hold of both of Peter's shoulders and tried to raise him up, talking to him all the time. After what seemed like ages, but was probably just a few minutes, Peter's eyes flickered open, looked at her with no signs of recognition, and then closed again.

Becoming really alarmed now, Sue pulled the bedclothes back fully and tried to pull Peter in a sitting position. He kept opening his eyes, and mumbling something, then closing them again and seemed to fall back to sleep. Sue knew something was wrong, and her instinct was to wake Peter. If he could only wake up properly, then she could assess the situation. Sue went into the bathroom and wrung out a flannel in cool water, came back to the bed and bathed Peter's face, eventually lying the cold flannel across his forehead. She kept on talking to him and urging him to sit up.

Eventually Peter was in an upright position, leaning against the headboard, and his eyes were more open.

'Oh, my head,' he said, squinting against the lights. 'I've got such a terrible headache.' Although Sue could make this out clearly, she noticed that Peter was having difficulty in breathing.

'Pete, you don't seem well. I think I'll call NHS 111, just in case they can suggest anything.'

Peter didn't say anything, just put his hand to his head, groaned, and tried to take some deeper breaths.

Sue picked up the bedside phone and rang 111. She went through the initial questions, giving her name, number and address, Peter's name and date of birth, explained her relationship to him, and then started to explain Peter's symptoms. Eventually the call handler said that he was going to transfer her to a clinician, and a brisk female voice came on the line. She asked Sue a few more questions, and then said, 'I'm dispatching an ambulance now. Don't be alarmed, but given your husband's underlying condition, I'm doing this as a precaution. I'd like to stay on the line with you until the ambulance arrives, which will be in a few minutes. Can you explain how your husband is now?'

Sue hadn't taken her eyes off Peter all the time she'd been on the call, and had seen him drift in and out of sleep, or was it consciousness? And his breathing was increasingly laboured. She explained this to the brisk woman, who said to try and keep Peter upright if possible.

It was 15 minutes until the ambulance arrived, but for Sue it seemed much, much longer, hours in fact. Peter seemed oblivious to what was going on, whilst she tried to carry out the brisk woman's instructions. Somehow, relaying Peter's condition back to this woman seemed to make it worse, a commentary on how ill he looked and how his breathing was getting increasingly laboured. Occasionally Peter would raise a hand to his head or his chest, but apart from that, he let Sue drag him around like a rag doll.

Sue was glad to hand over to the ambulance crew when they arrived, reassured at their matter-of-fact capability and cheerful manner as they talked loudly to Peter, explaining who they were and what they were doing. Eventually one of them turned to Sue and said, 'we think it's best if we take your husband to hospital. His breathing is very laboured, and we don't want to take any chances. Do you want to follow in your own car, so that you'll be able to get home later?'

Sue nodded, feeling her heart thumping in her chest. Peter would hate it in the hospital, but he looked so poorly, she couldn't say no. Sue went into the house to get her car keys and handbag, and when she came back Peter was on a stretcher and was being wheeled out to the ambulance. Sue locked up and went to the car. They pulled slowly out of the drive, and once they turned out of their cul-de-sac, she jumped as the ambulance's blue light and sirens came on. Sue's heart started thumping even faster and she gripped the steering wheel as she concentrated on keeping up with the speeding ambulance.

*****

It was nearly 8pm when Sue finally got home. She'd spent most of the day sitting around the hospital, waiting to be told something. Parts of the day she'd sat next to Peter's bed in one department or another, waiting for someone else to come and examine him. At other times she sat alone in a corridor, or waiting room, as Peter was examined, or moved around the hospital. She didn't know which was worse, sitting alone with Peter, who seemed to drift in and out of consciousness, and who looked slightly scary under an oxygen mask. Or sitting alone, not knowing what was happening, watching other relatives looking worried, getting angry, or sometimes upset and crying.

The house felt cold and empty when she got home. She quickly went around the rooms, closing curtains and turning on lamps. Since the fountain had been vandalised, Sue had never felt really safe in the house. She'd always thought of their back garden as a haven, not overlooked by anyone, but now it felt sinister. Not overlooked meant that no-one was watching out for intruders either. Sue shuddered as she looked out there, before double-checking that the doors were locked. She pulled the curtains tightly shut and turned on the fire to warm up the room.

Apart from something masquerading as coffee which she'd purchased from a machine in the hospital, Sue hadn't eaten or drunk anything all day, and she felt a bit shaky. She went out into the hallway and towards the kitchen but stopped short when she got to the tree and the carefully wrapped presents still underneath it. A black cloud of depression washed over her, and sighing, she headed towards the kitchen. She opened the fridge to find something to eat, and all the food she'd bought for the Christmas dinner was packed in there, unused.

Sue took her simple meal of cheese and crackers, a mince pie and a glass of wine into the sitting room. She sat down and despite the heat in the room, she shivered. Peter had a chest infection and respiratory complications, which are a common side effect of motor neurone disease. He seemed comfortable when she left, and the doctor she'd spoken with had seemed confident that he'd be fine in a few days. Sue flicked on the TV, not because she wanted to watch anything, but because she wanted to hear cheerful human voices. She'd never been on her own on Christmas day before in her whole life. She suddenly welled up with tears and despair. Was this what her life was going to be like in the future, relying on the TV for company, and crying into her wine? She put down her plate of food, curled up on the sofa, and gave into the tears that she'd been holding back all day.

CHAPTER 43

The cold and wet weather continued after Christmas, meaning that the boys were cooped up in the flat most of the time. The school holidays lasted for nearly three weeks, and as the boys got increasingly bored and restless, they started arguing with each other and misbehaving.

Lisa was finding it hard to cope with, as she was so tired all the time. Unlike her other pregnancies, where she had bloomed after the first trimester, during this pregnancy she had continued to be sick right through and felt lethargic and ill. She tried to describe how she felt to Gary, but the best she could manage was that it was like the feeling when you're just about to go down with flu, but it had lasted for months. Even minor tasks, such as washing the dishes, really tired her out, and for the first time she found the boys' incessant chatter irritating.

Les didn't turn up on Boxing Day, as he had promised. Sick of the boys asking when their Grandad was going to arrive, Gary had finally rung him, but he could tell by Les's slurred and quiet voice that he had been drinking. Gary told the boys that their Grandad was 'still not well' and tried to ignore the disappointment on their faces. Les did eventually turn up on 30th December, bringing some Christmas presents for the boys, and returning the box of Christmas crackers that they hadn't used on Christmas day.

'I'm sorry, we ate the food you'd brought over, I hadn't done any extra shopping,' he said apologetically to Lisa. Gary felt his jaw tighten at the thought of Danny eating the treats that they'd bought in for Christmas. He said nothing though, he didn't want to get into an argument.

Gary was finding it increasingly hard to be stuck in the flat. He felt as if the walls were closing in on him. He went out every day in the rain, looking for work, or visiting the Citizen's Advice Bureau. The letter from Unique Interior's lawyers was still adding to his worries, and it took several weeks to get it sorted out. Turned out it was a routine reminder that they issued every few months, in case debtors' circumstances had changed, and they hadn't renegotiated their repayment agreement. Through the bureau he provided a statement of his income and outgoings, and eventually they agreed that Gary's current payment should stay the same for the time being. Gary felt a bit more relaxed once he received a letter from the lawyers agreeing to this, but still wished he could pay more off the debt so that he wouldn't have to go through this rigmarole again in another few months.

Every day Gary went to the library to access the jobs' pages via the internet, and to the Job Centre. He started to apply for anything that he thought he could do, and not just for skilled jobs. He applied to a large construction firm who were advertising for general labourers. He hoped that if he was successful, and they could see he worked hard, then it might lead to some skilled work in the future. The interview seemed to go well at first. The foreman interviewing him was sympathetic about his business failing, sharing that his brother-in-law had experienced the same problems with cash flow when he'd set up for himself. Gary began to feel hopeful, but then he saw his interviewer look closely at his application form, and then he looked up at Gary.

'Mills, that's your surname?' He asked.

'Yes, that's right, Gary Mills.'

'Your business wasn't Mills Property Services was it?'

'Yes, it was,' Gary replied, suddenly feeling uncomfortable.

'Had a bit of bad publicity, didn't you?'

'Bit of a misunderstanding, that was all,' Gary replied, trying to smile.

But the man's demeanour had changed completely, and the interview was over within another couple of minutes and Gary found himself out on the construction site, looking enviously at the men busy working, earning a wage, being useful.

Gary kept replaying the interview over and over in his mind. It had seemed to go well, perhaps it wouldn't make any difference that he'd seen the bad publicity about his firm? After all he was overqualified for the job, and he was young and fit. He wanted to work. But if the foreman had believed the rumours about Gary taking wine from a customer's house, that might make a difference. This same discussion went around and around in Gary's head, over and over. After a week he couldn't stand not knowing any more, and he rang the firm to ask to speak to the man who'd interviewed him. The woman who answered the phone took his name, and he was left listening to music for several minutes before she came back on the line and said, 'I'm sorry, you weren't successful, and all positions have been filled.'

Gary couldn't even speak, he just ended the call, and sat staring into space. He had no other outstanding applications now, or any interviews lined up. He'd applied for all the relevant job vacancies that he'd seen, and everything just felt hopeless. At least if he had interviews lined up he felt that something could change, sometime soon.

He was roused from these thoughts by a thump and a crash behind him. He rose up and looked around, quickly taking in the scene in front of him. A football was on the kitchen work top, and the draining rack, which had held all this morning's breakfast dishes, was on the floor, surrounded by broken crockery. Jack was standing looking at it, with his hand over his mouth.

'Whoops,' Jack said, turning to Gary.

Gary felt his teeth grind together and a wave of anger rise from his stomach. 'How many times have I told you not to play football in the house?' he roared at Jack, and with two steps he went over to his son, grabbed him by the arm and smacked him hard on the bottom. He must have smacked him about four times, before he realised that Lisa, Jacob and Oliver were all shouting at him to stop. Lisa grabbed his arm as he lifted it to strike Jack a fifth time, and she pushed him away from the little boy.

Gary's anger left him as quickly as it had risen, and he looked down at Jack, horrified. The little boy's face was bright red, and he was sobbing uncontrollably. Noah had also started to cry, and Jacob and Oliver were looking at their brother, both white-faced, and close to tears too. Silently, they both went over and joined their mother in hugging Jack and trying to comfort him. Noah toddled over, and Jacob put his arm around him and pulled him into the group too.

Appalled at what he'd done, Gary tried to speak, but he couldn't find the words, so he took a step towards the group. Jack immediately started to sob more loudly, and Lisa turned to him, her eyes flashing, and her mouth set in a hard line. 'Get out, go on, go.' She hissed, and then turned back to her sons, holding them close and murmuring to them gently.

Gary snatched up his coat, and left the flat, feel totally ashamed and utterly wretched. He'd never hit one of his sons before. He'd even challenged other parents that he'd seen smacking their children. He kept seeing Jack's scared face in his thoughts, and he felt sick. He must have been terrified. Gary half-turned to go back to the flat, he just wanted to hold his son to him, tell him he was sorry and wipe away his tears. But he didn't know if he could face them all yet. In the end he just kept on walking. He didn't know how far he'd walked, or where he went. His thoughts were dark and upsetting. Jack sobbing and looking scared. Jacob and Oliver's silent and shocked faces. Lisa's anger. The face of the interviewer, looking closely at Gary's surname. His Dad's voice saying, 'Danny's come around, he's on his own.' Gary felt like he was going mad, how were they ever going to get out of this situation? That horrible flat where they were all cooped up and on top of each other day after day. No wonder Jack was kicking his football inside, there was nowhere else for him to play. Gary groaned inwardly, it was all hopeless. He'd wanted to create a perfect family, give them everything that he and Lisa didn't have when they were growing up. Instead he'd let them down, and now they were all suffering.

Gary sat on a seat in the town centre. It was still raining and bitterly cold, but he didn't even realise. He didn't know what to do. He was ashamed to go home and face his family. He had no money to go for a cup of coffee, and he didn't want to go to his Dad's house in case Danny was there. Despite all the walking that he'd done, he felt restless.

I've got to do something, Gary thought, *I think I might be going crazy.*

CHAPTER 44

As usual, Willow Drive was quiet during the day. All the houses had long driveways, so it was hard to tell if anyone was at home. When people did come out, it was usually in a car, and they sped away from the street quickly. Gary put his hood up and walked briskly along the street and in through the Robinsons' gate. There was no car in the drive and he couldn't see any lights on, despite the rain making the day dark and miserable. The curtains on the front window of the conversion were closed, but all the other curtains in the house were open and tied back neatly.

Gary walked as quietly as he could down the side of the house and into the back garden. He noticed that the fountain had been removed, and there was an ugly gap in the lawn where it had been. The pipes that supplied water to the fountain were still there, but they had been tied off and covered up, and just stuck up from the ground, looking odd and out of place. Not sure what to do, Gary looked around the garden for inspiration. He wanted to teach that bitch a lesson. Let her see what it was like to feel like your whole life was slipping away from you. Gary's eyes alighted on the shed, and he ran quickly towards it, keeping low, and as near to the trees as he could. It wasn't locked, and he slipped inside, shut the door, and looked around.

Like everything in the Robinsons' house and garden, the shed was immaculate and ordered. Garden tools hung in size order from special hooks on the walls. There was an expensive-looking workbench at one end, and above that a board containing a range of power tools. Opposite the garden tools were a row of sturdy shelves containing neatly stacked paint tins, and a row of plastic boxes, all with printed labels. For some reason, the tidiness and order made Gary furious. He wanted to disrupt it and smash it all up. But that would take too long, and they'd probably just think it was vandals. No, he wanted that bitch to know that she was being targeted. Make her feel some of the fear and despair that Gary felt each day.

An idea forming in his mind, Gary went over to the paint tins.

He scanned them quickly, dismissing the tins of emulsion. Instead he selected a tin of black metal paint, probably used to touch up the immaculate metal furnishings on the timber gates, and the fences that topped the walls around the front garden. He looked at the storage boxes and found one labelled 'paint brushes.' He opened it and selected a large brush with wide bristles. *No good*, he thought, *it won't fit into the paint tin*. He chose a smaller one instead, the widest one that would fit into the paint tin comfortable. In the box there was a special tool for opening paint tins, so he prised off the lid, and stirred the paint. He looked down at the gleaming blackness of the thick liquid and smiled.

Gary opened the shed door and peeped into the garden. Still no lights or signs of life, so carrying the paint tin in one hand, and the brush in the other, he ran quickly over to the back of the house and looked up at the pristine white render. He quickly started to paint a message onto the back wall of the house, reaching up as far as he could and then down low, so that the words were as large as he could make them.

When he'd finished he stepped back and looked at his work. Smiling to himself he picked up the tin and threw it as hard as he could at the kitchen window. There was a loud thud, but the window didn't break. The remaining thick black paint splashed out over the window, and then ran onto the windowsill, and down the wall. Gary was still smiling when he caught a movement out of the corner of his eye. The bi-fold doors of the conversion were opening, and then someone looked out. It was Peter Robinson. Gary turned and fled around the other side of the house, skirting the orangery, squeezing through the trees, and out into the front garden. He was sure that Peter would come out of the front of the conversion and tackle him, but when he burst into the front garden there was no sign of him. Gary ran quickly over the grass and out of the single gate. He then ran as quickly as he could along the street, expecting to hear footsteps running after him, or the sound of a police siren.

He kept on running until he was back in the town centre, then he stopped, bending over to get his breath and holding his hand to his side. He'd developed a stitch with running. There was no-one following him, he'd got away with it. Gary smiled broadly to himself, he felt better than he had for ages. In fact, he felt like whooping with delight and jumping up and punching the air. He settled for fist-bumping the bench, and then sitting back, letting his breathing return to normal. His face was aching he was smiling so much. He realised that he still had the paint brush in his hand, and in fact he'd been carrying it like a baton all the time he'd been running. He looked at his hands. He was wearing the thermal gloves that his Dad had bought him for Christmas, but they were covered in black paint, sticky and drying. He rolled them off, wrapping them around the brush, and deposited the whole lot in the nearest waste bin.

Finally, Gary felt able to face his wife and family again, and he turned towards home. For the first time in weeks the rain stopped, and some weak winter sunshine shone through the clouds. Gary looked up at the sky and smiled. *I think I've made the rain go away*, he thought and laughed out loud.

CHAPTER 45

PC Karen Docherty surveyed the house as she walked from her car to the front door. The occupants had reported an act of criminal damage, but she couldn't see any evidence of it out here. Everything looked immaculate. Karen rang the doorbell and waited. But instead of the front door opening, a door further along the property opened instead, and a tall man looked out.

'Hello, thank you for coming, I'm Peter Robinson, I made the call.'

Karen walked over to where the man was standing, and when she got there she realised why he hadn't come to the front door. He was standing upright with the aid of a walking frame, and his breathing was laboured. *What a shame*, Karen thought inwardly, *he doesn't look that old, I wonder what's wrong with him?*

'Good afternoon,' Karen replied brightly. 'I'm PC Karen Docherty, I understand you reported an act of vandalism.'

'Yes, I did,' Peter replied, 'come through this way and I'll show you.'

Karen stepped into a stylish and comfortable studio apartment, nicely furnished and surprisingly spacious. She thought about her room in a shared house and decided that something like this would suit her nicely.

'What a nice apartment,' she remarked. 'Do you live here?'

'Thank you,' Peter replied, turning to smile to her. 'Unfortunately, I do spend most of my time here. I do make it to the main house several times a day, usually in the evenings when my wife returns from work.'

He continued, 'as you can probably tell, I'm a bit decrepit. I've got this thing called Motor Neurone Disease, so we had this made so that my living accommodation is all on one level. Makes it easier. But it's a bit like being a lodger in my own home.'

Karen found herself warming to this man. His explanation was given without a trace of self-pity, in fact he laughed at the bit about being a lodger, and Karen could see that he must have been very attractive when he was younger, before his illness. Not that he was exceptionally handsome, but he had a charisma about him which was still evident.

'I'm sorry about your illness,' she said. 'Must be dreadful. Have you had to give up work?'

'Yes. I was a school teacher, and I loved it. I was planning on early retirement, but it was forced on me a bit earlier than planned. I couldn't have managed like this, but it does get a bit boring during the day. My wife still works full-time,' Peter explained as he slowly made his way across the studio. He stopped and sat on a chair at the table over in the kitchen area.

'Sorry, got to have a rest. We'll get there in a minute. Please do sit down.'

Karen smiled and sat in the seat he'd pulled out for her. 'Is your wife a school teacher too?' She asked.

'No, she's an accountant. Partner in a big firm on that new business park at the other end of town. She was always more practical than me, and cleverer too.' Peter smiled, and Karen detected real pride in his voice and face. She warmed to this man more and more.

'Do you want to tell me what happened to prompt your call?' Karen asked, pulling out her notebook and pen.

Peter took a deep breath and explained, 'it was just after 1.00pm, and I was lying on my bed, listening to an audiobook. I heard noises in the back garden, and I thought it might be the window cleaner, so I got up to go over to the big doors at the back. I was just going to poke my head out and say hello. Well, as you can see, it takes me a while to walk that short distance, and I was nearly over there when I heard an almighty thump. I thought he must have fallen off his ladder, so I went over and looked out. There was a young man out there, with his hood up, and when he saw me, he started running in the opposite direction, and then disappeared into the trees at the side of the house. I could see something on the ground, so I went out to have a look, see what it was. Probably best if you see for yourself,' Peter said, his mouth tightening, and his face growing serious. He struggled to his feet and walked over to the bi-fold doors and opened them. He lifted out the walking frame, and then stepped out himself, holding onto a handle attached into the wall. Once he was outside, he grasped the walking frame, stood upright, and smiled at Karen, inviting her to go first.

Together they walked along the back of the house, and Peter nodded at the back wall, outside what looked like the kitchen. Karen took in the scene. The words, "I'll make you pay, you fucking bitch," were painted in thick black paint on the back wall of the house. The message looked even uglier against the clean white of the wall. Karen took a sharp intake of breath.

'Watch your feet,' Peter advised, nodding down at the patio. Karen looked down and saw an empty paint tin, lying on its side on the patio, its contents spilling out and drying on the stonework. She followed the paint splashes up the wall, and onto the kitchen window, where there was a large splatter pattern, and a crack in the glass.

'I think the thump I heard was the paint tin being thrown against the window,' Peter said grimly. Karen looked at him, and she noticed that his hands were shaking violently.

'Are you OK, Mr Robinson?' she said, concerned.

Peter smiled thinly, 'just a spasm, thank you Officer, it'll pass. If you don't mind, I'll go back in the house. Just come in when you've seen enough of this disaster zone.' And he shuffled off to the back door of the house and stepped gingerly inside. Once he was through the door, he turned and looked out.

'I forgot to say, I think he got the paint from our shed. It looks like the metal paint we use for the fence at the front. The shed's just up there at the end of the garden.' Karen turned to look, and noticed the shed tucked away.

'Thanks, I'll just have a look around, then I'll take down some more details.'

When Karen had finished her investigation of the scene, she knocked on the back door of the house, and entered a beautiful airy kitchen. Peter was sitting on a chair at the far end, and he smiled warmly as she entered.

'Can I get you a tea or coffee?' he asked. 'Sue bought this machine that you put pods in. Means I don't spill anything, and the coffee is surprisingly good. I can do latte, cappuccino, hot chocolate, mocha, espresso, anything you want really.'

Karen was going to refuse, she didn't want to cause him any work, but he was looking at her hopefully. She replied, 'a cappuccino would be lovely, thank you, a real treat compared with the coffee down at the station.'

Peter busied himself with pressing buttons on the machine, and soon he had produced two steaming mugs of frothy coffee. 'Would you mind carrying the mugs over to the table?' he asked. 'You only end up with half a cup if I do it.' He joked, but Karen could see a sad look in his eyes.

The coffee was good, and Karen smiled and said, 'mmm, delicious,' which seemed to please Peter. He then looked serious. 'Did you find anything in the shed?'

'It all looks neat and tidy in there, although there is a box on the floor that looks out of place. It has paint brushes in it, so I think he must have taken a brush from there, to paint the words on the wall. I think we need to take some fingerprints from the shed, and from the paint tin, see if we have him on record. If you and your wife could leave everything as it is until we've done that, that would be great. I'll try and get someone over tomorrow.' Karen replied. 'Do you have any idea who might do this?'

Peter explained about the other two recent incidents; their car being scratched, and the damage to the fountain. 'We didn't think they were connected, just that we'd been unlucky. But with this, well, it's nasty, and seems targeted against Sue, my wife, so I wonder if they're all connected? We did report the first two incidents, but really there were no clues to go on, so very little could be done.'

Karen could see that Peter was really concerned, and that despite his attempts at humour, this experience had shaken him. She thought about how hard it must be to have your property attacked, and not be able to retaliate physically. She suddenly felt angry about whoever had done this. Who could target someone so ill as this nice, decent man?

'Do you have any idea of why someone might want to target your wife?' Karen asked.

'I do actually,' came Peter's surprising reply. 'But I'm not sure if I'm barking up the wrong tree, it's just a thought.' Peter then told her the story of the 'name and shame' website, and the subsequent publicity via local media. 'I imagine some of the firms that were named on the site might have a grudge to bear. But why they are acting now, I don't know, the site has been quiet recently. Sue doesn't have time to do much with it, and I think she's rather got it out of her system.'

'Would you be able to show me the site?' Karen asked, and Peter asked if she'd mind retrieving his iPad from the conversion. Karen brought it in, Peter found the site address, and handed the iPad to Karen, and sipped at his coffee while she looked through it.

'So really, although Mrs Robinson set up the site, the only firm that she personally names, was the one that did the work on your garage conversion. Mills Property Services.' Karen concluded.

'Yes, that's right,' Peter agreed. 'Sue and the young man who owned the firm, I think his name was Gary, they had words when we came back from holiday and saw the work that he'd done.

What was worse was there were some bottles of wine missing from our kitchen, and he had the empties in his van. And there was a wine stain on a rug in the sitting room. It looked like he'd been drinking when he should have been working. Shame really, young man, wasting his life like that.' Peter shook his head sadly.

'Did you meet this Gary Mills?' Karen asked.

'Yes, just the once, same time as Sue.' Peter replied.

'Do you think that could have been him in the garden today?'

Peter thought for a few moments and then said, 'I only saw him briefly. They were a similar build, very slim, average height, but I really couldn't be sure. The guy today had his hood up, and he ran as soon as he saw me.'

Karen left shortly afterwards, determined to try and find the perpetrators of this crime. Peter Robinson seemed like a decent man, and she'd really liked him. He wasn't demanding, critical or abusive like some of the people she came across in her job, and she could see that this incident had really shook him up. Mills Property Services seemed like a good starting point.

CHAPTER 46

When Gary walked into the flat, he found Lisa and the boys huddled under a blanket on a sofa, watching cartoons on the TV. They looked up at him warily, and none of them smiled. Gary took a deep breath and smiled at them broadly. He went over to Jack, crouched down in front of him and apologised for hitting him earlier that day.

'It'll never happen again Jackie, I promise. I've just been so upset with not having a job, but I shouldn't have taken it out on you. I'm really sorry. Are we friends?'

Jack nodded, but when Gary hugged him, the little boy flinched, and didn't hug him back. Gary felt dreadful, and vowed he'd try and make it up to him. He looked around the rest of the boys.

'And that goes for you all. I was wrong, I'm sorry, don't worry, I promise I will never smack any of you, ever.'

Gary turned to Lisa, who still wasn't smiling. He noticed that she looked dreadfully pale.

'Are you OK babe? You're looking a bit peaky,' he asked, suddenly concerned.

'Just tired, and I've been sick all day again. And I've got this awful itch, it's nearly driving me crazy,' Lisa replied, looking on the verge of tears.

'It's actually stopped raining outside, so why don't us boys all go to the park, and we'll let you have a rest?' Gary said, trying to sound upbeat and mask his concern. 'Do we have any stale bread we can take for the ducks?'

'We've got those biscuits that we bought in the sale, that none of us like. The ducks might eat them?' Lisa suggested, pointing over towards one of the kitchen cupboards.

The boys leapt up and started to pull on shoes and coats. 'Can we take the football?' Jacob asked, and Gary nodded.

'Course we can, we could do with a good kick around. Now then Noah, let's get your coat and shoes on, and we'll get away.'

It was cold in the park, but they weren't too bothered about it, because they played endless games of football, and the boys played on the swings and other playground equipment. The ducks did like the funny-tasting biscuits, and Noah squealed with delight every time a duck bobbed upside down in the water. It was probably the best afternoon they'd had for ages, and it was already dark when they returned home. The boys chattered happily as they walked back to the flat, and even Jack seemed to have forgiven Gary for his behaviour earlier in the day.

'Look, a police car,' said Oliver, pointing to the car parked outside the flats. 'There isn't anyone in it,' he added, sounding disappointed. Oliver often said that he wanted to join the police force when he grew up and was always fascinated when he saw a police officer in real life.

I wonder what's going on now? Gary thought as he let the boys into the house, wondering which of their neighbours had done something that warranted a visit from the police. Excited to tell their Mum all about their time in the park, the boys burst into the flat, and then stopped dead when they saw her sitting at the table opposite a uniformed police woman.

Gary's stomach lurched. *Has Dad got into trouble when he's been drinking?* He thought, feeling increasingly anxious. He looked at Lisa and then at the police officer, unsure of what to say. Lisa spoke first.

'This is PC Docherty. She's investigating a crime at that house where you and Danny did the conversion job. Something that happened earlier today.'

Gary felt himself flush. It was like the incident at the Robinsons' had happened at another time and had been done by someone else. It never crossed his mind that what he'd done would result in a visit by the police. He busied himself getting Noah out of the buggy and removing his coat and shoes.

'The Robinsons' place?' He said, trying to sound unconcerned. 'What's happened? And what's it got to do with me, it was months ago that I worked over there?'

The police woman spoke for the first time. 'Someone broke into Mr and Mrs Robinsons' garden earlier this afternoon, and committed an act of vandalism, including writing some distressing graffiti aimed at Mrs Robinson. It's the third similar incident that they've experienced recently. We are investigating anyone who may have reason to feel aggrieved with either Mr or Mrs Robinson. Your name came up in relation to a website that Mrs Robinson set up. I think you're familiar with what I mean?'

Gary smiled shakily at PC Docherty. 'Oh, is that website still operating? All just a flash in the pan I think. If you're in business, you always get your share of good and bad reviews. You say this incident happened earlier this afternoon? Well, it couldn't have been me, I've been in the park all afternoon with the boys. We went as soon as it stopped raining.'

'What time was that exactly?' Karen asked, looking down at her notepad.

'Shortly after one,' Gary replied quickly, and Karen looked puzzled. She turned to Lisa.

'I have written down that it was after 2.00pm that your husband and sons left for the park? That's what you said earlier.'

'Lisa's been asleep most of the day,' Gary interrupted, 'wouldn't know what time it was. It was definitely just after one, that was when the rain stopped. The boys are sick of being cooped up indoors, so I was waiting for a break in the clouds to get them out.'
Karen continued to look at Lisa, who shifted in her seat, scratched herself in several places, and then said, 'Gary's probably right, I've not been feeling well today at all, I must have thought it

was later than it actually was.'

'We had a fun time at the park,' Jack chimed in. 'We've been playing football, and we had the playground to ourselves, and the ducks liked those horrible biscuits Mum.'

'They gobbled them up,' Jacob added, 'and they tasted like puke.' Noah started giggling again, and clapped his hands, saying 'quack, quack' and bouncing up and down.

Karen smiled at the boys but turned back to Gary. 'So, let's make sure I've got this right. You left for the park just after 1pm, and you've been there until now? You haven't been anywhere else?'

Gary shook his head. 'That's right, we've been playing and feeding the ducks. We only came back now because it's dark.'

'Where were you earlier today?' Karen asked.

'I went for a walk into town this morning.' Gary replied. 'Had a look in the Job Centre, went into the library to look at some of the job sites, I'm unemployed at the moment, and then I came home.'

'So, you were not in the vicinity of Willow Drive at all today?'

Gary could feel his colour rising, but he tried to smile. 'No, I had no need to be in that part of town, it's a cul-de-sac, you can't cut through to get anywhere.'

Karen looked over her notes for a few moments, then decisively closed her notebook and stood up. 'Thanks for your time. I'll be in touch if there's anything else I need to ask you.'

Gary showed her out, and Karen walked slowly back to her car. *Something's not right here*, she thought, as she drove back to the police station. When she got back, she asked her Sergeant if he could spare her a few minutes. She told him about the situation at the Robinsons' house, and about the incidents with their car, and the fountain. She then recounted her meeting with first Lisa Mills, and then Gary Mills.

'The timings just don't add up. His children are quite young, one is just a toddler. It would be too cold for them to be in the park all those hours, even if they were running around playing. And Mrs Mills definitely said it was after 2.00pm when they left. She changed her mind to back him up, but I'm sure she was lying. I'd like to see if there is any CCTV on the route to the park, see if we can find out for sure when they actually went. If it was after 2.00pm, then he could have been responsible for the incident at the Robinsons' house, and got back in time to take the boys to the park.'

'You could do that,' her Sergeant agreed. 'But you're not going to. We have more serious crimes than this to investigate. And if it was him, you going around has probably given him enough of a fright for him not to do it again. If we get any fingerprints that we can match to him then that's a different matter. But he's not got a record, and his wife, and kids, are backing him up. Just leave it for now Karen, you've spent enough time on it.'

Karen sighed and nodded, but she wasn't happy. She'd promised Peter Robinson that she would investigate fully, and she thought that Gary Mills was lying. She made a note to check on the fingerprints the next day, see if they helped move the investigation forward.

CHAPTER 47

Peter was in the sitting room when Sue got home from work, and after they said hello he asked Sue to sit with him as he had something to tell her. Sue sat down, alarmed. She hoped Peter hadn't developed some new symptom, he did look dreadfully pale and was shaking more than usual.

'We've had another incident today Sue, another attack on the house. It happened just after lunch and I've had the police here this afternoon.'

Sue's heart started to thud in her chest. *Not again, who is doing this to us?* 'What happened?' she asked shakily, and then added, 'are you OK, you aren't hurt?'

'No, no, nothing like that,' Peter reassured her. 'Just felt such a crock, not being able to chase after him.'

'You mean you saw him? What did he do?' Sue asked, not sure if she really wanted to know.

'Daubed graffiti on the back wall of the house and threw the paint tin at the kitchen window. The window's cracked, and it's a bit of a mess.' Peter said, sounding subdued, but angry.

Sue stood up. 'I'll go and have a look.'

Peter held out an arm and tried to stop her, 'do you really want to look tonight? It's not very pleasant.' But Sue walked quickly into the kitchen and out of the back door into the garden. The sensor spotlights immediately lit up the back of the house, and she looked around to see the damage. When she read the message on the wall her hand flew up to her face. She felt sick. This wasn't just random vandalism, this was targeting her in particular. She took a few deep breaths of cold night air before she stepped back into the house, making sure the door was firmly locked behind her.

Peter had come out of the sitting room and was walking across the hallway towards the kitchen. Sue busied herself taking off her coat and waited to speak until he'd arrived in the kitchen and sat down at the table.

'Well, it's a bonny mess,' she said, trying to make light of it. She could see Peter was really shaken up. 'What did the police have to say?'

'They are sending someone out to dust for fingerprints in the shed tomorrow. That's where he got the paint and the brush from, so there may be some clues.' He paused for a few moments, then resumed. 'I showed the police woman the website, and she was going around to see that young chap who did the work on the conversion.'

'Gary Mills?' Sue said, immediately bristling at the mere thought of him. 'They think it's him who is doing this?' She could hear her voice becoming shrill and she tried taking some more deep breaths.

'No, they don't think that at all, they'd never heard of him,' Peter said calmly. 'I suggested that someone who'd featured on the website might have a grudge against you. They are starting with him because his was the only firm that you personally named, that's all.'

'But you got a look at him, didn't you?' Sue asked insistently. 'Did you think it was him?'

'It was impossible to tell Sue. It was a youngish man, and he was slim,' Peter began.

'Like that Mills creature,' Sue interrupted.

'Like lots of people,' Peter said gently. 'The person who did this had his hood up, it could have been anyone. The police woman just asked if there was anyone who could have a grudge against you, and that's all I could come up with.' Peter sighed and rubbed his face.

Sue immediately felt her anger subside and became concerned

for Peter instead.

'It must have been awful, seeing someone damaging our property like that. Were you scared?' she asked, laying a hand on Peter's arm and stroking it gently.

Peter laughed drily. 'I've got a disease that's killing me, what can be scarier than that?'

Sue was shocked, normally Peter was so matter of fact about his illness. He must be really shaken, she concluded.

'I wasn't scared, but I was frustrated. I wanted to run after him, catch him, not let him get away with it, but instead he was away before I even got out of the door. I felt so bloody useless.' Peter said, clenching his hand into a fist and thumping gently on the table.

Sue took hold of his fist and gently smoothed out of his hand. 'Why don't I take a couple of days off work, a long weekend?' she suggested. 'We'll bring in a firm to clear up that mess, make it as good as new. And while they're doing that we'll go out for the day, a drive in the country, or perhaps down to the coast? And we'll have lunch out. What do you think?'

'I think that sounds great.' Peter replied, smiling. 'Just what we both need.'

Sue checked all the doors and windows twice that night before going to bed. She'd always felt so safe in this house, but now it seemed an alien, frightening place, with shadows in every corner. When she went upstairs to bed, she felt even more alone than she usually did, and kept all the lights on for as long as she could. Even when she settled down to go to sleep she switched on the bedside lamp on what had been Peter's side of the bed, not able to face total darkness.

CHAPTER 48

Gary and Lisa slept very little on the night after Karen Docherty had visited them. Lisa was quiet all evening but did not ask Gary anything until after the boys went to bed, and she was sure they were all asleep. Then she turned to him and looked at him seriously.

'Gary, tell me the truth. Did you vandalise that house today?'

'Do you honestly think I'd do something like that?' Gary asked, feeling uncomfortable. He had never lied to Lisa before, but he didn't feel able to tell her the truth. To explain why he did what he did.

'I don't know Gary. You tell me. I didn't think you'd ever hit one of the children, but you did that today too. I know you lied about what time you went to the park.' Lisa said, sounding subdued and sad.

'I'm so sorry about hitting Jack, Lisa, I really am. I really don't know what came over me. If I could only get some work, I feel so useless.' Gary said, trying to move Lisa away from the subject of the Robinsons.

'It's hard for all of us living here. It's awful for the boys being cooped up all the time. They've been really good considering, you can't take it out on them Gary, you really can't.' Lisa shook her head and looked down at the floor. 'But you didn't answer my question. Did you do what that police woman said?' Lisa looked up at Gary hopefully. 'Please say it wasn't you.'

'Of course it wasn't me babe,' Gary replied, pulling her into a hug. *No point in worrying her with the truth*, he thought.

When they got to bed, Lisa couldn't get comfortable. She was itching all over, and her hands and feet had swollen alarmingly. She complained of a severe headache, and Gary could see that she was squinting in the direction of any light, even when it was quite dim. Gary rubbed her feet and hands, and massaged her back, not sure what to do to help.

'Do you think you should speak to the doctor, or your midwife tomorrow?' he suggested. And Lisa agreed that she would if she didn't feel any better. Eventually, in the early hours of the morning, Lisa fell asleep, exhausted.

Gary still lay awake, restless. He couldn't believe that the Robinsons had sent the police to his door. *Probably that vindictive cow*, he thought. *She obviously hasn't done enough damage to me and my family.* Gary thought about the satisfaction that he felt when he saw the ugly black letters against the startling white of the house wall. He wished he could smash up everything in their lives, just like she'd done with his life. When his anger subsided a bit, he began to get worried. *What if they could prove it was me? Do they send you to prison for something like that?* he wondered. *But how could they prove it was me anyway, I'd had my gloves on, so I wouldn't have left fingerprints? I don't think the husband got a good look at me, and Lisa and the kids backed me up about being at the park all afternoon.* Gary desperately tried to reassure himself, but he was still worried.

He started to drift off to sleep but was jolted awake by a replay of him grabbing Jack by the arm and smacking him. He felt so wretched and ashamed, and his heart began to thump alarmingly. *What is wrong with me?* he thought. *I've hit my son and lied to my wife. Every day I'm getting to be more of a loser.* Then he thought about the feeling of control and power he had when he threw the paint can at the Robinsons' kitchen window and he eventually drifted off to sleep, smiling to himself.

The next morning began badly. The rain had returned with a vengeance, meaning that once again they were all stuck in the flat with nowhere to go. Lisa was no better, she still had a terrible headache, and complained that her vision seemed blurred too. Gary rang the surgery and made her an appointment, but the earliest available was after the weekend.

Once the boys were up and dressed, Lisa went into their room and got into their bed in the hope of getting some more sleep.

They were all just finishing breakfast when there was a knock at the flat door. Gary opened the door and his heart sank when he saw Reuben standing there. The landlord was his usual brusque self.

'Saw the police here yesterday. I hope you're not in trouble? Don't want that sort of trouble in my house. If I see them here again you're out. Plenty more people want this flat. And keep those bloody kids quiet.' He spoke and turned to go before Gary could offer an explanation, or even reply. Gary was tempted to slam the door to make a statement towards Reuben's retreating back, but instead he closed the door and briefly laid his head against it.

Gary tried to keep the boys amused by making up games all morning. But by lunchtime he was running out of ideas, and the boys were restless and starting to squabble with each other.

'Come on,' he said, 'we're going for a walk. Get your coats and shoes on.'

Jacob turned and looked out of the window. 'But it's pouring down,' he said, looking at Gary as if he'd gone crazy.

'There is loads of washing needs done,' Gary replied. 'We'll go to the launderette and you can help me fold it up.' The boys all groaned.

'Never mind groaning,' Gary said, 'you're all back at school on Monday, and you need clean uniforms.'

Doing the laundry at least diverted the boys for a while. Gary treated them to a cup of hot chocolate from the vending machine whilst the washing was going around. An elderly woman, waiting for her washing to finish, chatted to the boys and gave them all a bag of sweets.

Noah insisted on walking rather than riding in his buggy on the way back, which meant progress was extremely slow. Noah could walk perfectly well, but like many toddlers, he liked to stop and look at everything on the way, and nothing could persuade him to get a move on.

They had stopped while he watched a leaf floating in a puddle, when Gary noticed Jacob's friend James on the other side of the road, walking along with his parents and another boy. James had been Jacob's best friend since they both started at pre-school, and they loved to spend time with each other. Gary suddenly realised that Jacob hadn't caught up with James throughout the school holidays, which was very unusual.

'Jake, look there's James over the road, do you want me to give him a shout?' Gary asked, tapping Jacob on the shoulder and pointing. Jacob shook his head, turned away and started walking in the direction of home. Puzzled, Gary putting the washing bags in the buggy, picked up Noah, and carrying him in one hand, and pushing the buggy with the other, he hurried after his eldest son.

'What is it Jacob, why don't you want to see James?' Gary asked. Jacob just looked down on the ground, kicking at a twig with his foot.

'They're not friends anymore,' Oliver said quietly.

'When did that happen?' Gary asked, wondering why he hadn't know about this.

'It's because I don't go to judo any more, and then I didn't get the transformer for Christmas. James sees Nathan all the time now, that's who he's with. He says I'm no fun.' Jacob said all this in a quiet voice, not looking up.

Gary's heart went out to his son, and he remembered how upset he'd been on Christmas day when he didn't get the gift that he'd asked for. Now he understood why.

'Why didn't you tell me this son?' Gary asked gently.

'What good would it have done?' Jacob asked, sounding angry now. 'I still wouldn't have been able to go to judo, I still wouldn't have got the stupid transformer for Christmas. I'd still be no fun. What's the point?' Jacob said, turning and walking determinedly in the direction of home.

Gary turned to Oliver and Jack and put Noah back on the pavement. 'Come on boys, let's get out of this rain,' he said. *My God, what's happening to us all?* He thought as he resumed the long walk back to the flat.

Gary spent another restless night. Events kept going around in his head. The police woman looking at him suspiciously. Their landlord making threats. Jack's frightened face, and Jacob's hunched shoulders as he'd walked away, avoiding his once closest friend. Gary got up and sat at the table. He hated this flat and felt like the walls were closing in on him. Everything just seemed black and hopeless. Gary sat up, watching the clock tick round, until it was time to wake the boys and start another day.

As soon as breakfast was over, Gary took advantage of a break in the rain to take the boys to the park. It was so cold outside though that they didn't stay long. Noah was crying because he was cold, and when it started raining again, they headed for home. Gary made everyone a drink, but as soon as he'd finished his coffee he felt restless again, and knew he had to get out of the flat.

'Do we need anything at the shops Lisa?' he asked hopefully.

'We could do with something for Sunday lunch, and we don't have much in for tea tonight.' Lisa replied. Almost before she'd finished speaking Gary had snatched up his coat and was heading off downstairs.

Gary took his time shopping, going to several different shops to get the best prices. It saved very little, but it gave him an excuse to be out of the flat a bit longer. Once he had all the shopping that he could afford, he walked around town, looking in shop windows, and then headed out of town, just for something to do. Gary wasn't really paying attention to where he was walking, but he wasn't surprised to find himself around the corner from Willow Drive. Knowing he was taking a risk, he pulled up the hood of his coat, and turned casually into the street. There was a car driving slowly along the street and he shrank back as he recognised the dark silver BMW that he'd last seen in the supermarket car park. As it drove past he noticed that it had been resprayed, and that both Robinsons were inside. *She* was driving, and Gary got the impression that she was laughing as she passed him. Gary felt his hands clench and a flush rise to his cheeks. *I'll give you something to laugh about*, he thought furiously.

Gary slipped into the now-familiar gate and tucked his shopping bag under a bush. He didn't have any gloves on, so he'd have to be careful what he touched. Feeling confident as he knew the Robinsons were out, he made his way slowly into the back garden. He looked at the wall that he'd attacked last time he was there and saw that it was in the process of being cleaned. *I hope it never comes off*, he thought, and then looked around to see what else he could do. His gaze alighted onto the flower beds. Although it was winter, they were still colourful, with lots of expensive-looking shrubs with various coloured leaves and even some flowers. Gary felt a surge of energy and stamped into one of the beds. He started trampling down the bushes, and tugging at some of the smaller shrubs, trying to pull them out of the ground. He was so intent on causing as much damage as he could, that he didn't realise he wasn't alone until there was a shout from the other side of the garden. Gary looked up, startled, and saw a group of four men, all dressed in overalls, coming around the side of the house. Gary turned and fled, taking the same route as he had when Peter Robinson had nearly caught him. He could hear footsteps behind him, and a hand grabbed at his coat. Gary held onto his coat with both hands and kept on running, and he felt the coat slip out of the man's hands. He rushed into the front garden to see another two men appear around the other side of the house and start running towards him. Gary ran diagonally across the lawn towards the single gate. The other men were older than him and bulkier, but even so they nearly caught up with him. Gary flung open the gate and nearly fell out onto the pavement. He ran straight across the road and up the street, not stopping to look behind. His heart was thumping, and not just from the exertion. Every second he expected to feel another hand grab him.

Gary had reached the end of the road when he heard an engine behind him. He glanced back as he turned the corner and saw a white van coming along the street. It must be the workmen, they were following him in their van. Before the van could turn the corner, Gary ran through an open gate into another garden, and lay down on the ground behind the wall. He glanced at the house, which was detached, like all the houses around here, with a large front garden and long driveway. There were lights on downstairs in the house, indicating that someone was at home. Gary prayed silently that they wouldn't look out and notice him. He heard a vehicle drive past and assumed it was the van. When the engine noise disappeared, he crawled along the ground, keeping behind the wall, then got to his knees and peeped along the road. It was all quiet, so he rose to his feet and started running again. He was back in the town centre when he remembered that he'd left his shopping in the Robinsons' garden.

Gary sat down on a seat in the town centre to catch his breath. He was shaking, and not only from the physical exertion. That had been a close call. The workmen must have been cleaning up the mess in the back garden. They hadn't been there when he arrived, probably on a lunch break or something. Gary realised that he'd been very lucky to get away. *It must stop now*, he thought. *I'm really going to end up in trouble. But it feels so good when I'm teaching them a lesson, when I'm fighting back. But I can't risk the police coming around again. I wonder if any of those guys would recognise me again? They only saw me for a minute, surely they couldn't get a good look at me?*

Despite all his concerns, Gary couldn't feel any regret that he'd gone to the Robinsons'. He just wished he'd had time to do some more damage before he was interrupted. It made him feel so alive and in control when he was punishing them. Sighing, he resigned himself to letting it go from now on.

CHAPTER 49

Gary shivered and pulled his coat more closely around him. He couldn't continue sitting on this bench. But how could he go back to the flat without the shopping? He'd have to wait until the workmen had left for the day and then quickly retrieve it from under the hedge. Which meant that he couldn't go home just yet.

After thinking for a few moments, Gary pulled out his phone and scrolled down until he found his Dad's number. Les answered the phone after only a couple of rings. He sounded pleased when Gary asked if it was OK if he called around for a coffee.

'Is Danny there?' Gary asked.

'No son, he's not. I'm not expecting him over today,' his Dad replied. Gary said that he'd be over within the next half an hour and he stood up and started walking in the direction of his Father's house.

On the way Gary devised a plan. He'd stay at his Dad's flat for the rest of the afternoon. It was the weekend, so he didn't think the workers would be at the Robinsons' house later than 4.00pm, or 5.00pm to be safe. Of course, the Robinsons themselves may have just popped out for a short journey. But all he had to do was open the gate, reach around for his shopping bag, and then get out of there as quickly as possible. It would be unlikely they'd see him from the house. It would be dark then too, so that would be to his advantage. It was risky, but he didn't have any more money for shopping. He didn't want anyone finding it and tracing it back to him. The shopping receipts were in the bag, showing where he'd been that day. All the supermarkets had CCTV, they might put two and two together. Gary started to feel anxious at the thought of returning to Willow Drive again today, but he really had no choice.

Les looked delighted to see Gary when he opened his front door, and Gary was glad that he'd thought of coming here. They chatted about the weather as Les bustled about making coffee and a sandwich. When they had finished eating and were relaxing and drinking mugs of coffee, Les turned to Gary and spoke.

'I'm sorry about Christmas Day Gary. It must have seemed like I was choosing to spend it with Danny rather than you. But he turned up here drunk – his drinking is out of control at the moment. I didn't think it would be right for Lisa and the boys to see him like that. His temper gets out of hand when he's been drinking. He's not a happy drunk like I am,' Les added with a short laugh. 'I'm sorry son, I feel awful about it.'

Gary felt a warm glow. This was one of the few times his Dad had ever apologised for anything, and it was certainly the most heartfelt apology he'd ever heard from him.

'I was a bit upset Dad, but well, it's done now, and I understand, you couldn't have done anything else.'

'I wish you and Danny could make things up,' Les said wistfully. 'I've tried talking to him, explained your situation. But he doesn't want to hear it.' Les shook his head. 'He might feel differently when he's not drinking so much. I've begged him to get help, but he doesn't want to stop, that's the trouble.'

Gary could see that his Dad was worried about Danny and said, 'you know yourself Dad, no point forcing someone to stop, he'll have to do it in his own time. He's been sober before though, so he will be again.'

Les looked down at the carpet. 'I know he gets it from me, the drinking. Must be something in the genes I think, because he didn't see that much of me when he was growing up. Not like you, and you don't touch a drop. You're lucky that way Gary. It's hard to explain what it's like, you know it's bad for you and you know you should stop. But when you're drinking, nothing else feels as good. You don't care about anyone or anything, just want to keep that feeling. But then when you stop drinking everything's just awful. I suppose it's hard for you to understand?' Les said gloomily.

Gary thought about how he felt when he damaged the Robinsons' house, and suddenly realised, for the first time, what it must be like for his Dad and Danny when they drank.

'I think I do understand Dad, you want that good feeling more than anything. And it must be great while you've got it. And crap when everything goes back to normal.'

Les looked at Gary for a few moments and then smiled. 'Aye son, that's it exactly.'

'Let me know when Danny's sober again and I'll have another go at making it up with him,' he promised. Les smiled and looked pleased.

For the next couple of hours Gary and Les sat watching sport on TV and chatting intermittently about nothing in particular. Gary was just thinking that it would be safe for him to go back to retrieve his shopping, when his mobile rang. He saw Lisa's number flash up on the screen, and he felt guilty that he hadn't been in touch since he left the flat earlier that day.

'Hi Babe, I'm just at my Dad's,' he started, but instead of Lisa's voice, Jacob's voice came on the line, sounding a bit tearful.

'Dad, can you come home? Mum's not well, there's blood ...' Jacob said, his voice quavering.

Gary was immediately alarmed. 'OK son, I'm at Grandad's, and I'll be back very soon. Tell Mum I'm on my way, and don't worry about anything.'

Gary jumped up and grabbed his coat from the radiator where his Dad had put it to dry. As he did so, he explained the situation to his Dad.

'Shall I come too?' Les offered. 'If you have to go to hospital, I can look after the boys.'
'I'll get back quicker on my own thanks,' Gary replied. 'But if you follow on at your own pace, then if everything's OK when I get there I'll ring you on your mobile and you can turn around.'

And with that plan in place, Gary left his Dad's house and started running towards the flat.

When Gary entered the flat, all four of the boys were sitting on the sofa in the living room, looking scared. Gary hugged them briefly and said, 'where's your Mum?'

'Bathroom,' answered Jacob, his eyes filling with tears.

Gary rushed into the bathroom and found Lisa sitting on the toilet. She looked pale and was sweating. Before either of them had a chance to speak, she doubled over in pain, and moaned loudly.

'Is the baby coming?' Gary asked, feeling alarmed.

'I thought my waters had broken, but it was blood, and I've got a pain Gary. It's not like contractions. And I haven't felt the baby move since yesterday,' Lisa said with a sob. 'Oh Gary, I'm so scared.'

Gary went over and hugged her. She was burning up. 'I think you've got a fever,' he said, growing increasingly alarmed, but trying to keep it under control. 'I'm phoning an ambulance. My Dad is on his way over, he can watch the boys.' Lisa nodded, tears streaming down her face. Gary went into the bedroom and rang 999. After listening to all the information, the operator said they would send an ambulance straight away, and Gary went back into the bathroom and helped Lisa to stand and get cleaned up. He then helped her to lie down on the bed to wait for the ambulance arriving.

There was a knock on the flat door and a few seconds later he heard Jacob say, 'Grandad!' with a sob in his voice, and when Gary went into the sitting room, his Dad was hugging all the boys, and saying, 'come on lads, I'm here now, it'll be alright,' in a reassuring way.

'We think the baby might be coming,' Gary said, to everyone. 'There is an ambulance on its way, so we'll have Mum sorted out in no time. The doctors and nurses will look after her. I'm going to go too, but Grandad will look after you all, is that OK?'

The boys nodded, still looking scared. His Dad said, 'have you had your tea boys?' And four little heads shook to say that they hadn't. 'Well how about pizza?' Les asked. 'We could ring and have some delivered, how about that?' This brought some faint smiles and all four heads nodded. 'Right then, what sort will we get?' Les added, and Gary went back to Lisa, grateful that his Dad was there.

There was another knock on the door, and Gary heard his Dad say, 'come in, she's just in here.' Gary felt himself relax a little as the ambulance crew entered the bedroom.

CHAPTER 50

The nurse slipped quietly into the hospital room, carefully carrying a tiny bundle, wrapped in a pale pink blanket. Gary turned to look at her from his seat alongside the bed, still keeping hold of Lisa's hand.

'I've brought baby for you,' the nurse said gently. 'It often helps to spend some time with a sleeping baby. Perhaps take some photographs, a reminder for later.' She spoke kindly and held out the tiny bundle towards Lisa. Lisa snatched her hand out of Gary's grasp, and without speaking, turned over on her side, so that her back was towards the nurse.

Gary looked up at the nurse, not knowing what to say. She smiled sympathetically and said, 'what about you Daddy? Would you like to hold baby?' Not able to speak, Gary held out his arms, and the nurse gently handed him the little bundle. 'I'll leave you alone, ring if you want anything, and take as long as you want.' And the nurse turned and walked quietly out of the room.

Gary looked down at the baby in his arms, feeling a bit scared of what he would see. But she was just perfect. Very tiny, but with lots of dark curly hair, a perfect rosebud mouth, and a sweet little heart-shaped face. All the boys had arrived in the world with bright red faces, but his daughter was pale, lying there with her eyes closed. Gary felt himself unconsciously rocking her, and he carefully moved back the blanket when it fell over her face. She was so beautiful, you'd never know, except that she was so still. Babies were never still like this, they always twitched their eyelids, or moved in their sleep. And when his finger touched her little face he was shocked at how cold she was. 'Sleeping,' that's how the nurse had referred to her. That's the term they used instead of 'stillborn.' Gary had found that out at some point in the past few hours. He couldn't remember now who'd told him.

Still rocking his daughter, Gary turned to Lisa. 'Lisa love, don't you want to hold her? She's so perfect, there's nothing to be scared of.'

Lisa sat up angrily. 'Why would I want to hold a dead thing? It's not going to bring her back to life, is it? All that effort and pain, and for what? Nothing to show for it. I blame you for this Gary, if we hadn't had all that worry, and had to move to that awful flat, then we'd be holding a live baby now. Our baby girl, not that thing. Take it away from me,' Lisa ended, with a sob, and then turned her back to Gary and the baby and again laid down.

Gary felt himself pull the baby closer to him. He wanted to protect her from Lisa's harsh words. Not knowing what to say in response to Lisa's angry outburst, he continued holding the baby, rocking her gently.

Poor Lisa, it had been a terrible 24 hours. When they got to the hospital they couldn't find the baby's heartbeat. Eventually they broke the news that the baby had died. Because Lisa was so near to full-term, she had to go through a full labour and delivery. It had gone on for hours and hours, much longer than with any of the boys, who had seemed to slip out easily. All along Gary had secretly hoped that the hospital staff had been wrong, and that when the baby was born it would be alive. When she was eventually delivered, Gary held his breath, waiting to hear the cry, but the minutes ticked slowly by and there was nothing. They'd offered the baby to Lisa then, but she'd become almost hysterical, screaming at them to 'take it away.' So, they had, and Gary had only managed a glance at the top of her head as they'd hurried her out of the room. He'd felt so empty, he couldn't imagine how Lisa must feel.

The hours passed by and Gary continued to cradle the baby while Lisa slept fitfully. He thought about Lisa's words. She was right of course, all the stress over the last few months had affected the pregnancy. Lisa hadn't been well all the way through. He realised that tears were running down his face. He'd let them all down, and especially this poor little thing. He held his daughter up to his shoulder, cradling her head and her tiny body. He rocked her gently and sobbed quietly. Things could have been so different, they should be taking her home to a princess bedroom, pink with unicorns. Instead, what? Would they have to leave her here? Put her in a tiny coffin? A wave of pain rose up from Gary's stomach. He didn't think he could bear it. It was all so pointless. Their problems were caused by a few bottles of wine and some unfinished plasterwork. His pain was replaced by a blind rage, and as Gary looked again at his daughter's perfect little face, he vowed to get revenge on the cause of all this. That evil cow, Sue Robinson.

CHAPTER 51

Eventually the kind-faced nurse came back into the room, and asked Gary if he wanted her to take the baby away. 'Or I can leave her in the cot in case Mummy does want to see her when she wakes?' she suggested.

Gary looked down at his daughter. He didn't think he could bear to leave her. The thought of never seeing her again was just too much to bear.

'What will happen to her?' he asked, his voice sounding hoarse.

'You can spend as much time with her as you want, some families choose to spend a few days with a sleeping baby. When you're ready then we'll arrange a funeral.'

An involuntary sob escaped from Gary at the mention of a funeral. She was so tiny, so helpless.

'Do you have other children?' the nurse asked, speaking softly.

'Yes, we have four boys.' Gary answered flatly. 'They're at home with my Dad,' he added, unnecessarily.

'You can bring them in to see their sister too if you like.' The nurse suggested.

Gary didn't know what to say. 'I'll think about it, discuss it with Lisa tomorrow,' he eventually mumbled.

The nurse smiled at him kindly. 'Why don't you go home now? Your wife needs her rest, and you've been through a lot. Go home and see your boys, they'll be wondering what's happened. I'll take baby and bring her back when your wife wakes up. You can see her again when you come tomorrow.' Gary felt his eyes fill up again at her kind words and concern. He looked up and she was holding out her arms. Gary reluctantly handed over his daughter, gazing longingly at her lovely little face for as long as he could.

It was good to be out in the fresh air after the heat of the hospital. Gary should have been tired but instead he felt restless, and full of hate and regret. Lisa and he should be bringing their baby home. Not to that awful flat, but to a nice house, with a nursery all ready for their little girl.

Gary knew he should go home and see the boys. He'd texted his Dad a few times over the past 24 hours, and he'd got brief replies, 'all asleep,' 'having breakfast,' 'going to the shops,' 'all OK.' It sounded like everything was under control. Gary pulled his coat collar up, looked around him, and decided. He was going to give that Sue Robinson a piece of his mind. She had to understand what she'd done.

Suddenly he couldn't wait to confront her, and rather than walk as he usually did, Gary caught a bus outside the hospital that would take him to the other side of town. On the bus he sat brooding, rehearsing what he was going to say. It was dark outside, but it wasn't that late, he was sure they would still be awake. But he didn't care whether they were or not, he'd kick the door down if necessary. He could feel energy surge through his tired body, he was going to make her realise what she'd done to him and his family.

The bus took Gary just a few streets away from the Robinsons' house, and he ran the rest of the way, needing to do something to avenge his daughter's death and all the other hurts his family had suffered over the past few months.

Gary let himself into the familiar front gate. There were lights on in the front of the house, but the curtains were closed. Gary made for the front door, but then changed his mind and went around to the back of the house. He let himself into the shed and looked around. He needed something to show he was serious. He had no definite plan, except he needed to intimidate her enough so that she would listen to what he had to say.

Looking frantically through the boxes, Gary picked up a long, sharp chisel, a Stanley knife, and some garden twine. Then he went over to the back door and banged on it as loudly as he could. Despite lights coming on in the hallway and kitchen, he banged again angrily. A woman's voice reached him through the door.

'Who is it? What do you want? My husband is calling the police.'

Yes, they would be calling the fucking police, wouldn't they? Gary thought, growing increasingly furious.

'It's Gary Mills,' he shouted back, 'I have to talk to you, so open this fucking door.'

There was a silence, and Gary was just about to start banging again, when Sue Robinson spoke. 'I don't think we have anything to say to each other, so I think you'd better just leave, if you don't want to end up in trouble.'

'If you don't let me in I will break every window in your house. I just want to talk to you, you stuck up cow. Open this door.'

There was a rattle on the other side of the door, and the door opened slightly. Sue Robinson's furious face appeared in the gap.

'Get away from here, you horrible little man. The police are on their way and you're going to be in serious trouble. We know it's you who has been vandalising our property ....'

She stopped talking when she noticed Gary raise his hand, which held the Stanley knife. As she stared at it, wide-eyed, Gary took his opportunity and pushed the door hard, sending Sue flying backwards. She toppled, but as she was still holding onto the door handle, this stopped her from falling onto the floor.

'I'm not doing anything you tell me, you vindictive bitch,' Gary spat at her. You're going to listen to me for a change. Where is your husband?'
Sue's eyes involuntarily flicked towards the hallway. Gary moved the knife to his other hand, grabbed her arm and dragged her along the hallway and into the sitting room. Peter Robinson

was sitting on one of the armchairs at the end of the room, next to the bookcases, and he had the phone in his hand. Gary rushed over, and knocked the phone onto the floor, and then brandished the knife.

Peter Robinson looked alarmed but sat calmly looking at Gary. Sue Robinson opened her mouth, but Gary screamed at her, 'shut the fuck up and sit down in that chair. You're going to listen to what I have to say, or I will cut you.'

Sue obediently sat down in the chair and reached for Peter's hand.

'Do you know where I've just been?' Gary asked. 'I've just come from the hospital. For the last few hours I've been sitting nursing our new baby. Our new dead baby. She died in the womb and my wife, my beautiful wife, had to go through hours of labour and give birth, to a dead baby. And it's all your fault,' he screamed, pointing the knife at Sue. 'Because you wouldn't let me finish the job I lost my business, and we got behind with our rent, and lost our home, and the boys have nowhere to play and they've lost their friends. We have no money, and I can't get a job because I've got a bad reputation. And I never drink, so I didn't steal your fucking wine. And you're sitting here with all this space, and your fancy car, and your month-long holidays, and you have no idea what you've done to me and my family. Going on the radio and saying I was crap, my Dad heard that, how do you think that made me feel? You don't know how fucking lucky you are, with everything you've got here.' Gary was sobbing now, he was so angry.

Sue Robinson interrupted angrily, 'you don't know what you're talking about, you know nothing about us and our lives, what we've had to go through, what we're still going through.'

Gary went over and slapped her around the face with the back of his hand. 'I told you to SHUT UP. I'm talking, it's my turn.'

Sue sat quietly, looking frightened, and Peter grasped her hand.

'Say what you have to say Gary,' he said quietly. 'We'll listen.'

'Too right you'll listen,' Gary said. 'We are trapped you see, stuck in a damp, crummy flat with four little boys. They have nowhere to play, and we have no money to take them anywhere. I owe so much money to Unique Interiors, and in rent to our old landlord. And I can't get a job, and every day is the same, it's just hopeless.'

Gary didn't know what else to say. When he'd rehearsed it on the bus coming over, it had all sounded so good, they'd understand what they'd done. But now, he just couldn't find the words. He looked down at the rope in his hands. He might not be able to explain it, but he could show them.

He moved quickly over to Peter's chair. 'Put your hands on the arms of the chair,' he said.
Peter looked alarmed, 'what are you going to do?' He asked, his voice sounding a little less calm.

'Just do what I fucking tell you.' Gary screamed, and Peter put his hands on the chair arms. Gary noticed that his hands were shaking, and he felt a surge of satisfaction. He quickly tied Peter's hands to the chair arms, and then bent over and tied his feet. Sue looked as if she was going to speak again, but he held the knife towards her and she fell silent. Gary cut the rope with the Stanley knife, and then gestured to the arms of the chair that Sue was sitting on. She immediately obeyed and placed her hands on the arms. Gary quickly tied her up too.

'Now you'll know what it feels like to be trapped, just like we are,' he said. He threw down the chisel, knife and what was left of the rope into the corner of the room and picked up the telephone. Then he looked Sue in the eyes and uttered one word, 'bitch,' and he left via the front door, leaving Peter and Sue securely tied up in their own sitting room.

CHAPTER 52

Sue and Peter sat still for a few moments after they heard the front door slam, but the continued silence indicated that Gary had really left, and they both started to struggle to release their ropes.

'Must have been a boy scout,' Peter joked, 'strong knots.'

'I can't budge an inch,' replied Sue. 'I hope it doesn't cut off my circulation.'

'Keep wiggling your fingers,' Peter said, 'if you can move a bit you should be OK.'

They both struggled a bit longer, and then eventually Peter relaxed and looked over at Sue. 'It's no good, we're not going to be able to get these ropes undone. I'm afraid we're stuck here for the foreseeable sweetheart.'

Sue gave a final wriggle and then she relaxed too. 'Well this is a turn up for the books. How are we going to get help?' she said, with a tremor in her voice.

'Worst case scenario is that we'll be stuck here until morning,' Peter replied. 'The carers come in first thing, so they'll untie us then.'

'But what if he comes back?' Sue said, 'he looked quite mad to me.'

'I think he got it out of his system,' Peter said reassuringly. 'And he'd struggle to get in the house, he gave the front door a good slam. And all the other doors and windows are double-glazed and have strong locks on them.'

'I'm not sure if the back door is shut, and it's definitely not locked,' Sue said. 'He forced his way in and then made me come straight along here.'

'Why on earth did you unlock the door?' Peter asked.

'He made me angry,' Sue confessed, 'I wanted to confront him.' She looked so shamefaced that Peter gave a small laugh.

'Another fine mess you've got us in,' he joked. Then he sat thinking for a few moments.

'Despite the fact he's vandalised our property, threatened us, swore at us, and left us here tied up so we'll probably pee ourselves before morning, I can't help feeling a bit sorry for him.'

Sue sighed, 'Oh Pete, you are a softy. But I did feel sorry for them losing their baby. And a little girl too, after all those boys. His poor wife.'

'Yes, that's an awful thing for anyone to go through. It sounds as if they've had a hard few months. Can't be easy, living in a small flat with four young boys. And no job. But I don't know how he can blame us for it all? He did a poor job, and there's still the business with the wine. All we did was complain that we hadn't got the standard of work that we'd paid for.' Peter replied, sounding puzzled. 'It's like he doesn't see his part in it at all.'

Sue nodded, agreeing with Peter. 'I'd feel sorry for anyone in that situation, but he must see that his own actions have contributed to it. Perhaps losing the baby has driven him nearly crazy?' she suggested.

But Peter shook his head, 'this must have been building for some time, otherwise why has he done all the other things? I think we can safely assume it was him who did the other stuff.'

'Oh yes, I think so,' Sue agreed, 'not unless I have another crazy man wanting revenge against me for standing up for my rights as a consumer!' She laughed briefly and then said, 'but I'm not sure how he can blame me for his children losing their friends? I wanted to ask him to explain that but thought I'd better not.'

'Good move,' said Peter. 'I don't think he was in the mood for questions.'

'Wish he'd left the whisky a bit nearer,' Peter said, indicating the decanter on a coffee table which was out of their reach.

'Wish I'd gone to the loo before I opened the door,' Sue said. 'And made some sandwiches.' They both laughed.

'We are going to have to report him to the police, and they'll have fingerprints this time, from the knife and the chisel,' Peter said, nodding towards the corner of the room where Gary had put the weapons. 'He must have had gloves on before.'

'I suspect there will be fingerprints in the shed now too,' Sue replied. 'I'm sure they are our tools, and this is our garden twine, so he must have been in there. And he touched the back door.'

'I wonder what will happen to his family if he goes to jail?' Peter said, and they both fell silent for a few moments.

'What will the charges be?' Sue asked, 'breaking and entering? Kidnap? Threatening behaviour, vandalism? Do you think you get a jail sentence for any of those?'

'Not sure,' Peter replied, 'if it's his first offence, perhaps not, but I don't really know. I would think tying people up and threatening them in their own home would be considered quite seriously.'

As the night moved on, it became increasingly uncomfortable in the armchairs without being able to change position. The room also became cold, as the central heating was on a timer, and it had switched off earlier. Sue wished they'd had the fire on, but it had been warm enough with the radiators, so they hadn't bothered. She looked over at Peter and saw that he was dozing. He'd been tired and was about to go to bed before this all happened, so he would be exhausted now. Deciding there was nothing she could do, Sue got as comfortable as she could and tried to doze too.

Sometime later she awoke with a start, her heart thumping. *Was that a noise?* She was afraid that Gary Mills had come back. She could hear a 'beep, beep, beep, from another part of the house, and she recognised it as a smoke alarm. *Where is it coming from?* She suddenly felt afraid, *the kitchen? No, further away, the conversion perhaps? Oh God, has he set the house on fire?* Sue was sure she could smell smoke, but was she just imagining it? She began to struggle desperately against her bonds, whilst shouting at Peter to wake up.

CHAPTER 53

Gary remembered to collect his shopping from under the hedge as he left the Robinsons' house. He felt quite calm now, but also a bit disappointed. Confronting them hadn't really resolved anything. If only he'd been able to explain things more clearly, make them see what they'd done. He wasn't sure that they'd understood anything.

When he got back to the flat, he let himself in quietly, and found his Dad asleep, wrapped in a blanket on the sofa. Leaving him sleeping, he tiptoed into the bedroom and sat on the floor with his back to the wall. He stayed still, just watching his boys sleeping. It was good to see their pink flushed cheeks and hear them breathing. He put his head in his hands as he began to realise that his actions tonight could only lead to even more trouble.

Suddenly Oliver stirred and sat up, then half asleep he got up and went into the bathroom. He didn't notice Gary sitting on the floor until he was on his way back to bed.

'Dad, you're home,' Oliver said, looking delighted, and he rushed over to hug Gary. Gary held him close, revelling in the warmth of his little body. 'Do we have a new baby? Is Mummy OK?' Oliver asked, looking worried.

'Mummy's fine, she's resting,' Gary said, pushing Oliver's fringe out of his eyes. 'But the baby came too soon I'm afraid, she's with Jesus now.'

Oliver looked sad, and then said, 'she must have been very special if Jesus wanted her back so quickly.' Gary nodded, and hugged Olly to him, to hide the tears in his eyes. 'What was she called? The baby.' Oliver asked, and Gary thought for a few moments.

'Julia, her name is Julia. Like my Mum, she's called Julie, so Julia is like that.'

Oliver nodded, still looking serious. 'Julia,' he said, trying out the name. 'Why do we never see Grandma Julie? Does she not like us?'

Gary wasn't sure what to say, but luckily, he was spared from having to think up an answer by Jacob waking up and looking over at him. 'Is the baby here?' Jacob asked immediately, and Gary repeated what he'd told Oliver, about the baby arriving too early and being with Jesus.

Gary was shocked when Jacob immediately burst into tears and started sobbing uncontrollably. Gary stood up and lifted Jacob out of the bed, and sat back down on the floor, rocking him and holding him close. Gary remembered just how young his son was, he always thought of him as being grown up, as he was the eldest.

'Sshh, it's alright, don't be upset. Mum's fine, she's resting, and baby Julia looked ever so peaceful, she didn't feel anything.'

Through hiccoughing sobs Jacob said, 'but Mum's been so unhappy, I thought it would make her happy to have another baby. And I was going to help her look after Julia. And now I'll never have a sister.'

'You might have a sister one-day Jake,' Gary said, 'and you do have Julia, she'll still be with us in our hearts. You can go and see her if you want, she's really pretty.' Gary wasn't sure what to say to make Jacob feel better.

Jacob sat on the floor next to Gary, who put his arm around him, then Oliver sat at the other side, and he held him close too. Jacob continued to cry, and Gary could feel his shoulder was wet with Jacob's tears. When the sobs eventually subsided, Gary knew he should get the boys back into bed. They had to go back to school in the morning, it was the first day of term.

'How about a story?' he suggested, leaning over to a pile of books on the floor at the bottom of the bed. Both boys nodded, so he picked up a book of short stories and read them a fable about a fox and a crane.

A FOX AND A CRANE

Once a fox and a crane became friends. So, the fox invited the crane to dinner. The crane accepted the invitation and reached the fox's place at sunset.

The fox had prepared soup for his mate. But as we all know that foxes are cunning by nature, he served the soup in flat dishes. So, he himself lapped the crane's share with his tongue enjoying its relish a lot. But the crane could not enjoy it at all with his long beak and had to get back home hungry. The shrewd fox felt extremely amused.

After few days, the crane invited the fox to dine in with him. The fox reached his place well in time. The crane gave him a warm welcome and served the soup in a jug with a long and narrow neck.

So, the crane enjoyed the soup with great relish using his long beak. The fox's mouth couldn't reach the soup through the narrow neck of the jug. He had to return home hungry. Now he realized that he had been repaid for his behaviour with the crane.

By the time Gary had finished the story, Jacob had fallen asleep, but Oliver was still awake.

'The fox and the crane are both silly, aren't they Daddy?' he said sleepily. 'If they'd both tried to help each other then they would have had two good meals each.'

'Yeah, that's right Olly, they would,' Gary replied, lifting Jacob up and laying him back into bed. He then turned back the covers so that Oliver could get in.

As Gary slipped quietly out of the boys' bedroom he reflected on his behaviour with the Robinsons and recognised that he'd acted like the fox or the crane, or both, and he realised he'd have to go back and set them free.

CHAPTER 54

Gary tiptoed around the sitting room, so that he didn't disturb his Dad, still asleep on the sofa. He picked up his coat and made his way quietly down the stairs and out into the street. The walk back to Willow Drive seemed extra-long in the dark, and Gary felt dizzy with tiredness and lack of food. He knew he had to do the right thing, and thinking about it now, he didn't know why he acted as he did. What good had it done after all? It couldn't wipe out what had happened over the past few months. And it certainly wouldn't change the situation, in fact it would make it worse. *I'll be going to jail now for sure*, Gary thought, and his footsteps slowed. He thought about the police woman who'd come to the house and wondered if she would be on duty? He wasn't sure if he could face the Robinsons again tonight. Perhaps he should just ring Karen Docherty, and let her sort it out? But if he did that then they'd take him in for questioning, and he wouldn't be there to get the boys ready for school in the morning. But if he set the Robinsons free then they'd ring the police straight away. Perhaps he'd say that he'd release them only if they didn't ring the police until the next day?

As he continued to walk, Gary argued with himself about the best thing to do. A couple of times he nearly turned back, but he knew that he couldn't leave the Robinsons tied up all night. The consequences were going to be bad whatever he did, but he had to try and reverse how badly he'd acted earlier.

Eventually Gary found himself back at the familiar gate, and with a deep breath, he opened it and stepped into the garden once more. His eye was caught by a strange light coming from the conversion. It was flickering, and there was an incessant, but faint, 'beep, beep,' noise coming from somewhere. In a split-second Gary realised what this meant. The conversion was on fire.

Gary ran around to the back of the house, hoping that the back door didn't automatically lock. He tried the handle and felt relieved when it opened under his grasp. He stepped into the kitchen, but was immediately engulfed in a cloud of thick, acrid smoke. Gary stepped outside again, wondering what to do. He had to get the Robinsons out, they could die in there. The spotlights came on again over the patio as he moved, and he looked around. There was an outside tap further along the wall, next to a neatly coiled hosepipe on a holder attached to the wall. Gary ran over to the tap, stripping off his coat as he ran. He soaked his coat as much as he could then ran back to the back door, covering his nose and mouth with the wet coat before he stepped inside. His eyes were streaming, but he could breathe more easily as he made his way across the hallway, and into the sitting room.

The lights were still lit, although everything looked eerie with the cloud of smoke that had already reached the room. Peter Robinson was slumped over in his chair, he seemed to be unconscious. Sue Robinson was sitting bolt upright. She looked terrified and was coughing violently.

'Don't worry, I'll get you out.' Gary said, trying to sound reassuring. He strode over to the corner of the room and picked up the Stanley knife and headed over to Sue. She shrank back in the chair, her eyes widening in fear, despite the smoke. 'I'm going to cut the ropes,' Gary said, 'keep still and I'll have you out in a tick.' It seemed to take ages to saw through the ropes, but eventually they broke free and Sue started to rub her wrists unconsciously, and said, 'we must get Peter out, he's got breathing problems anyway.'

Gary was already sawing through the ropes holding Peter's feet, and then he moved up to his hands. Peter didn't move, and Gary glanced at him, feeling increasingly concerned. The older man's breathing was laboured, and Gary could see through the smoke that he was a ghastly colour.

When he was free, Gary spoke to Sue, his voice sounding urgent. 'We'll make for the front door, that's the nearest. You get one side, try and put his arm around your shoulders. I'll get the other side, and we'll move as quickly as we can. There's a lot of smoke out in the hallway.'

Sue moved quickly, if a bit stiffly, around to the side of Peter's chair. 'Right, I'll count to three then we'll lift,' Gary said, lifting Peter's arm and placing it round his shoulders. Sue did the same, and then Gary said, 'one, two, three,' and they both heaved. It took three attempts to get Peter upright, and he was much heavier than Gary would have imagined. He seemed to be totally unconscious, and so was a dead weight between them. It seemed to take ages to half walk, half drag him across the rug to the door. Then there was the problem of how to get out of the room. Gary had closed the door behind him to keep the smoke out, but the door opened into the room, and they would have to open it and then try and get out as quickly as possible.

'I'll hold him up, you open the door, and then grab your side again, and we'll go straight through and towards the front door.' Gary said, manoeuvring himself in front of Peter, so that he could grab him under both arms as soon as Sue let go. 'Right, ready,' he said, as he grabbed Peter firmly. Sue moved towards the door, but Peter slumped and started slipping to the floor. Sue reached the door, but then looked back, saw what was happening, and ran over to help. Gary's legs were shaking with the effort of keeping Peter upright, but in the end, he had to give in and let him slip to the floor. 'He's just too heavy,' he said desperately to Sue.

'What are we going to do?' Sue said hoarsely, and Gary could see she was on the verge of tears. He suddenly had a thought. 'Have you got a blanket or something? We could lie him on it and drag him along. It'll be much quicker.'

Sue thought for a moment, and then said, 'there's a travel rug in the car, would that do? All the others are upstairs.'

'Where are the keys?' Gary asked quickly.

'They're in the drawer in the kitchen.'

'Which one?' Gary said, moving over to pick up his coat. His eyes were streaming again, and he was starting to cough now. They had to get a move on and get out of here.

'The drawer under the microwave,' Sue said, 'I always put them in there.'

Gary wrapped the coat around his nose and mouth and headed back across the hallway and into the kitchen. The smoke was even worse now, and Gary could see flames licking at the door from the conversion into the kitchen. He couldn't see to find the drawer that he needed, so he opened the back door and waved his arms outside, so the spotlights would come on. He didn't dare turn on a light inside the house in case it sparked something and made the situation worse.

Luckily the blinds in the kitchen were open, so the spotlights lit up the inside enough so that he could find the drawer. Mercifully it was practically empty, and very tidy, so he spotted the keys straight away. Gary turned and ran as quickly as he could manage back across the hallway and towards the front of the house. Sue was peeping anxiously out of the sitting room door, and Gary held up the keys as he went past. His legs felt like jelly and he was struggling to breathe, so it was a relief when he made it outside into the fresh air. Gary fumbled with the remote control of the car as he stumbled towards it and was eventually rewarded with a beeping noise and the car's lights flashed. *Where will they keep a travel rug?* he thought desperately and decided to try the back seat. It was empty. He held onto the car to propel himself around to the boot. He couldn't work out how to open it, there seemed to be no obvious catch. He fumbled with the remote control again, pressing all the buttons, and eventually there was a slight 'click' and the boot lid started to rise smoothly. Nearly in tears with frustration now, Gary peered inside, and there, neatly folded, was a large tartan rug. Gary snatched it up and leaving the car as it was, raced back to the house. Sue had disappeared, and when Gary got back into the sitting room, he found her leaning over Peter, talking to him softly, in between her frequent coughing fits.

'Quick, help me spread out the blanket, get it as close to him as possible.' Sue stood up immediately and started to help. Gary realised that she'd moved a coffee table out of the way while he'd been out at the car. This gave them a larger space to spread out the rug, which luckily was big and thick. Getting Peter onto the rug was a painfully slow process, involving rolling him this way and that, and tucking the rug under his body. Eventually the rug was underneath him from head to knees, with plenty of spare material at each side for them to grasp onto. Sue started to cough violently and seemed to swoon a bit.

'Are you Ok?' Gary asked, concerned that she was going to pass out. Sue nodded, unable to speak for coughing, and then she stood upright and went to one side of Peter's body and picked up both ends of the rug. Gary went over, opened the sitting room door, and hurried to the other side of the rug. He nodded at Sue, and they grasped the rug and pulled. Once Peter started to move, they were soon at the door. Getting through the door was a little difficult, as there wasn't room for all three of them to get through at once.

'I'll do this bit, you go and open the front door and then come back.' Gary said to Sue, and she headed off towards the front of the house. Gary stood behind Peter's head and pulled both sides of the rug. He pulled as hard as he could, and just when he was about to give up, the rug moved slightly and started to move Peter across the floor. Gary kept tugging as hard as he could, and inch by inch, he dragged Peter out into the hallway. Sue had returned and as soon as there was space, she grasped the side of the rug and started pulling too. Gary's muscles were shaking with the effort, and the relief at having someone else's help was fantastic. Once they were out into the hallway, they progressed much more quickly on the marble floor. They had a similar problem at the front door as they'd had with the sitting room door, but it was even worse as the front door had quite a high threshold.

'Let's just get his head out into the fresh air,' Gary said. Sue nodded, and they pulled Peter's head and shoulders out onto the front step.

Gary fished into his coat pocket and pulled out his mobile phone. He handed it to Sue, and said, 'you phone for a fire engine and ambulance.' I'll get the hose and try and put the fire out.

'No Gary, don't,' Sue said, placing a sooty hand on his arm, 'it's too dangerous.'

Gary patted her hand. 'I'll be careful,' he said, trying to smile. And he set off around the front of the house, and into the back garden, rather than risking going through the hallway again, with its choking smoke.

Sue's hands were shaking, but after two attempts she managed to ring 999, and, between coughs, explained what had happened, and what assistance was needed. Then she sat down against the front wall, and talked gently to Peter, who still hadn't stirred.

Gary stepped into the back garden, grateful again for the spotlights which lit up as soon as he turned the corner from the side of the house. He ran over to the tap, and again wetted his coat, and then tied it, using the arms, around his face. He then turned the tap on full and started pulling at the end of the hose. Luckily the holder was well maintained and moved easily, as Gary felt exhausted and he didn't think he could have managed if it had been stiff. The hose uncoiled smoothly, and by the time Gary reached the back door, it was already fattening with water.

Gary stopped for a second, then took a deep breath and headed into the kitchen. The door from the conversion was now totally alight, and Gary started spraying it with water, dousing the flames. The smoke was terrible, choking him, and Gary coughed, despite the coat tied around his face. He couldn't see anything, and his eyes streamed incessantly. He just kept pointing the hose, and dowsing the flames, determined not to let them get into the house and down the hallway to the front door, where Peter was lying helpless. He stood there for what seemed like hours, depressing the hose every time he saw the flicker of fire. Eventually he heard the far away sound of sirens. They grew louder, and he heard the unmistakable loud thrum of a large vehicle outside. *Thank God*, Gary thought, as his knees finally buckled, and he fell to the floor.

CHAPTER 55

'Ok, Mr Mills, you're fine now, you can go home. Just make sure to make an appointment at your own surgery, get the nurse to have a look at those burns. And if your cough gets worse, call NHS 111 immediately.'

Gary looked down at his dressings before he started to get up from the treatment couch. He still wasn't sure how he'd managed to burn his hands. He couldn't remember it happening, and he didn't think he was close enough to the fire to burn, but perhaps he'd grasped something hot in the panic? He remembered receiving oxygen in the ambulance though and feeling almost instant relief from the terrible coughing that had wracked his chest. *God, I'm tired*, Gary thought, trying to remember when he'd last slept. He was on his feet now, and the nurse nodded and smiled at him, then he picked up some notes and turned to leave the cubicle.

'Wait,' Gary said, holding out a hand, 'how are Mr and Mrs Robinson? The people I came in with.'

The nurse turned around again and said, 'Mrs Robinson's fine, she's been discharged. Mr Robinson is still in treatment as far as I know.'

'Thank you,' Gary said, feeling relieved that Sue was OK, but still feeling concerned about Peter.

The nurse stopped again and said, 'Mrs Robinson's in the waiting room down the corridor actually, just along there on the left, if you want to say hello. She doesn't want to leave until she gets some news about her husband.'

Gary smiled and nodded, and after hesitating for a few moments, he headed gingerly along to the waiting room. Gary had no idea what time it was, probably the early hours of the morning, he thought. He didn't know where his mobile phone was, so he couldn't check the time on that. He slowly opened the door to the waiting room, expecting to find a few people waiting for patients, but there was only one person there, sitting against the back wall of the room. It was Sue, who looked up eagerly when the door opened. When she saw Gary, her shoulders slumped a little, but she smiled at him and spoke.

'Hello Gary, have you been discharged? How are you?' And then, noticing the dressings on his hands, she added, sounding concerned, 'did you have burns? I hadn't realised that.'

Gary walked over the waiting room and sat down heavily opposite her. 'They're nothing, just minor burns, from the heat I guess. How are you? Are you feeling OK?'

'Yes, I'm fine,' Sue replied, then gave a brief smile. 'Feel a bit dirty and dishevelled, and my chest is a bit sore, but I'm sure that will pass.'

'What's the news about Peter?' Gary asked tentatively.

Sue rubbed her hand over her face. 'He's still in treatment, he is struggling to breathe and hasn't fully regained consciousness yet. I thought I'd wait here until he does.'

Gary sat silently, not quite sure what to say. After a few moments, Sue continued speaking.

'He was admitted here on Christmas day with respiratory problems. He'd only been home a few days, so that's why he's been affected so badly.'

'Did he have a chest infection or something?' Gary asked, 'it must have been bad if they admitted him to hospital.'

'He has Motor Neurone Disease, he was diagnosed last year. Respiratory problems are a side-effect of that.'

'What is that?' Gary asked. 'I think I've heard of it, but I'm not sure what it is.'

Sue sighed, and her shoulders slumped. 'It's a disease that

affects your central nervous system. You gradually become more and more disabled, and it cuts your life short. They told Pete he'd have between 3 and 10 years at best. But the disease, in his case, has progressed quickly, so we're not really sure.'

Gary felt a wave of sympathy, and swallowed before he said, 'I'm so sorry, I didn't realise.'

'Why would you?' Sue replied, looking him full in the face for the first time. 'That's why we needed the conversion you see. As you know, Peter is a tall man, and he would struggle with the stairs, even if we got a lift installed. We thought him all being on one level would be better. We didn't think, well, I didn't think, that we'd need it so quickly, but he moved in there a few weeks ago.'

Gary and Sue sat in silence for a few moments. Gary thought about what Sue had said. It explained a lot of things that had puzzled him, such as why Peter hadn't resisted more when he'd tied him up, or why he hadn't chased him when he saw him vandalising the back wall. The man was ill, dying. Gary closed his eyes, suddenly feeling totally ashamed of himself and his actions.

Sue cleared her throat and spoke softly. 'Gary, I have to ask you something. Did you set fire to our house?' She looked him straight in the eye.

Gary was appalled and replied quickly. 'No, honestly Sue, I didn't. I wouldn't do that. The other stuff, well it was just getting back at you. But I wouldn't do anything serious like that. I really don't know how the fire started.'

Sue stared at him for a few moments, then she relaxed. 'I believe you. I'm sorry I had to ask. But I had to know. There will be an investigation into the fire you see, for the insurance.'

Gary nodded and looked down on the floor, he didn't want to leave her here on her own, but he didn't know what to say. He looked up as Sue started to speak.

'I'm sorry about your baby. How is your wife coping?' She

looked so sad and sympathetic that Gary felt tears fill his eyes.

'She's not doing too well. The midwife said it was best if we saw the baby, so that we could remember her. But Lisa doesn't want to look at her, won't hold her. Her little heart stopped beating you see, and she was nearly full-term. Lisa had to go through a full labour and ...' Gary stopped, sobbing now. He put his head in his hands, and then felt two arms grasping him around the shoulders and gently rocking him and rubbing his back. Gary put his arms around Sue Robinson's waist and he cried unashamedly. Sue didn't speak, just kept rocking him and rubbing his shoulders.

After several minutes Gary's tears stopped, and he pulled back and looked up at Sue, rubbing his face with his sleeve. He was surprised, and touched, to see that she was crying too. She patted his shoulder and went back to sit down opposite him.

'Did you hold your baby?' Sue asked quietly.

Gary nodded, 'Julia, I called her Julia, after my Mum. She is just so perfect, such a pretty little thing. I held her for hours, I know it's stupid, but I thought she'd wake up and start crying. She looks like she's sleeping. That's what they call them you know, 'sleeping' babies, stillborn ones I mean. I didn't know that.'

'No, I didn't either,' Sue replied. 'I hope your wife, Lisa, I hope she does hold her and see her, so that she can remember her. You don't forget babies, just because they aren't with you anymore.'

Sue looked wistful and Gary suddenly blurted out, 'Did you lose a baby? You and Peter?'

'Not in the same way as you and Lisa, not like Julia. We couldn't have any babies naturally, left it too late I think. We had IVF, and we had some embryos, a few of them had taken. They were ours, mine and Peter's, they just made them outside of us. They kept planting them in me, and I got pregnant, but I couldn't keep them, could never hold onto one. When I didn't get pregnant with the last one, I sort of collapsed. I still think of them as my potential children, and although the pain does get less, there still isn't a day when I don't think what might have been.'

'Why did you wait to have a family?' Gary asked. 'Did you marry late?' He suddenly felt he wanted to know more about this woman and her life.

'No, we met in the sixth form, and we married as soon as we graduated from university. We were only 21. We planned on having a big family. We're both only children you see, and we liked the idea of a squad of children.' Sue smiled, remembering. 'I took my professional accountancy exams, and Peter qualified as a teacher, we bought the house, house prices were cheaper then, and then a baby was next on the list. But my Father became ill, so we helped my Mother nurse him. He died, and then Peter's Father had several strokes, and his Mother was ill too, and she ended up in a wheelchair, she had to have her leg amputated. We were helping out there too. We kept putting it off, waiting until the time was right. The time is never right. I was well in my thirties when we tried for a family, and when I didn't get pregnant naturally, you have all these tests and things, and we were too old for IVF on the NHS, so we had to pay privately. Peter's Mother had died too by then, and we inherited her house, so we were able to sell it and pay for several rounds of IVF with the money. When the money ran out, we were going to sell our house to fund some more. But the consultant talked us out of trying again, he said we'd be wasting our time. We were looking into adoption, but my Mother had Alzheimer's disease and she needed more and more support to stay in her own home, so we decided against that.'

'How long were you looking after sick parents?' Gary asked, touched by Sue's story.

'Thirty-two years,' Sue said, with a bitter laugh. 'My Mother died last year, she'd been ill for 17 years. She didn't even know who I was in the end. And she thought Peter was her husband.' She stopped, thinking. 'We've never regretted looking after them, I don't want you to think that,' she said, looking directly at Gary. 'We were lucky with our families, and we both had great childhoods, but it did rather take over our lives. We couldn't even have a dog, because we were always at work and then at our parents' after work. I always wanted a dog.' Sue added wistfully. Then she resumed her story. 'Once my Mother died, we realised that we were finally free. We had such plans, early retirement for both of us, selling the house, moving to the coast, holidays, eating out. But then Peter was diagnosed, and suddenly it was happening all over again.'

Sue looked up at Gary. 'I'm so sorry about the fuss I made about the conversion, and the website and everything. I just didn't want the conversion, you see, because it meant that Peter was ill, that his illness was real. I didn't want it to be. And then when you said we were lucky, well, I think I flipped a bit. I'm so sorry.'

Gary looked at her sadly. 'I think I flipped a bit too, I blamed you for everything, but I see now that a lot of it was my fault. I started my own business, but I'm not a natural businessman. I'm too soft, I let people take advantage of me, and I run whenever anyone shouts. It means that I never do things properly. I was already having cash-flow problems when I took on your job, and I depended too much on the fee I was going to get for it. I wasn't paid anything from Unique Interiors in the end, because the contract said it had to be finished to the clients' satisfaction, and I still owe them for the replacement tiles and things.'

Gary stopped and sighed, he felt exhausted. Suddenly he had a thought, 'I didn't drink your wine,' he said. Sue looked puzzled, and Gary carried on speaking, 'I didn't drink it, my half-brother, Danny, did. He was helping me out on the job, doing the labouring. He's an alcoholic, and he'd been on the waggon, but I should never have left him alone where there was alcohol. He just can't resist it. I should have realised that. I couldn't say anything before because I would have got him into trouble.'

'It wasn't about the wine,' Sue said, 'it was just the thought that you'd been drinking our booze when you should have been working. If it had been finished, then Danny could have had the whole case!' she added, with a short laugh. 'I'm sorry I jumped to conclusions, but when I saw the empty bottles in your van, well, it seemed pretty damning.'

'Yes, I know, I probably would have thought the same,' Gary admitted. 'I struggled to find labour for the job, and my Dad asked if I'd give Danny some work. I was glad of the help, and we worked well together, but I should have realised about the wine. You're lucky you had any left at all.'

'What made him an alcoholic?' Sue asked, looking genuinely interested.

'Our Dad is an alcoholic too, I guess it runs in the family. I'm lucky, it skipped me, I don't like the taste of alcohol and rarely touch a drop.'

'That must have been hard when you were growing up,' Sue said, 'did your Dad drink then?'

'Yes, he's always gone on benders, his whole life,' Gary replied. 'I lived with my Mum when I was very small, and I didn't see much of Dad. Then when I was eight my Mum married, and she moved away, so I went to live with my Dad then. It was OK, but when he did go on a bender I had to go into care. It wasn't much fun, I never knew where I was going to be from one month to the next. It all depended on whether Dad was drinking or not.'

'But that's dreadful,' Sue said, sounding shocked. 'Did your Mother not come back and take her to live with you when she saw what was happening?'

Gary shook his head, 'I've never seen or heard from her since the day she went on her honeymoon and left me at Dad's.'

Sue stared at him, tears welling up in her eyes again, and she shook her head sadly.

'It could have been worse,' Gary said, trying to sound cheerful. 'Lisa, my wife, her Mum put her up for adoption when she was five. But she wasn't adopted, she was in children's homes and foster homes all the time, she never knew her family at all. At least I did spend time with Dad, and he did his best.'

He went on, 'Lisa and I met in a children's home. Right from the start we knew we'd get married, and we did, before I'd even finished my apprenticeship. Jacob, our eldest, was already on the way, we didn't want to wait to have a family. We have four boys now, Jacob, Oliver, Jack and Noah.' He smiled at Sue. 'They're great kids. Do you still have my mobile? I'll show you a photo.'

Sue rummaged around in her pocket, and pulled out Gary's phone, and handed it to him. He fiddled with it for a while and then said, 'flat, never mind, I'll show you another time.'

Sue looked at Gary and started speaking, 'you think we're lucky because we have a big house and nice things. I think you're lucky having your boys. They are much more important than things.'

'Thanks,' Gary replied. 'But I feel I've let them down. We used to rent a nice house, just a little terraced house, but it had space, and a garden. Now we live in this awful flat in a shared house. There is nowhere for the boys to play, and the landlord is always threatening to evict us if they make a noise.' He looked down at his phone. 'My eldest, Jacob, he was really good at judo, loved it, but we can't afford for him to go any more. And he fell out with his best friend over it. It's not much of a life for them.'

Sue shook her head sympathetically. 'But hopefully you'll get a job soon, and then you can move somewhere nicer?' she suggested.

'It's not that easy,' Gary explained. 'We would have to put down a bond, and rent in advance, and even if I get a job it'll take months to save that much up, probably years. And I have to get a job, at the moment my reputation as a radio star, wine thief, and poor workman is going before me.'

Sue looked down to the floor, 'I'm sorry Gary, I'm going to take down the website as soon as possible. I hope that will help a bit.'

'Thanks,' Gary said, 'I hope it will too.' He paused and then said, 'Lisa blamed moving to the flat for Julia being stillborn, she said it was the stress. Do you think that'll be true?'

'People with lovely comfortable homes and few worries have stillborn, sleeping, babies too Gary, I really think it's just one of those things. You can't blame yourself.'

'But we don't even have a proper bed, we have to sleep on a sofa bed, that can't have been good for a pregnant woman. And it's damp and cramped in the flat.' Gary said, his voice sounding slightly tearful through the hoarseness.

'I still don't think that would have made a difference, I really don't. All you can do is work for a better future, focus on that. No point worrying over what might have been.'

Gary looked at her and smiled, and then they both turned as the door of the waiting room opened. A doctor came over and said, 'Mrs Robinson?'

'Yes, that's me,' Sue replied, sitting upright and looking concerned.

'I'm Dr Culvert, I work in the respiratory ward. I think we met when your husband was an inpatient recently?'

'Yes, sorry, I didn't recognise you,' Sue answered, sounding flustered. Dr Culvert turned and looked at Gary, who started to rise. 'This is a friend of ours, Gary Mills, he rescued us from the fire.' Sue said, 'please don't go Gary.' Dr Culvert nodded at Gary and then turned back to Sue.

'Peter regained consciousness, but we've given him something to help him sleep, it's probably for the best after an ordeal like this. His breathing is still laboured, of course, but I'm not too concerned at this stage. It will probably be best if you go home, and come back tomorrow, he'll be awake then.'

Sue's whole body relaxed, and she said, 'thank you Dr Culvert, I am rather tired and shaken up. I think I'll do that.'

The doctor left the room and both Sue and Gary stood up wearily. 'I'm getting a taxi home,' Sue said, 'there is a rank outside. Let me drop you off.'

'But it's in the opposite direction,' Gary protested, but Sue waved a hand at him.

'Don't worry about that, least I can do.'

'Is it Ok if I just run up to maternity? I'll say hello to Lisa if she's awake.'

'Yes, of course, please do,' Sue replied, 'I need to find the ladies' room anyway. I'll meet you at the taxi rank, out by the main outpatients' entrance?' Gary nodded, and hurried as quickly as he could up to the maternity ward. He rang the bell to gain entry, and luckily the nurse who came to the ward door recognised him. She noted his dirty and dishevelled appearance and looked at him quizzically.

'Sorry, I've just rescued some friends from a fire, I've just been discharged, and thought I'd pop by in case Lisa is awake. I'm sorry, I know it's late.'

'Are you and your friends OK?' the nurse asked in a loud whisper.

'Peter, the husband, he's having to stay in, but Sue and I are OK. I can go if you think it's too late to visit.'

'You're here now,' the nurse replied with a smile. 'Just peep in the window on the door, and don't disturb her if she's asleep.'

Lisa was in a single room, away from the mothers who had live babies, and Gary walked up quietly and peered through the window in the door. Lisa was sitting up in bed, and Gary started when he saw that she was holding a little pink bundle. His eyes filled with tears as he realised that Lisa was quietly singing to Julia, the same little lullaby that she'd sang to all their babies. He turned to the nurse who was standing behind him, also witnessing the touching scene inside. 'Don't think I'll disturb her,' Gary said thickly, and the nurse nodded her agreement.

It was good to be back in the fresh air, and he quickly found Sue, who had hailed a cab, and was looking out for Gary. Once they got inside, she asked Gary to give his address to the driver, and she pulled up the privacy screen.

'We need a story for the insurance, and perhaps the police or fire service or whatever.' Sue said, suddenly business-like. 'An explanation of why you came to our house so late at night.'

Gary looked at her, his mind was blank, and he didn't know what to suggest which would explain the circumstances.

'How about this?' Sue said, 'you came around earlier to ask me to remove your firm from the website, as it's stopping you getting a job. We chatted, and I said I would, as your business is no longer operating. You left your phone at our house by mistake, and because your wife is in hospital, you came around to get it, in case the hospital needed to get in touch. You came back, saw the fire, and looked for a way in. The back door was unlocked, so you rescued us. Does that sound OK?'

Gary nodded, not sure what to say. He'd put this woman through so much, and now she was coming up with a plan to protect him. 'You don't have to do this Sue, I was wrong, it's only right that I'm punished.'

'And what good will that do? Just promise me you'll never do anything like this again.' Gary nodded, and Sue said, 'did you use your phone after you left our house the first time, until you came back? Think carefully, because it's very important.'

Gary thought hard, it all seemed such a long time ago. 'No, I went straight home and read the boys a story. I didn't call or text, I'm sure of it.'

'That's good then, so remember, stick to that story, repeat it back to me, just to make sure,' Gary obediently repeated the scenario that she'd outlined.

Sue sat back, and Gary did the same, he felt exhausted. He looked out of the window and realised that they were turning into his street. The taxi pulled up outside the flat, and Gary turned to Sue.

'I'm sorry for everything, I really am.'

'Me too,' Sue said, and held out her hand for Gary to shake. He looked at her hand, and then leant forward and gave her a brief hug, before he stepped out of the taxi and started walking up the path.

CHAPTER 56

Lisa and Gary walked hand and hand out of the crematorium, not speaking, but holding onto each other as if their lives depended on it. The hospital had made all the arrangements, and after many late-night discussions, they had decided that only the two of them should attend Julia's funeral. If the boys had been older, they would have taken them along too, but they felt it best to keep them in school, and to say goodbye to their daughter quietly.

The day after the fire, Lisa was able to come home from hospital, and when Gary had gone to collect her, they had spent some time with Julia, and had taken photographs. One of the midwives had taken tiny footprints and handprints for them to keep. The day after Lisa came home, Gary went into town and registered the birth, and death, of Julia Rose Mills.

Gary got some prints from the photographs that they'd taken of their daughter. When the boys got home, they all made a memory box, which held the photographs, the handprints and footprints, Julia's hospital tag, and a lock of her hair in a little trinket box. The boys all did drawings, which they placed in the box too. Lisa sat for a while, quietly, with the box on her knee. Then she stood up and stored it away in the wardrobe.

Later in the week Les offered to babysit and gave them some money to go out for a meal, just Lisa and Gary. Neither of them really felt like going but they enjoyed it much more than they thought they would. And in the quiet corner of the restaurant, Gary told Lisa all about the Robinsons, what he'd done to them, and about the fire.

Lisa looked shocked, but then she grasped his hand. 'Life is awful now Gary, but it will get better as long as we stick together. We have to focus on the boys, and on each other, and keeping the family together. That's all that's important, isn't it?'

Gary nodded and pulled her into an embrace. *I'm so lucky*, he thought, *I don't deserve her.*

The funeral ceremony was mercifully short, the tiny coffin looking unreal as it lay there, surrounded by flowers. Lisa stifled a sob as the curtains closed, and the vicar said the final words. Gary squeezed her hand and realised that he was crying too.

As they walked towards the bus stop, Lisa turned to Gary and said, 'shall we walk back home? It's a fine day, and I don't feel like being stuck with other people in a bus.'

Gary nodded, and they turned in the opposite direction and headed for home. They were both quiet, lost in their thoughts, but they kept holding hands all the way. When they were nearly home, Lisa turned to Gary and said, 'no more babies for a while. Not until we can move somewhere bigger.'

'If you're happy with that?' Gary said, looking at her closely.

Lisa nodded and said, 'we're young, we can wait. The boys need our attention now anyway. I'll sort something out when I go to the doctors for my check-up.'

The flat was quiet and still when they got home. The three older boys were at school, and Noah was staying at his Grandad's house until Lisa and Gary got home. They picked up the post on the way up to the flat, and Lisa opened it whilst Gary made some tea. There were several more condolence cards, and Lisa picked one up and took it over to Gary. 'Look,' she said, handing him the card. Gary took it and read the words inside. It said, 'Lisa, Gary, boys, so sorry to hear about your loss. Thinking of you. Danny.'

'That's nice,' Gary said thickly, glad that his brother had made this gesture.

'Yes, it is,' said Lisa, 'he could have easily not bothered.'

They turned around as they heard a noise at the door. Lisa walked over and opened it, and there was Noah, standing outside. Lisa opened her arms and he ran into them and she hugged him close. Gary looked out to see where his Dad was and saw him struggling up the stairs with the buggy.

'I'm glad Noah can walk up,' Les remarked, as Gary went to help him. By the time they got into the flat, Lisa was bringing a tray over to the table and setting out cups of tea and some juice for Noah.

Les sat down and got his breath back, then said, 'how was it? The service?'

Lisa looked down at the table, so Gary replied for them both. 'It was a nice service, but, well, it was sad, obviously.'

Les nodded sympathetically, then he sat up straight and rubbed his hands together. 'Well I've got some news that might just cheer you up. I bumped into an old friend of mine yesterday, Geoff, a good bloke, straight as they come. Done well for himself Geoff, and he's the boss of a big construction firm, he's the manager of it. I was talking to him and he said he's having difficulty finding skilled tradesmen. I told him about you Gary, and he said he's got a job for you if you want it. I explained about the baby and the funeral, and he said to go either today or tomorrow, whenever you felt up to it.'

Gary and Lisa looked at each other, stunned at Les's words. 'You must go straight away,' Lisa said, 'show him you're keen.'

'Are you sure you'll be OK?' Gary asked, excited, but concerned for Lisa.

'Yes, I'm fine, go, your Dad will stay a bit, won't you Les?' Lisa said, turning to her Father-in-law.

'Of course I will honey, I'll stay as long as you want. And I can go and get the boys for you if you don't feel up to it.' Les offered. Then he rummaged in the pockets of his coat and pulled out a piece of paper. 'Geoff gave me this, it's his details, so you can find him alright.' He handed the paper to Gary, looking pleased.

'Thanks Dad, I'll head off now,' Gary said, taking the piece of paper. He kissed Lisa and Noah and rushed out of the door, studying the paper as he went.

Forty-five minutes later, Gary was sitting in the reception area of a large construction firm on the outskirts of the town. On the walls were pictures of housing developments that they'd constructed, as well as industrial buildings and office blocks. This was their Head Quarters, located in a fairly new business park. It wasn't luxurious, but the phones rang constantly, and they seemed busy. The receptionist had told him that it would be half an hour before Geoff O'Rourke would be able to see him, so he tried to relax as he waited.

About 20 minutes later a burly sandy-haired man in his mid-forties strode into reception and held out his hand to Gary. 'Geoff O'Rourke,' he said in a booming voice, 'and you must be Gary Mills, I can see a resemblance to your Dad.'

Gary shook hands firmly with Geoff and followed him across the reception area and into a large untidy office. Geoff gestured towards a seat and Gary sat down.

'Before we get started Gary, your Dad told me about your baby, and I just wanted to say how sorry I am for your loss. Dreadful thing that, going through all those months, and ending up with nothing at the end. Bad business. How's your Missus coping?' Geoff asked, genuine concern in his voice.

'Thanks, she's coping OK I think. It was the funeral this morning, so that was a bit hard.'

'Yes, thanks for coming along today. I would have understood if you'd wanted to wait until tomorrow.' Geoff said, smiling sadly at Gary.

Gary smiled back and said, 'I'm desperate to get back to work, so I didn't want to scupper my chances.'

Geoff smiled more broadly and said, 'tell me about your experience, your qualifications, and how you ended up out of work.' He then sat back and waited for Gary to speak.

Gary took a deep breath and went through the work he'd done as an apprentice, and at George's firm after he qualified. He then explained about how he'd been made redundant when George sold up, and he took the chance to set up his own business.

'But setting up on my own was a mistake, I see that now,' Gary continued, 'I was too inexperienced and naïve, I didn't know how to price work up properly, or run the business side of things, and I let people take advantage of me. And I thought I could spend time with my family during the day *and* work, and that's a recipe for disaster.'

Gary then continued, explaining about taking on the job for Unique Interiors and employing Danny and how it had led to his firm going under.

'I've learned my lesson now though,' Gary said, looking Geoff squarely in the eyes. 'If you give me a chance I won't be answering my phone to the family during the day, and I'll work really hard and do what I'm told. I'm a good worker, I'm just not a good businessman.'

Gary sat back, suddenly wondering if he'd said too much.

Geoff smiled at him broadly. 'I appreciate your honesty, thank you for telling me that. Sounds like you've learned from the experience, and that's why we have challenging times in life, so we can learn. Now, there is one thing I need to ask you, and don't be offended. I like your Dad very much, but we both know that he's a drinker, and you've just told me that your brother is too. I can't have any drinkers working for me. Your Dad says you never touch a drop, is that true?'

Gary looked Geoff in the eyes, 'yes, that's right, I've never acquired a taste for alcohol, think I saw enough of it when I was growing up, can't see the appeal. You have no worries there.'

'That's good enough for me,' Geoff said. 'I'll start you on a two-month trial. I do that with all new workmen, it's standard procedure. If you do OK, and I don't see why you shouldn't, then there's a permanent job here for you. How does that sound?'

'It sounds fantastic,' Gary said, 'I can't wait to tell Lisa, and my Dad.'

'That's great,' said Geoff, 'I'll tell you a bit about what we do here, and then I'll take you through to our Human Resources department, and they'll get everything set up. Can you start on Monday?'

When Gary got back to the flat, he ran up the stairs and burst through the door. His Dad and Lisa were sitting on the sofa, and Noah was playing with some toy cars on the floor.

'I start on Monday,' Gary said, his eyes shining. 'Two months trial at first, they do that with everyone, and then there's a permanent job if I want it. Thanks Dad, you're right, he's a good bloke, Geoff. And it seems a great firm to work for.' Gary looked at Lisa, who was watching Noah, and he waited for her to say something. But she remained silent. Slightly hurt, Gary said, 'well, I think I'll get changed, time to pick the boys up.'

'I'll have a walk along with you son,' his Dad said, 'are we taking the little-un?'

Lisa spoke then, and said, 'no, leave Noah with me, he's busy playing with his toys. He can help me set the table for tea.'

When they finally got the boys to bed that evening, Gary turned to Lisa, who was still quiet and withdrawn. Gary was disappointed that she hadn't said anything about him getting a job, but he assumed it was because of the funeral, and that she was thinking about Julia. Sadness about his daughter still swept over him in waves, but this was interspersed with relief, and excitement, because he was finally going back to work.

'Are you OK babe?' Gary asked. 'I know it's been a tough day. But aren't you pleased that I've got a job?'

'I hate this place,' was Lisa's unexpected reply. 'It only has bad memories for me, and it's going to be months, even years before we can get away. We need to save up a deposit and advanced rent, and you'll need a permanent job. And once we have more money coming in then you'll probably have to pay more off our debts.'

Gary felt a bit wounded, and he said, 'but it's still the best news we've had for ages.'

'Yes, I know, sorry if I seem negative. But I've been thinking, Noah will be going to nursery soon for two or three days a week, he's entitled to a free place now that he's two and a half. Why don't I look for a job too, see if I can find something that will fit around school times? That way we'll get out of here quicker.'

'But don't you have enough today already, looking after me and the boys?' Gary asked.

'There isn't much work to do here, and I nearly go crazy when the boys are at school. I think it will be good for me, good for us all if I can get a job. We depend on you too much, it's not fair.'

Gary thought about it for a while, and then started to warm to the idea. It would be good not to have to rely on his wage alone, and the extra money would make life a bit sweeter.

'That's a great idea Lisa, get yourself down to the Job Centre tomorrow!' He smiled to show he was being flippant, and Lisa smiled back and threw a cushion at him.

CHAPTER 57

Sue looked around the penthouse critically before she picked up the car keys and headed to the hospital. She'd been living here for a week now, but Peter had still been in hospital, so he hadn't seen it yet. She wanted it to look nice for him coming home. She'd chosen this particular flat because it was all on one level, so it would be easy for Peter to navigate. Sue picked some dead petals off a flower in a vase, plumped up a cushion on the sofa, and then headed off to the hospital.

As she drove across town, she thought about her visit to the house that morning, and the discussion that she'd had with the insurance assessor and a representative from the fire service. They'd discovered that it was the dishwasher in the conversion that had started the fire. Sue was surprised, she knew tumble driers, and sometimes washing machines, could cause fires, but didn't know that dishwashers were a leading cause of house fires too.

The house looked in a sorry state. There was extensive smoke damage everywhere, the conversion needed to be gutted and totally refurbished, and the kitchen was waterlogged. After she'd left the hospital on the night of the fire, she'd gone back, locked up, packed a bag and went to a hotel. She'd slept for a long time, then woke up, rung room service for a meal, and made a list of everything that she needed to do. Finding a short-term rental property had been easier than she'd imagined. There were several local businesses that kept apartments for visiting executives, and she'd had a choice of a few modern, bland properties. It would do until they could move back home.

Now that the insurance assessor had been, he'd given the go-ahead for the work to start. She had a firm on standby. They'd been recommended by a client of hers and specialised in properties that had been damaged by fire or floods. Sue had looked around the house in despair, there seemed so much work to do, but the representative from the firm, a smart young woman in incredibly high heels, had been so matter of fact about it all, that she'd felt immediately reassured. 'We see worse every day of the week, this is nothing,' she said breezily, teetering up and down stairs in her spindly heels.

The man from the fire service had told her that the house would have been even more damaged if Gary hadn't stopped the fire from spreading further into the main body of the house. 'It was a bit risky, but it's stopped things from being a lot worse,' he said seriously.

Sue managed to find a parking space at the hospital surprisingly easily, for a change. She carefully removed the folding wheelchair from the car boot and fiddled to assemble it. She was sure it would get easier in time. *I hope Peter will like it*, she thought, as she hurried over to the main entrance. She had ordered the wheelchair after Peter had a session with an Occupational Therapist. She said it would help him to get around but that he wouldn't need to use it all the time. Sue had picked a lightweight folding chair, in a bright red, from the huge array at a mobility superstore. She could lift it in and out of the car easily, meaning they could go out together, which would be nice as spring would be coming in soon.

Sue was looking forward to leaving the hospital with Peter, instead of leaving him there as she had over the past couple of weeks. He was still struggling to breathe, but the doctors said that now this was related more to his Motor Neurone Disease than the fire.

Peter was sitting in a chair by his bed when she walked on the ward. He was dressed in the clothes she'd brought in for him, and she noticed that they were slack, he must have lost weight over the past few weeks. He smiled broadly when he saw her and tried to get up.

'Just you stay there for a moment Mr,' she said, admonishing him. 'Might as well check we've got everything before we make the great escape.' Sue bent down to kiss Peter, and he put his arm around her and hugged her to him. 'What do you think of your new wheels?' Sue asked, pointing at the wheelchair.

Peter examined the wheelchair. 'I think it looks marvellous,' he finally pronounced. 'How fast does it go?'

Sue smiled, and went off to the nurses' station to check if it was OK to take Peter home.

The wheelchair was still easy to push, even with Peter in it, much easier than Sue had feared. She remembered to apply the brakes when they got to the car, and Peter was able to stand and, holding onto the top of the wheelchair, transfer into the car seat. Sue deftly folded the wheelchair and placed it in the boot, not confessing to Peter how many times she'd practised when on her own.

The lift to the penthouse flat was large and silent, and they both maintained the silence as they travelled upwards. It was a dedicated lift and it went straight into the hallway of the flat. When the lift doors opened Peter wheeled himself out, using the large back wheels of the chair to push himself forward. It moved easily over the tiled floors of the penthouse, and he headed over to the large curved windows which dominated the living room.

'What an amazing view Sue, it's stunning.' The flat looked out over the town, and there was always something new to watch. Sue had suspected that Peter would find it fascinating.

'Would you like to see the rest of it?' Sue asked, but Peter shook his head.

'Perhaps later,' he replied, 'for now I'm just going to enjoy the view.'

Sue sat down on the large leather sofa, lay back and relaxed. Peter was out of hospital, the house was being repaired, and suddenly everything seemed OK.

CHAPTER 58

The Portakabin was already full of men when Gary arrived at lunch time. He'd been busy plumbing in a bath and wanted to finish it before he broke for lunch, so he was one of the last to arrive. He was glad that they always had somewhere warm and dry to come for their breaks though, and he found a seat near the door, and sat down and opened his lunchbox.

He was six weeks into his new job and it was going well. In fact, Geoff O'Rourke had spoken with him only two days ago, and said that he would be making him a permanent member of the team. The paperwork was being sorted out now, and he would have a contract of employment before his two-month probationary period was up. Gary smiled to himself when he thought about it. A permanent job, it meant they could really start planning for the future.

Gary tucked into his sandwiches, and listened to the other men on his table, who were talking about football. Gary wasn't really interested, and he fished out his mobile phone and switched it on. He always turned it off when he was working now, and only checked it at break times, in case there were any emergencies. He'd given the office number to Lisa, and to the boys' schools, so that they could always get in touch if it was urgent.

The phone pinged, indicating that he had a new text message. It was from Lisa, so he read it eagerly. It said, 'Hi babe, fantastic surprise for you when you get home. So exciting! Love you, L xxx'

Intrigued, Gary was tempted to phone Lisa to find out what she meant, but he'd vowed to only concentrate on work during his working day, so instead he switched off his phone and put it back in his pocket. *Something to look forward to when I get home*, he thought, and picked up another sandwich.

One of Gary's colleagues dropped him off near home, so he

was back in good time that evening. He was starting to feel excited about Lisa's surprise and wondered what it could be. Perhaps Lisa had a job? She'd been looking for the past few weeks and had submitted some applications. But she hadn't had any interviews yet. Perhaps she had her first interview. But would she be so excited about that?

Gary raced up the stairs and into the flat. Lisa and the boys stopped what they were doing and turned to him, all smiling broadly.

'I got your text,' Gary said, smiling back, 'I don't think I can stand the excitement any longer, what is it?'

'A letter,' Jack blurted out, unable to contain his excitement any more.

'A letter?' Gary said, puzzled. Then he noticed that Lisa was holding out an envelope, looking excited. He took it and sat down at the table. The envelope was handwritten, but he didn't recognise the writing. The postmark was local.

'Open it, for goodness sakes,' Lisa said impatiently, looking at him, exasperated.

Gary felt into the envelope, and pulled out a card, with a tasteful art picture on the front. He opened the card and found a cheque inside. He picked up the cheque and looked at it. It was made out to Mr and Mrs G Mills and was for a considerable sum. The names at the bottom of the cheque were P Robinson and S Robinson. Gary looked up at Lisa puzzled, and then he looked back at the card. There were only a few words written in it, and the simple message read, 'children need space to grow, please take this so you can move to somewhere bigger.'

'Isn't it marvellous?' Lisa asked. 'We can move as soon as we find somewhere, no waiting for months or years. With this money we will be able to pay the bond and the advanced rent on somewhere decent. We will even have enough left over to hire a van to get all of our stuff out of the storage unit.'

Gary looked at her, shaking his head, 'I know it sounds great, but can we really take this Lisa? I don't deserve it.'

Lisa looked dismayed and said, 'but they want us to have it Gary, when will we get another opportunity like this? We can't stay here, I can't stand it and it's not good for the boys.'

Gary realised that the boys were crowding around him, and he turned to look at them.

'Will I be able to have my own room?' Jacob asked.

'Me too,' added Oliver.

'Will we have a garden?' Jack said, his eyes shining.

'Paddling pool,' added Noah.

Gary looked at the boys, and back at Lisa. Seeing them so happy made him realise just how miserable they had looked over the past few months.

'Well, we'll see what we can do to meet all of those requirements. What would Mummy like in her new house?' he asked, looking at Lisa.

'I'd like a proper kitchen, with room to cook, and a real bed instead of a sofa bed. And my own front door instead of sharing one with other families.'

'In that case, put this cheque in the bank tomorrow, and get yourself around some letting agents.' The boys cheered, and Gary felt himself joining in. *Thank you, thank you, I don't deserve it*, he thought, hoping that the Robinsons would know just how grateful he   was.

CHAPTER 59

Sue was heading out to the terrace with her morning coffee when she heard the thud of something falling through the letterbox. She looked out into the hallway and saw that a bulky envelope had been pushed through, so she went to pick it up. The envelope was hand-written, but she didn't recognise the writing.

'I wonder what this is Teddy, it feels thick,' she said to her black Labrador retriever, who ran up and tried to wrestle the package out of her hand. 'Stop it, you daft dog,' Sue said, holding it higher, 'it's not for you, it's addressed to me.' She put the package on the tray with her coffee and a plate of biscuits and went out through the kitchen door. She put down the tray and sat down, and as she always did, she looked out over the beach and the sea beyond, not really able to believe that she lived here.

'If I ever take that view for granted Teddy, you have permission to nip me on the ankles.' Teddy came over and put his head on her knee, and she stroked his silky head. She talked to him all day long and he always responded, either coming to her, or putting his head on one side as if he was listening intently. She suddenly hugged him to her, and he reciprocated by licking her on the side of the face.

'Right, I'll drink my coffee while it's still hot, and then we'll see who's been writing to us,' she told Teddy, who was looking hopefully at the plate of biscuits.

Sue looked at the writing on the envelope again before she opened it. It was addressed only to her and had a Kent postmark. 'Probably turn out to be some junk mail forwarded from the old house Teddy, and I'll just have to put it in the bin.' Sue opened the envelope and shook out the contents. There was a letter, folded over neatly, a card which looked to have been made by children, and a couple of photographs. She picked these up first. The first one was a family portrait and Sue looked at it, puzzled, until she recognised the smiling face of Gary Mills standing at the right-hand side, with a baby in his arms. On the left-hand side there was a pretty woman, with long dark curly hair, and she also held a baby.

Between Gary and his wife were two young boys, and in front of them another two. They were all smiling broadly. Sue smiled, and looked more closely at the photograph. Gary had filled out a bit since she saw him last, and he looked healthy and happy.

Sue picked up the next photograph. It showed two identical babies, dressed in frilly pink dresses, and rather sweetly, holding hands. They were very small, and Sue realised that they mustn't be very old. She then picked up the card, which had the words 'thank you' written in glitter on the front. There was also a picture of a house, drawn in the usual childish way with the door in the middle and windows at each side, both upstairs and downstairs. Inside the card read, 'To Mr and Mrs Robinson, thank you for our new home, we love it. From, Jacob, Oliver, Jack, Noah, Ava and Ella xxx.' Each of the boys had written his name himself, and they ranged from very neat (Oliver), to a scrawl (Jack), and large printing (Noah).

Sue finished her coffee and shared a biscuit with Teddy before she opened the letter. It was quite long, so she sat back and took her time reading it.

Dear Sue,

First of all, we want to say how sorry we were to hear about Peter's death. We called around to the house to see you both, and the new people living there told us that you had moved after Peter had died, and they didn't have a forwarding address. We went to the Estate Agents who sold the house, and met a nice lady there, Charlotte, who offered to forward this on for us. Apparently, Peter taught Charlotte when she was at school, she remembered him very well and wanted to help.

You must think that we are awful not thanking you for your generous cheque before now. But we wanted to tell you that your generosity had turned our lives around, and it has, so the time seemed right. We are only sorry that Peter will not know how grateful we are to you both. I didn't deserve such kindness after the way I treated you.

Just before we got your cheque I was offered a job, and I've been there a couple of years now. I work for a big construction company, we build housing estates and office buildings. They are a good firm to work for, and I've recently been promoted to supervisor. I learned my lesson though, and when I'm at work I concentrate only on work. And when I'm at home I concentrate on my family.

We found a nice house in West View. I don't know if you know it? It's a quiet area, and it has good schools within easy walking distance. The couple who owned the house were downsizing to a retirement flat and decided to rent out their family home. They were foster parents for many years, so the house is geared towards children. It has five bedrooms, so Jacob and Oliver, our two eldest, have rooms of their own, which they guard fiercely from their brothers, and the younger two boys share a room. We also have two attic rooms, which Lisa uses, but more about that in a minute. The house has a large garden, and three reception rooms, so we have a playroom for all the toys, meaning we can sit down without stepping on Lego or a toy car!

The boys are all doing well, growing like weeds, as you can see from the photograph. Jacob went back to judo, and he represents the county in the under-eleven category. Oliver is still a book-worm, reading all the time. Jack, who was always the liveliest of the boys, has taken up gymnastics, which is great as it burns off his energy. Little Noah has started school and he already has a girlfriend. We think his hobby is going to be breaking hearts.

Lisa is well, and as beautiful as ever. She decided to get a job after Julia died, and was lucky enough to find a part-time job in a shop that sold fabric. Lisa learned to sew from one of her foster families, so that helped her to get a start. The shop runs sewing classes, and she started to help with them, and she's a natural at it. She does that part-time now, instead of working in the shop, and she loves it. She had also recycled some of the boy's clothes into baby dresses for Julia, and she took them in to show the shop's owner, who offered to display them for her. They sold within days and she started receiving orders for more, and now she's built up a nice little business, selling through the shop and online. Lisa has turned out to be much better at business than I was, and she's worked with the local small business support team and set things up properly. She has taken over our two attic rooms and has her sewing machine in one (we call it her design studio) and her office in another. It's grown so much that over the past two months she's had to outsource the actual sewing to other people, and she concentrates on designing new items, keeping the books, and dealing with the online shop and orders. It's funny to think of Julia Rose designs shipping internationally and being worn by children all over Europe and America. And if that wasn't enough, Lisa has also managed to create not one, but two, new members of the family. We welcomed our twin girls, Ava and Ella, two months ago, and we couldn't be more delighted. They are like two peas in a pod, and so far, only Lisa, me and Oliver can tell them apart.

And the final piece of news that I wanted to tell you, and the reason why we're getting in touch now, is to say that last week we finally paid off all the debt we'd built up when the business went under. It's so good to be debt-free, and now we're going to start saving, and perhaps have a little fun too.

So that's our news, and as you can see, life is good, and we are thriving. We couldn't have got as far without your help, and we really are truly grateful to both you and Peter. It was so much more than I deserved. We hope that you are well, and that you are also having good luck. You deserve it. If you do have time to write, or email, or call, it would be great to hear all your news.

With our love and thanks, the Mills Family.

CHAPTER 60

Sue put the letter down on the table and thought for a few moments. 'Well Teddy,' she said, looking down at her dog. 'What would we say if we replied to this letter?' Sue stopped and stroked Teddy's head, and he looked up at her as if he was waiting for her to continue.

'First of all, we'd thank them for writing, congratulate them on the safe arrival of the babies, say it was good that everything had worked out. You see Teddy, you must get the niceties out of the way first. Then I'd give them a rundown of what's happened since I last saw Gary Mills. Something like this ...'

Although Peter's death wasn't unexpected, it did happen quicker than we thought. I found him one morning when I went to wake him up, and he'd slipped away peacefully in his sleep. I suppose that's the end we all hope for. He had grown increasingly frail and disabled, and was finding it hard, so for him it was a welcome release I think.

Several months before he died, Peter traced an old friend of mine through social media. Pat and I were the closest of friends at university, but we lost touch afterwards as life got in the way. Pat is divorced and lives in York, but we started speaking, then she came to stay, and it was just like all those years had never happened, and we were as thick as thieves again in no time. She came immediately when Peter died, and I don't think I could have managed without her help and support.

When Peter was still alive, Pat and I took a short walking holiday in Northumberland. I'd never been that far north before, and I fell in love with the place. I'd always thought that when I did finally move to the coast it would be to Devon or Cornwall, but instead I live in a Northumbrian fishing village now, and I love it. I put the house on the market immediately after the funeral and retired from work. The house sold quickly, and I rented a house in Northumberland for a while until I found my perfect place. And this is it, Cliff Cottage. It's actually two cottages knocked into one, making it spacious and open. It has an open plan kitchen/dining/sitting area, and two bedrooms with en-suite bathrooms. There is a pretty cottage garden at the front and sides, and at the back there is an unusual stone terrace with an arched stone roof. I've had windows (triple-glazing) installed to keep out the sea breezes, and had radiators and a fire put in there. It has the most magnificent view of the beach and the sea, and so every morning I have breakfast looking at the changing seasons. It's quite breath-taking.

Pat and I spend two weekends together a month. One in York and one up here. It makes a nice contrast. We've also pledged to see as many countries as we can while we're still fit enough. We spent our first holiday in New Zealand, visiting Pat's son and his family. We were very courageous, renting a huge camper van and driving around the country on our own. It was quite an adventure! This year we have been to Dubai and Rome, and we have booked a cruise for the autumn.

The day that my offer for Cliff Cottage was accepted, I was sitting on a seat admiring the sea view, when a chocolate-coloured Labrador dog ran up to me as if I were a long-lost friend and placed her head on my knee. I got chatting with her owner (did I mention that people in the north east are so friendly and welcoming?) She told me that the dog, Poppy, was pregnant, and so I put my name down for a puppy at once. I went to view them with the intention of picking a chocolate-coloured girl puppy, like Poppy. But I ended up falling for a jet-black boy, and so Teddy came into my life, and he's an absolute joy. I'm sure Peter would have loved him.

I am steadily ticking off the list of things that Peter and I had planned for our retirement. Move to the coast, tick; get a dog, tick; travel, tick; eat out, tick. Pat and I have a list of the 'best restaurants' in both the north east and Yorkshire, and we are working our way through them. I am also pursuing my ambition to be an artist. This house is too small to have a studio, so I rent one in an artists' collective here in Northumberland. This has turned out to be a good move, as I've now got a new group of creative friends. One makes items by fusing glass. Another makes hand-made musical instruments, another is a jewellery-maker, well, you get the picture. We have open studio events, Christmas sales, that sort of thing, and we go to exhibitions and classes together too. I go to my studio three days a week usually, and I have sold a few pieces now, which means, I think, that I can call myself an artist.

I sold the BMW and bought a convertible instead. Totally impractical for this climate, but I'm not sensible Sue the accountant now, I'm bohemian Sue the artist and I just get wrapped up and put the hood down anyway.

So, life is good, thank you. I am settled here now, and have made friends amongst the creative community, the dog-walkers, and my neighbours. I miss Peter dreadfully of course, and I do get lonely, but life as a widow isn't the hell that I imagined.

'And then Teddy, we'd sign off, wishing them well etc. Because that's what you do when you end a personal letter like that.

Sue sat holding the letter and thought about the things she wouldn't include. How some days the only thing that gets me out of bed is Teddy begging for a walk. Those are the days when Peter not being there seems not only unbelievable, but unbearable. How I once followed a man from York Railway station half-way across the city, convinced it was Peter. He wasn't the least bit like him once I saw him from the front, and I could have cried with disappointment and shame. I won't tell them about the days that I only eat toast because I can't bear to cook another meal for one. Or about how I sleep with a nightlight on like a child, because I'm afraid of the dark.

Teddy's cold nose pushed against her hand, and she smiled and looked down at him, 'another thing I wouldn't do is tell them how rich we are, because that would seem like boasting.'

And I am rich, Sue thought, *thanks to Peter*. And she thought again of the day when she'd gone to the solicitors, in those dark days after Peter's death. She recalled the solicitor's words, 'the will is straightforward of course, everything is in joint names anyway, and the money in Mr Robinson's personal account is left to you. But what you don't know about, as far as I'm aware, is the life insurance policy.'

'What life insurance policy?' Sue asked, puzzled.

'Your husband took out a policy many years ago. He didn't want you to know, wanted it to be a surprise if you ever had to redeem it. It's for a considerable sum. He sent me this note for safe keeping, after his diagnosis. He asked me to give you it after his death.'

Sue took the note but didn't read it until she was alone. She couldn't quite take in how much money she was going to get under the insurance policy. With that and her pensions, and the money from the sale of the house, she would never need to worry about money again, and she could do anything she wanted, go anywhere.

She sat in the car and opened the letter, addressed to her in Peter's familiar handwriting.

'My darling, if you are reading this, then it means that I'm no longer with you, and for that I am sorry. Sorry to leave you alone, but also sorry that we are not getting the chance to grow old together.

You will also now know about the insurance policy, which I hope has come as a pleasant surprise. You are probably wondering why I've never mentioned it, and I thought I'd leave this note by way of explanation. I took it out many years ago, when my Father and Mother both became ill. I somehow suspected, with our luck, that we might need it one day, and I thought if I ever had to leave you, then I wanted to leave you comfortable. I didn't tell you because I thought you'd think I was being morbid, and it was a lot of money each month, which at times we could ill-afford. But I'm glad that I persevered, especially now that I've got this awful disease.

So now that you are protected financially, and finally free from caring responsibilities, live for both of us. Do all the things that we have talked about. Move to the sea, get a dog, paint, travel, and most of all, my darling, be happy.

And remember, no lame ducks.

I will love you for ever, thank you for the happiest times in my life. Peter.'

Sue sighed, she had read that note so many times, still did occasionally, although she knew every word off by heart. And she had taken the words to heart, and tried to be positive every day, determined to live for both her and Peter. She was sure that it was this attitude that had helped her to cope and to carry on, even when she thought she couldn't bear it, and there seemed no point.

'Come on then lazy bones, time to get some fresh air and exercise,' Sue said, and Teddy jumped up, his tail wagging. Sue picked up the package and her tray and went through to the kitchen. She pulled on her coat, snapped on Teddy's lead and went out through the front door. But instead of heading straight out of the garden, she detoured around the side of the house to where she kept her dustbin. She lifted the lid and threw the whole package inside, and then headed off towards the beach.

CHAPTER 61

Gary looked up at the blue sky, enjoying the sunshine on his face and shoulders. This was the first warm and sunny day this year, and he hoped it was the sign of things to come. He was sitting on the patio, reading the Sunday papers, and relaxing with a cup of tea. The boys were playing a riotous game of football on the lawn, and the babies were lying in the shade in their double buggy, kicking happily in the warmth of the day. Lisa had just gone indoors to get changed, before they all headed out for Sunday lunch.

Gary's thoughts drifted to Sue Robinson, and he wondered if she'd received their package yet? He was a little disappointed that they hadn't received a call or an email from her. Perhaps she would send a letter instead? He had intended to visit the Robinsons months ago, but he wanted to go in with his head held high, a different man from the last time he'd been there. Gary tried not to think about that terrible night of the fire. He must have been crazy, and he was never going to get that desperate again.

When he paid off all his debts he'd felt the time was right, and he'd put the girls in their pram and pushed them down Willow Drive with his heart thumping. But when he knocked on the front door a strange woman opened it and asked if she could help him, before she started making a fuss of the babies, cooing at them with a smile on her face. He explained that he was an old acquaintance of the Robinsons, and her face grew serious.

'Oh, I'm sorry,' she said. 'Mrs Robinson sold the house to us, after her husband died. She's moved away, and we don't have an address for her. You could try the estate agents, Smith and Parker, in the High Street.'

'Peter's dead?' Gary had said, sounding dismayed. He didn't think it would have happened so quickly. He stayed and chatted with the woman for another couple of minutes. He noticed that there was a ramp coming from the front door of the conversion, which hadn't been there before. He commented that it was new, and the woman said they'd had it installed.

'Our son has Cerebral Palsy. This house is ideal, as he has his own little flat in there. He's in his teens now so it gives him some independence.'

'I'm glad it's being used,' Gary replied, and headed away. Later he did call into the offices of Smith and Parker, and was lucky enough to be greeted by Charlotte Flynn, a petite and very pretty blonde, who knew exactly who he was talking about when he mentioned the Robinsons.

'I can't give out Mrs Robinson's new address, confidentiality and all that. But I will post something on to her for you if you like? Mr Robinson was my form master when I was at school. I got into a bit of trouble and he helped straighten me out. I remember him saying that at the end of the day we're all responsible for our actions and we must do what we think is right. We can't blame other people, we all make our own choices. And if we make the wrong choices, that's OK, realise they're wrong and learn from them. He was kind, a real gentleman. I was sad to hear that he'd died, I owe him a lot.'

'Me too,' said Gary, and he handed over the package.

*****

Lisa tapped Gary lightly on the shoulder. 'Are you ready?' she asked, 'you look miles away.'

'I was just thinking how lucky I am,' Gary replied, and went to round up the boys for lunch.

The End

AUTHOR'S NOTE

The Fox and The Crane is one of Aesop's fables, and the moral of the tale is that if you treat someone badly, you can expect them to retaliate and treat you badly in return. The lesson you can take from this is that you should treat others as you would like them to treat you.

I don't think anyone would really argue with this, but I wanted to show in 'Hurt and Revenge' that people's motivations for action aren't always clear-cut, even to themselves.

When an animal is hurt, it will lash out at anyone or anything it sees as a threat. Humans, in my experience, operate in the same way. And this can lead to all sorts of problems.

These are some of the themes that I explore in Hurt and Revenge, hence my inclusion of the tale of the Fox and the Crane.

Deborah E Oxberry

ABOUT THE AUTHOR

Deborah Oxberry is a business woman, author, wife, sister and dog-owner, who aspires to be an artist, musician and secret agent.

Her working life has taken place mostly in mental health services, and she has degrees in psychology and related subjects. This has made her even more confused and curious about how people think and why they act as they do.

Deborah writes for a living, through her business, Mercury Business Development (www.mercury.ventures), and she is the author of two popular non-fiction books.

Hurt and Revenge is her first novel, and it explores several themes, but mostly it's about trying to understand why people act in sometimes bizarre and unexpected ways. It is inspired by real events, observation, and sleepless nights puzzling about other people and why they do what they do.

Deborah loves to connect with other people, so if you would like to join her mailing list, then please visit her website and sign up. Emails will be infrequent and brief, and will only contain exciting information, such as the publication of a new book, or discovery of the world's most delicious chocolate. (Although, would she want to share that? It might sell out.)

www.deborahoxberry.com

Thank you.

Deborah doesn't really do social media, but will reply to enquiries, questions, or 'hellos' from readers. Contact her on:

deborah@deborahoxberry.com

24161295R00167

Printed in Poland
by Amazon Fulfillment
Poland Sp. z o.o., Wrocław